THE
PRINCELING

Ed Zhao

I AM SELF-
PUBLISHING

@iamselfpub
www.iamselfpublishing.com

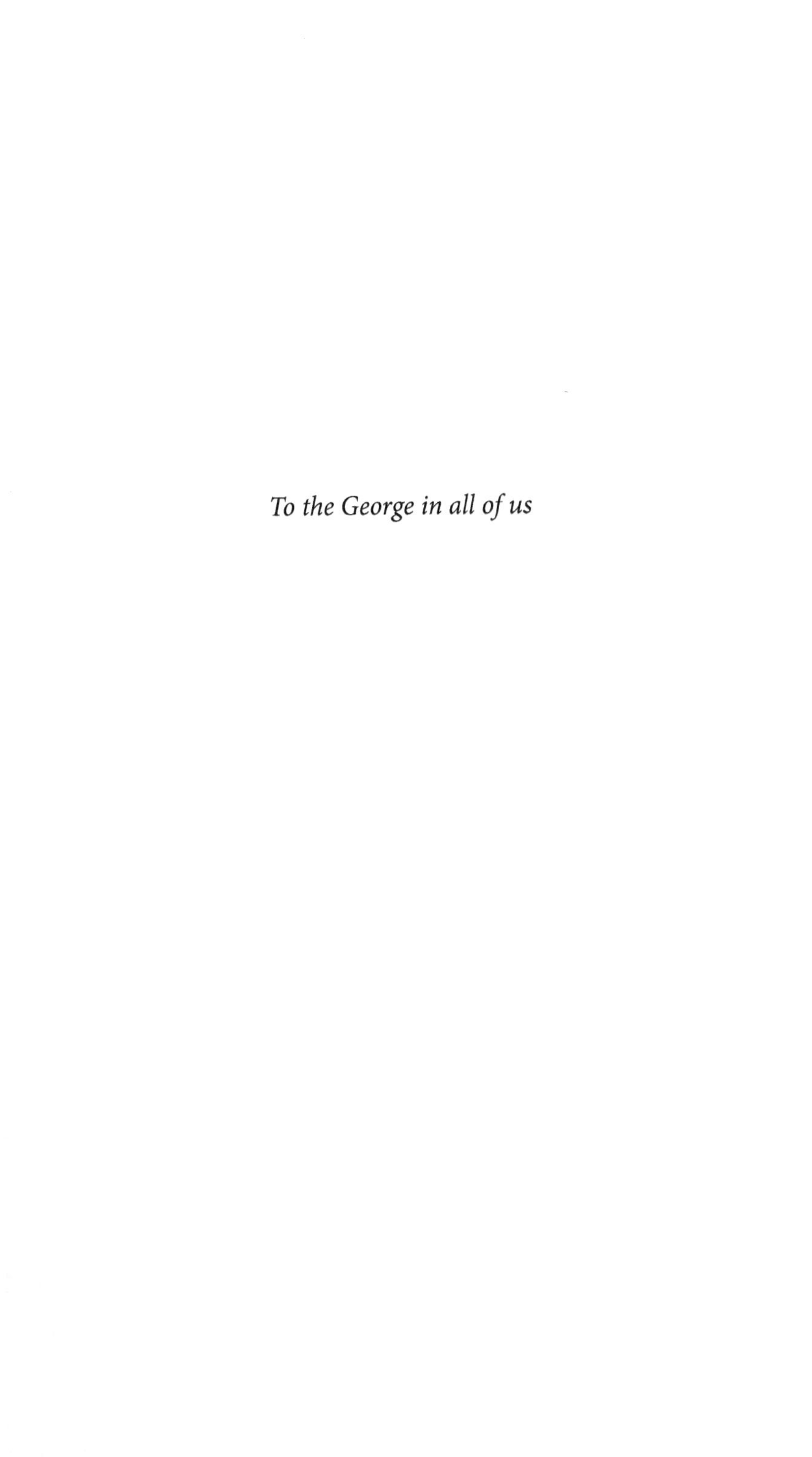

To the George in all of us

THE
PRINCELING

Ed Zhao

Oh angel, beautiful angel,

The fragrant flowers are no match for you.

You are so delicate and beautiful, and your beauty is beyond words.

Gulbita, your words are sweeter than honey.

Your red lips intoxicate me, Gulbita.

CONTENTS

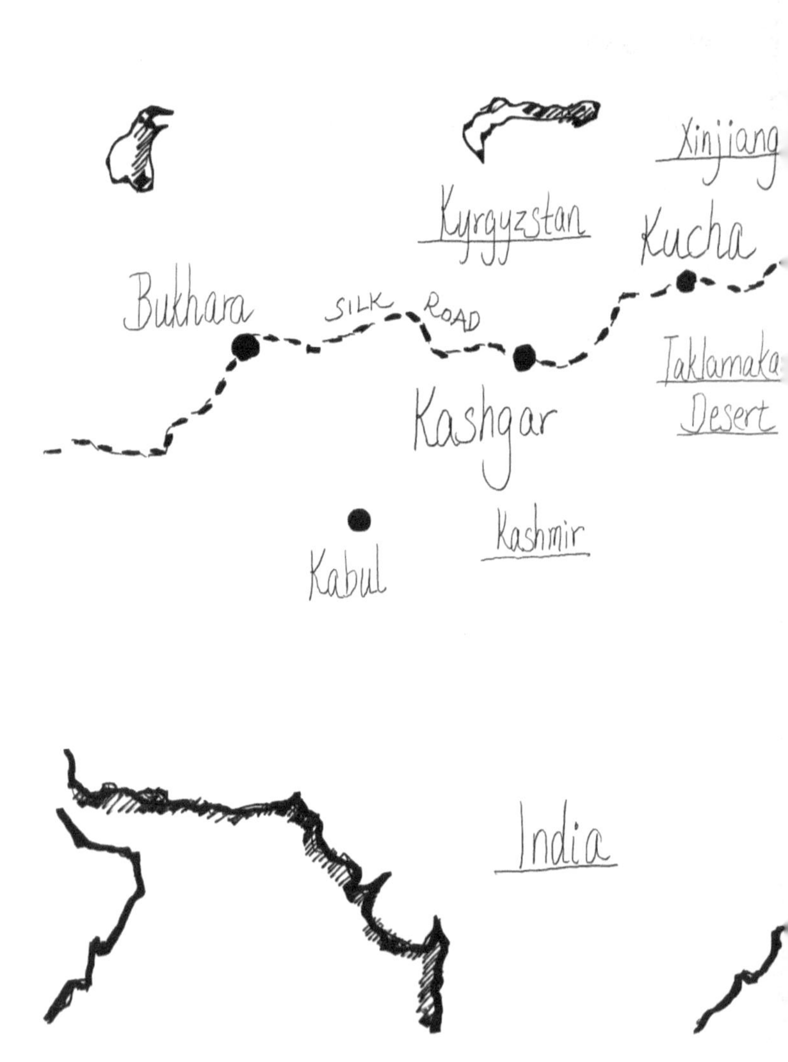

Xinjiang
Kyrgyzstan
Kucha
Bukhara
SILK ROAD
Taklamaka Desert
Kashgar
Kashmir
Kabul
India

Mongolia
Manchuria
Turpan
Beijing
Gobi Desert
GREAT WALL
Dunhuang
Central Plains
Xi'an
Shanghai
et
Hong Kong

PART ONE

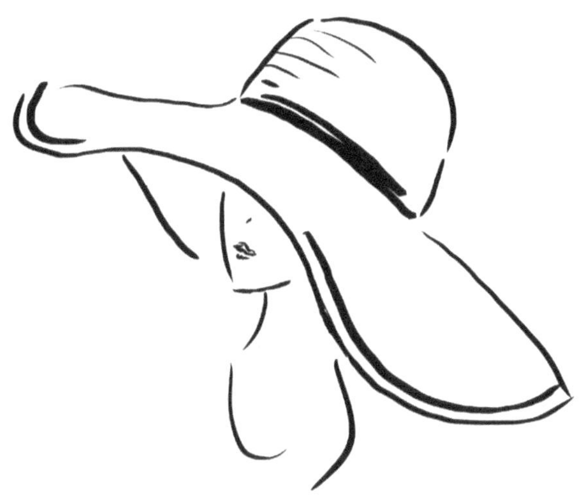

1

Three syllables… I repeat them under my breath. The first one… that is when I first saw her… The second… that is when we were alone… The third… that is when I left… There is no fourth. Her name… I repeat those three syllables under my breath…

You see, my soft-hearted reader, I have seen someone, just now, on Clapham Common. The warm summer sun is softly kissing the tender grass. The gentle breeze lovingly caresses the green leaves. And there is me, standing with my backpack on my shoulders, frozen… Then, there… there…

A girl. In the slight distance. The hem of her dress sways with each step she takes, lifted by the gentle breeze. The soft fabric of summer. The smell of grass and the warm sun. Yellow flowers in bloom. Her slender, honey-coated legs. The rim to the sides of her large straw hat droops down, as if to hide her from unwanted attention.

She looks briefly in my general direction. Thin nose. Slightly upturned upper lip. Arched eyebrows, as if she is intrigued by the world's business. She turns away and continues walking. Each step takes her further away from me, as the sun kisses her bronzed, bare flesh and the breeze touches her tender body through the thin fabric of her light blue dress. She leaves the lawn behind and walks under the shade of the majestic trees. She turns… Gone. Yet, there I stand, perfectly still, as if waiting. Waiting. Waiting. For what? I do not know.

Go. I hear my own voice. *Go. Let go…*

Where am I going? I do not know. Perhaps I will know, one day. Just not now. Now, all I know is how to repeat her name, in three syllables. All I know is that the present is empty and the future does not exist. All I know is the past… The past when I burned…

Looking back, maybe it was all a matter of fate, yet maybe fate is merely the recollection of all the crossroads a man has encountered. With each crossing, he takes a path of no return. Hindsight can hurt him or make him wise. Whichever way a boy chooses, he will become a man.

I know myself better now. Not that I have changed or perhaps become a different and better person, but I can see myself more clearly. I am perhaps even willing to accept who I am. I laugh at the person in the mirror; he is a pile of ashes, a hologram of a man. A hollow man. A man who has lost his heart, five thousand miles away, in the East...

Come. Come with me on this journey. This journey of change, of love, of consternation, of procrastination, passion, delirium, and of discovery... to my world, and another world...

2

"A journey of ten thousand miles begins with a single step," Confucius said. Yes, I have travelled more than ten thousand miles. My first step was taken in London's East End, in the late 1980s. I have no recollection of that toddler's step, instead my earliest memories were of good friends, jerk chickens, lamb curries… I spent a lot of time at Jameel's house. There was a picture hanging in the middle of the wall in his living room – a big black block surrounded by people dressed in white.

"It's in Mecca. It's a holy place." Jameel was knowledgeable. "If you walk in a straight line from here," he said, pointing to the corner of the room, "then you'll get there." I looked at the tens of thousands of people in the picture and this empty living room. I thought to myself, "Where did all the people start their journeys, if not from here?"

Jameel's next door neighbour also went to our primary school, a girl whose name was written somewhere on my collage of memories at some point, but has since disappeared. I can still recall that early evening having supper at Jameel's, when I saw her walking past the living room window, following her father who had an impressive beard. She was wearing a colourful dress, decorated with tiny mirrors and beads. To me, she looked like a princess from a mythical land. She turned and saw me looking at her. She smiled. I froze, then quickly turned to Jameel, "What's this we are eating?" Jameel said it was called Kashmiri lamb. That smile could have lit up all the valleys of Kashmir.

My paternal grandfather sometimes visited us. "What's your neighbour cooking this evening?" he would ask when he stepped into our flat, as the smell of our neighbour's cooking penetrated the walls. He would walk carefully, sometimes pausing to figure out where to land his feet in our cramped, rented flat, with my toys everywhere. Once he nearly fell over while trying to avoid stepping on my fire engine. His hand reached to the wall to steady himself, but alas, the wallpaper was loose and he ripped a large piece off. Later, I recognised our wallpaper on TV, in Del Boy and Rodney's flat.

All these fragments of memories were full of colour, as if they were sharp crystals in a kaleidoscope. When did my parents decide to move me out of my kaleidoscope to the Cotswolds countryside? Was it after the gun shot on my street? Was it after they heard me swearing like some of my schoolmates? By the way, Jameel never swore – he was a good kid. Was it when they took me to a friend of my dad's place in the countryside, where there was a fountain in front of their mansion, and I screamed, "Dad, dad, *coul'dai* go in *da wo'er*?"

Whatever the reason, we moved to the countryside, to a place where the land had been deserted by people. On summer nights, with my windows open, I would struggle to fall asleep, as the noise of the rustling leaves dwarfed the noise of London's traffic. The trickling stream down the garden deprived me of my sleep – it was a thousand times louder than our London neighbour's bass-heavy music. When I walked to the bus stop in the morning, the smell of cow dung hit me. It was so unbearably potent that I thought the happy people in the countryside had no sense of smell – otherwise, surely, they would have moved out a long time ago.

Sometimes I felt lonely, as I did not make new friends at school quickly. I could not say why that was. I used to think that perhaps if I walked from the corner of my house, I could reach Mecca and see Jameel on the way there. When I looked out of my bedroom window, gazing at the gentle valley down below, I used to reminisce about that girl's smile, which could have lit up all the valleys of Kashmir.

It seemed that I had moved to a different world, even though my new home was only a couple of hours' drive away from my old home. I missed my old home, my kaleidoscope of coloured crystals, which had disappeared, along with the whole world's car alarms, the half-eaten fried chickens on the pavements and my Cockney-accented swearing.

The Cotswolds was a mild and gentle place with its tender and harmonic colours, rolling hills and houses of pale stones. A tint of yellow, the fields of barley. A dash of red, the poppy flowers. An expanse of blue, the sky decorated with soft white clouds. All these reminded me of Werther's Originals, Cadbury's hot chocolate, plain roast chicken with gravy, boiled potatoes and Brussels sprouts.

3

Our move to the Cotswolds brought us closer to my grandparents, who had lived in the area for years. I often visited them in their grand house. Grandpa used to show me the photographs he had taken of distant lands; some featured people that looked like Jameel and the girl who lived next door to him. And there were others – some black as coal and bare-chested, some narrow-eyed and expressionless, some pale with monstrously large beards, others wrinkly-faced with feathers in their hair. He had a vast collection of odd things – a samurai sword on the desk in the study, a large sea turtle shell on the bathroom wall, a leather shield painted black and white in the corner of the living room, a blue and white plate on the mantelpiece, next to which stood a small statue of a red-faced Chinese warrior with a long beard.

I loved my grandfather's stories from different countries. Perhaps they inspired me, unconsciously preparing me for my own exotic adventures. He often sang to me, playing his ancient piano… *"In the Philippines, they had lovely screens… In the Malay states, there were hats like plates… In Hong Kong, they struck a gong and fired off a noonday gun…"* Sometimes, he looked sad as he told me stories or showed me photographs from his travels, but he never allowed himself to drown in sorrow. *Snap.* He would click his fingers and return to the land of joy, where I was waiting for him to tell me more about the people and places of the east, west, north and south – eating shark fins, using chopsticks, searching for white elephants, visiting the burning ghats and being enchanted by sight of the Taj Mahal under the moonlight…

My grandparents often visited us at the weekends, bringing random gifts. My mother would greet the aged with her usual broad smile, as if all this was part of some theatre production, "Ah, good morning! Which part of your attic have you cleared out for us today?"

One day, the aged turned up with that Chinese warrior statue for me. I quite liked it at first, but soon left it standing in the corner of an unmemorable room. However, somehow, I was always aware of its existence somewhere in the house.

While I became closer to my grandparents, I saw less of my dad. It was quite horrible at first, but I got used to it. Dad was a stage actor. There were not many stages in the countryside, so he had to go on tour a lot, leaving Mum, me, my two younger brothers and my little sister at home. As a nurse, Mum sometimes had to work nightshifts. I suppose I had to grow up quite quickly to help her look after my siblings. I always told them that I was the big guy, because I was born and raised in the tough East End. They did not know the East End. So, I showed them films, such as *Batman*, and when I was slightly older, *The Godfather*. This worked – that was until they grew old and wise enough to burst my bubble of pride with their own knowledge of Dot Branning, Phil and Peggy Mitchell of Albert Square.

4

I went to a comprehensive school in the local town, a few miles away from my village. I had just started secondary school. It was strange how similar the pupils looked at first. Despite having different coloured hair, almost everyone had the same complexion and the same shaped eyes. They shared the same accent too, mostly. Well, there were perhaps a couple of kids with darker complexions and another guy who I thought looked Chinese. The South Asian kids were not in my year, but the Chinese guy was. I was vaguely friends with him. The only lesson we shared was history.

I was quite good at geography and, to a certain extent, history too. Our geography teacher was quite surprised that I knew Kashmir was an actual place rather than simply a fabric spelt with a 'c'. He was also impressed when I talked in class about Mecca and the pilgrims. My classmates simply stared at me with blank faces, as if they weren't looking at me at all.

I was not particularly interested in British history. Things that had happened close to home somehow seemed less exciting than those that had happened in distant lands. Maybe I had my grandpa to thank for my desire to learn and fantasise about the far-flung corners of the world. The Chinese guy once gave a presentation on Chinese history. For the most part, I found it hard to follow the names of bygone dynasties and supposedly illustrious emperors. However, a few things were imprinted on my mind: the Forbidden City in Beijing, with its roofs of golden tiles, and the Great Wall that stretched from the eastern shores to the desert that marked the furthest point from the sea anywhere on Earth; the Silk Road on which camel trains travelled carrying silk and tea to the West, and brought back grapes, carrots, pomegranates, musicians and dancers from Central Asia, merchants and soldiers from the Middle East, Buddhists from India, Christians from Syria, Zoroastrians from Iran, and later Muslims from Arabia. Everything came to life as he showed us photos of China. What I found most fascinating was how the people in his photos looked. Those from the eastern parts of China looked more like him and those from the western parts looked more like Jameel or even me. Who were these people? All sorts, Wooo-something or another, Taj-something or another, Uzi-something or another.

I had a large world map on my bedroom wall. After the Chinese guy's presentation at school, I gazed at my map, imagining the Great Wall, which was over ten times longer than the distance between London and Edinburgh. Then there was the Silk Road. Shown as a dotted line, this stretched from Xi'an to Turpan, Kucha and Kashgar within the borders of today's People's Republic of China, and then onwards to Kabul, Bukhara, Isfahan, Baghdad, Damascus, Istanbul, Venice... Back to the east, I looked at the marker for Beijing and imagined the Forbidden City – the emperor's palace that covered an area greater than our local town. If I was the emperor, then the whole town would be my residence. I would not have to share a bedroom with my brother. There would be no queue for the shower. I would host a banquet with amazing dishes, including Kashmiri lamb cooked by Jameel's mum, and there would be dancers twirling round and round, dressed in beautiful clothes with little beads and mirrors sewn on... Dazzling. Simply dazzling... A kaleidoscope of wonders...

I daydreamed about all of this, as I sat at home gazing at my map, or standing at the bus stop waiting for the school bus in the rain, the smell of cow dung in my nostrils... Have I always been a dreamer? Perhaps. Otherwise, there would not be this book.

5

Once a year, my grandfather would organise a cricket match. It was always his family and friends against the people who lived in the same village as him. Not all members of my clan would turn up every time, as many of them were scattered in other Anglo-sphere countries, such as *Sauth Efrika* and *Straya*. The younger members of the spread-out clan enjoyed mocking each other's accents.

My grandfather travelled extensively with the Foreign and Commonwealth Office before he retired. He often invited old colleagues and acquaintances from far away to our annual game. I vividly remember an old turbaned man with a big, white beard who joined us one year. I thought he was the Indian Army's answer to Father Christmas. He was a devilishly fast bowler. I simply saw the ball coming, and before I could swing my willow, my fortress was destroyed in a flash to the cheers of the villagers, as well as my own teammates. More memorable than that though was one summer, a couple of weeks before the end of the school holidays. It was a warm cloudless day.

I was not in my clan's Eleven. However, I was occasionally called up for a bit of catching, throwing and batting. It all depended on how my team was performing and how my grandfather felt – as he decided which of his many little grandchildren should see a bit of action. However, most of the time, I was among the spectators, sitting in the pavilion.

A Land Rover pulled up and out jumped an old man, older than my grandfather. He wore a blue blazer, with brass buttons that caught the sunlight. He had a white moustache, which made him look like an old gunboat captain – far more fierce-looking than Captain Birdseye. A girl followed him with a large straw hat, pale blue dress, and legs that were slim and honey-coated. Honey-coated, like her bare shoulders and arms. Her hair was braided. Two plaits. One resting on each shoulder. Brunette.

They walked over to my grandfather, who was sitting at the other end of the pavilion. They exchanged pleasantries. After planting a kiss on the girl's cheek, my grandfather invited her grandfather to sit beside him, and she was set free.

It was the first time I had seen this girl. She did not speak to anyone as she strolled towards me, while playing with one of her plaits. As fate had it, all the seats were taken, apart from the one next to me. As she walked, the hem of her dress swayed with each step. A gentle breeze lifted the edge slightly. The soft fabric of summer. The smell of freshly cut grass and the warm sun. The flowers in bloom.

She looked at the players in their dashing cricket whites. The rim to the side of her large straw hat dropped down, as if to hide her from unwanted attention. Her face would only be revealed if she chose to face me.

She faced me. Slight freckles. Thin nose. Slightly upturned upper lip. Her eyebrows arched, as if she was intrigued by the world's business, puzzled by what the fuss was all about. She sat down next to me, turned towards me, gave me a smile, and then turned away. Her face was hidden by the rim of her hat again.

I gazed at her, or rather at the rim of her hat, wanting to penetrate it with my gaze. I must have looked like a fool, just transfixed like that. I heard no leather on willow, no cheers, just my heartbeat…

She lifted her left hand and bit her nails – blue painted nails, with evidence of habitual biting. With her every bite, my heart pounded faster and louder, until I felt there was thunder in my chest. I was worried that others might hear; that the world might hear; that she might hear.

I did not know how long this torment lasted, but it was interrupted when she suddenly jumped up, waved her arms and cheered her grandfather onto the pitch. Her grandfather gave her a resolute wave, as if he had already scored a victorious six. I rubbed my temples with one hand, my eyes fixed on her slim long legs as she jumped. My other hand fidgeted, fiddling with the edge of my T-shirt.

Then, suddenly, she sat down and I quickly diverted my attention to the game.

"Were you looking at me?" She suddenly turned to me, leaning in towards me, her plait almost brushing my shoulder. Her arched eyebrows suggested that her accusation was in jest.

But still, what was I to say? Yes? How would she take that? No? But, in all honesty, I was. And why would she ask me if she already knew that I was not looking at her?

She laughed slightly, noticing my anxiety. "Don't worry." She gave my thigh a gentle slap, "Let's get something to drink. I'm thirsty. Aren't you?"

Yes, of course I was. So thirsty, so anything, so... whatever she said I was!

She jumped up. The edge of her dress took a slight flight due to her sudden movement and the timely breeze. She tossed her plaits back, nearly slapping me in the face, as I followed her closely.

"Orange squash please," she commanded, putting her hat down on the bar.

"The same please," I said, softly.

She took the straw to her mouth and sucked the glass dry in one go.

"One more please." She slammed the glass down.

She did not rush her second drink, and we did not rush back to the pavilion.

Her name was Isabel. My name was George. Her grandfather was an ex-colonial officer in Hong Kong. Mine too. Her father was a banker, first in Hong Kong, then in London. My father was an actor.

"An actor?!" she screamed. "Which films has he been in?"

"None."

Disappointment.

I explained that he was a stage actor. She was not paying me any attention at this point, as she put her index finger on one end of the straw and held it there, while lifting the straw up above her head. She tilted her head back as far as she could and opened her mouth, aiming the end of the straw into her wide-open mouth. Her index finger let go. Drip...

She went to a school in Exeter, very far from here. It was a very old school, quite creepy in parts and the hall was always cold. She boarded there, and had some really good friends, who shared many of her interests, such as swimming, horse-riding, tennis... The previous winter, they had gone skiing in Switzerland. She asked me whether I had ever been skiing.

"Oh, our school organised a ski trip too," I answered, "to France, by coach. In fact, even if the school trip was to Mongolia, it would have been by coach as well." I thought I was being quite humorous. But if she did think I was funny, she hid it pretty well. Her silence meant that I did not have to explain I had given the school trip a miss. I did not think it was worth my parents' hard-earned money for me to go up a hill only to slide back down again.

There was a long moment of freezing silence. Well, perhaps in reality it lasted only a second or two. "Oh, all right," she uttered, then suddenly flicked her straw at me. "Bull's eye!" She giggled.

We chatted, while she continued to invent new games with her straw – standing it on her finger, the back of her hand and on her upper lip while watching it with her eyes crossed, keeping it balanced... What did we talk about? This and that. Kids' talk, perhaps. I have no recollection of our conversation. All I can remember was her lips moving, like a little flower in the summer's breeze – opening, closing, drinking the fresh dew of the morning. Moist.

Her glass was empty. I emptied mine. She put her hat back on. We went back to the pavilion. Our chat continued there. Every now and then, she turned to me, permitting me to adore her face, which she revealed between the dropped corners of her hat. She bit her nails every now and then, and played with her plaits. The soft ends of her hair brushed against her skin. I wished they were brushing against me, painting a picture of fantasy...

The game ended. A draw, just like last year and the year before. I wondered if anyone bothered keeping the scores at all once the tea had been replaced by alcohol, with plenty being supplied by a brewery from Hook Norton, a neighbouring village.

Then, her grandfather stood up from his seat in the pavilion. When did he stop playing? I had not noticed, but his rising from his chair meant only one thing. Oh, no… Never mind.

We said goodbye, and that we would meet again. She was fourteen. I was twelve. And a half.

6

Before we parted, Isabel gave me her e-mail address and said it would be fun to write to each other. Pleasantly surprised, I was only too eager to agree.

Given that the ball was in my court, I had to play the first serve. But I just sat there in front of my computer that very night after everyone had gone home. I could not bring my hands to the keyboard for the fear of a return volley that was so strong I would not possibly be able to return it. No, actually, what I feared was there being no return volley at all. What would I do then? Serve again? Or just admit my defeat of fifteen love. Fifteen to me, but my defeat nevertheless. The shame. The agony. Love? A joke.

So, I stood up and did not serve at all that night, nor for a few nights thereafter. Two weeks later, two weeks of anxiety and nerves, I finally plucked up the courage to face the computer – so what if my serve would not be returned at all? No serve, no game.

"Dear Isabel…"

No. Backspace, backspace…

"Hi Isabel…"

No. Backspace, backspace…

"Hi…"

No. Backspace, backspace…

"Dear Isabel. It was wonderful…"

No. Backspace, backspace…

"It was good…"

No. Backspace, backspace…

"It was really nice to have met you that day at the cricket. I hope you enjoyed your time with us. I'm sorry if I seemed a bit quiet – it's just that before you arrived, I played quite hard…"

What bullshit! But how else could I explain my awkwardness? No. Backspace, backspace…

Just like that, I spent most of that evening fighting with myself, wrestling with words. In the end, as the clock ticked towards midnight, and my mum nagged me to go to bed, my half-baked e-mail was sent.

"To hell with this." I said to myself, "Whatever it is, it is… So be it…"

The next day was my first day back at school. I quickly checked my e-mails in the morning. Nothing.

First lesson, maths… Did I write too much? Too little?

Second lesson, English… Were there any grammatical mistakes? Was it well-written? Not enough of a 'come on'? Too plain? Too uninviting? Too nervously composed? Would she see straight through it all, as someone who's older than me? Would she laugh?

Third lesson, history… Perhaps I had written too soon? Or not soon enough? Perhaps she was just being nice when she gave me her e-mail address?

Science… Was that her little experiment? To see if this idiot would write to her?

I came home. E-mail. None.

So, my days went by… One… Two… Three… Nothing… Nothing… Nothing…

Then, finally, her e-mail came!

"Hi! It was wonderful to have met you too. Shame that I didn't see you scoring your six – I'm sure it was an amazing strike…"

Okay, okay, so I did lie about my cricketing skills – adding five to the only one ordinary run I scored in that game. Lying or not, just like that, Isabel and I became pen friends. We did not write to each other every day, as much as I wanted to. Following some unsaid protocol, I held myself back from replying to her immediately, and waited for as many days as it had taken her to reply to me previously.

We wrote about all sorts of things – school, family, friends, music, sports… It seemed that even though we were not the same age and went to different schools in different areas, we were not a completely different species after all. I set up a special folder for her e-mails, and wondered if she had done the same for mine.

7

I cannot say whether I felt the time had gone by quickly or slowly. Yes, when I waited for her e-mails, time seemed to have stood still. However, each time I read our exchanges and re-read them, time flew by. Soon, it was the summer holidays again. Isabel came to stay with her grandfather, a few miles away from me.

She called me on my landline, using the 01608 local code. This was at a time before mobile phones were widely available. I was excited when my mother handed me the receiver. I could hear my heartbeat.

"Hello Isabel."

"Hi George. It's a nice day. Do you want to meet up?"

"Of course!"

"I'll come over, all right?"

"Of course!"

"Maybe you can meet me halfway?"

"Of course!"

"I'm setting off now."

"Of course! See you halfway, I'm heading off now."

My love for her got the better of my vocabulary. I hastily put my trekking sandals on and ran out of the front door. "Take some water with you, George!" my mother shouted behind me. I had no time to turn back for water.

A single winding road of four country miles, over rolling hills, linked my house with Isabel's grandfather's house. I was never a runner, but I found my energy and endurance this time. The sapphire sky was above me, with the sun glowing joyfully. The cotton-like clouds shaded me every now and then. I gazed into the distance, to the golden fields of wheat and barley, as birds flew up into the sky, chirping away. My heart sang with them.

Alas, I gradually found my legs were unable to cope, and I had to slow down. I sweated and puffed, out of breath. I knew I had covered more than two miles. There was no sign of Isabel, so I decided to walk at a reasonable pace and cool down.

I carried on, all the time thinking that I would see her distant figure after the next bend, or that her silhouette would suddenly appear on the horizon, but there was still no sign of her. I carried on. My mouth was dry, my throat burning. If only I had listened to my mother.

The midday sun was beating down mercilessly, while the sound of my grandfather singing *Mad Dogs And Englishmen* echoed in my head. This mad dog was exhausted and each step became a struggle. I felt like sticking my tongue out to see if this dog's habit would work for humans as well when it came to cooling down. Finally, I threw myself on the grass by the side of the road, and put my arms over my face to provide me with a bit of shade from the sun. I listened to the birdsong with my eyes closed. I was not far from Isabel's now, maybe just a mile or so. "Get up. Get up," I said to myself. "Isabel won't want to see you as a loser, George. Get up!" My mind screamed at my body, but it refused to listen and went on strike…

"Get up George." I heard Isabel's beautiful voice and my body sprang up. My eyes had been closed for so long, it was difficult to open them at first because of the strong sunlight. However, I managed to squint open my eyes and saw her beautiful smile. I smiled, rubbed my eyes and was full of energy again.

We walked back to my house. Isabel wore a short white dress and the same large straw hat that she had worn when I first saw her. As we walked, the hem of her dress swayed with her each step, although I tried not to look down. It did not matter, in reality, as the drooping edge of her hat meant she had no idea where I was looking. I had no idea where she was looking either. She turned to me occasionally, and each time I saw her face, my heart skipped a beat.

"What have you been up to at school?" I asked her.

"Not much… Oh, we invented a game."

"What sort?"

"Hangman."

"That's not a new game you invented." I was thinking about the word-guessing game.

"Not that sort, you geek. It's for real," Isabel said dismissively. Then she explained how her version of the game involved tying a bedsheet around a girl's neck until she couldn't take the suffocation anymore, then you released her after a second or two. It gave everyone a massive high.

I felt a lump in my throat, and fell quiet. Isabel did not say anything either for a while, then she laughed at me. "You'll understand one day, George… maybe." I was not sure whether I wanted to. I had no desire to dance with death like that. Was I a coward?

After we arrived at my house, and my mother had exchanged some pleasantries with Isabel, we went to my room. My brothers and sister were all at my grandparents', and my father was touring again. Mother was cooking downstairs. She loved spending time in the kitchen.

"What should we do now?" Isabel asked. She threw her hat on the bed, then let her beautiful long brown hair loose. She was like an angel, who had just landed on Earth from the heavens; an angel who wanted to break free from the gods and experience life with common mortals.

"Let's play a game," I said. Then quickly added, "Not your hangman game, please, but an acting game."

"Oh?" said Isabel, intrigued.

So, I explained to her how my game worked. We would agree a scene and a set of characters, then act it out. There was no script beforehand and you just developed the characters and stories as you went along. You could base it on some known work of fiction or invent new stories entirely.

"Okay," Isabel smiled, "you suggest one."

I looked around and put my mind to work. "What is Dad doing now? Which play? Oh yes!" I thought.

"Romeo and Juliet!" I suggested.

"Ugh!" Isabel clearly did not like that, "we are studying that at school. No way!"

"Sorry…" I tried to think of an alternative romance. Of course, it had to be a romantic story! "Captain Smith and Pocahontas!"

"Sure!"

I breathed a sigh of relief.

So, we played it out, creating our own version. The captain's ship capsized and he was washed ashore. He was dying. The native girl saw him and wanted to save him, and so she dragged him into her tent. She fed him bread and gave him water. And he was so thankful. He fell in love with her, and she fell in love with him. They were about to kiss…

"Supper is ready," my mother said, knocking on my door.

The end.

8

Isabel and I never picked up the remainder of our Captain Smith and Pocahontas play. I was thirteen and a half and she was fifteen by then. In retrospect, maybe I was terribly lucky that a maturing teenager had entertained me as she did. We met again a few times that summer, during her stay at her grandfather's. We saw each other again over Christmas, then the next summer. I can remember it all, but I will not bore you, my eager reader, with all the details. Suffice to say that whatever happened between us was all trivial kids' play. However, I will never forget the summer three years after our first meeting. I was, fifteen and… okay, let's say sixteen, and she seventeen.

An uncle of mine had a house in Snowdonia. It was filled with my clans people during the school holidays, but was otherwise empty. The local farmer kept an eye on it. He and his wife, and the railway stationmaster, were the only permanent residents for miles around. The station was only used every now and then by trekkers.

My uncle arranged for a few other uncles and cousins to stay at the house for a couple of weeks over the summer holiday, for some hill climbing and bog walking. The lists of stuff to bring were distributed to the visitors to ensure there would be enough food and drink to last the entire stay.

I was looking forward to this trip, as I had always enjoyed family gatherings. It was all planned for mid-August.

In mid-July, I received a phone call. It was Isabel. She asked me if I would like to go on holiday in a couple of weeks' time with her and her grandfather.

"Yes, of course," I felt my heart racing, "Where to?"

"Madeira."

After the phone call, I dashed to my map and found that little green dot off the sandy northwest coast of Africa.

Why me on this holiday? I pondered. Just me, Isabel and her grandfather. Was this her invitation for something more serious? After all, we had been friends for quite a while now.

Perhaps she just wanted company. She was her grandfather's only grandchild, and so there were no cousins. Perhaps she was not allowed to take any of her school friends on this holiday. Perhaps her grandfather did not like any of them, but he liked me, which would be a welcoming endorsement. Perhaps it was an invitation from her grandfather, rather than from her. Perhaps... perhaps...

That night, I tossed and turned in bed, imagining all sorts of scenarios – some happy, some sad – as if I was about to go into a negotiation room over some multi-billion-pound deal, or a diplomatic wrestle over the fate of millions of people... The responsibility over billions of pounds and millions of people crushed down on me. I suffocated in bed on that hot summer's night, tortured by the continuous trickling of the stream outside my window.

9

After he retired, Isabel's grandfather continued to travel all over the world, as if he had not been to enough places during his time with Her Majesty's diplomatic and colonial service. Eventually, however, the Andes and Himalayas became too challenging and long-haul flights to Pacific islands wore him out. So, he bought a little cottage by the sea in the fishing village of Camara de Lobos on the south coast of Madeira, where Winston Churchill used to have lunch and paint his watercolours. Hills rose steeply from the shore, behind the village. To the east, several miles away, was the old capital of Funchal, which was the only clearing in the forest when the Portuguese first arrived at the beginning of the fifteenth century. The Portuguese arrived here en masse when there was a war against Spain, to populate this island safely tucked away from the European mainland, and grow crops for the war...

Sitting on the plane between Isabel and me, the old man went on and on, informing us of various Madeira facts – its history, vegetation, industry and birds. Some of his words went in, but most of them simply went in through one ear and out of the other, as I imagined the forthcoming courtship wrestles, and strategised how I could turn this holiday into the ultimate victory: making Isabel my girlfriend.

Isabel openly showed her lack of interest in his monologue, as she page-turned her gossip magazine and played with her plaits, the ends of which occasionally brushed against her cheeks, gently tickling my fantasy...

10

The holiday cottage was painted white on the outside. Inside, there was some rattan furniture. It was south-facing, with half-closed shutters to keep out the midday sun. This was typical of the Mediterranean style and so different from our Cotswolds living room, which was centred around the fireplace. I looked around in excitement and saw little boats anchored in the harbour. "What are they for?" I pointed to the distance.

"They are for scabbard fishing," the old man informed me, then added, "I'm a little tired, so I'll have a nap. You two can go to the beach."

"Let's go for a swim!" Isabel was excited.

Of course. I quickly changed into my swimming trunks and stood in the hallway, waiting for her. I opened the shutters a little bit and let the sun in. It was raining when we left England, so I fancied a bit of Mediterranean sun. I pulled the windows open too and enjoyed the gentle breeze, the smell of the sea, the rhythmic sound of the waves and the sight of the white foam, as the blue waves pushed and caressed each other gently.

Her door opened. Her large straw hat, which I had first seen at that cricket game, rested on her head. Two plaits, one on each shoulder. The straps of her bikini top were tied behind her neck. Her body was wrapped in a loose-fitting, yellow, slip-on dress, which ended halfway down her thighs. As the sun came through the widows, her dress became semi-transparent and I saw a hint of blue underneath the light fabric.

"Do I look okay?" She gave a twirl.

"Yes..." I picked my jaw up off the floor, metaphorically. "Of course... Lovely." I tried to hold back from any overt demonstration of adoration. I must play it cool, or so I told myself.

She giggled, as if having seen straight through me. So uncool.

"Come on, let's go," she commanded.

"Are we not taking a towel?" she said as we walked out of the door.

I rushed to the bathroom and grabbed one – as quickly as I could, so as not to waste a single second. I only had one week to secure her true feelings for me.

We flip-flopped along the promenade – me with that towel over my bare shoulders, and she under her straw hat. The sea was in clear view to our right. In the distance, I could see a few boats floating. They were so far away from the shore they looked almost stationary. They were, perhaps, stationary, waiting for enough fish to swim into their nets. Then, in one big pull, all sorts of fantastic creatures would be caught. Delicious. But until that moment arrived, they would just have to wait, under the midday sun, hallucinating over the thoughts of black scabbard, blue marlin, blue fin tuna, swordfish… ouch! Blue shark!

She walked to my left, her face hidden by the dropped rim of her large straw hat, only permitting me to adore it when she chose to face me. And that was quite rare as she faced straight ahead, hardly ever looking at me. Perhaps the cliffs in the distance provided a more intriguing view than my face, which was becoming over familiar to her.

To our left, the hills were covered in green. A few terracotta-roofed and white-walled houses decorated that jade blanket. The hilltops were hidden in the clouds. What was up there? How could I tell? As much as I wanted to know, there was little I could see from the shore. I could not blow away the clouds to reveal it all. Perhaps I just had to wait, for that moment of revelation to arrive, and for nature to take its course. Just wait…

We walked for miles at a leisurely pace, first on the promenade, then on the black beach of volcanic ash – the remnants of the particles that had been propelled to the surface of the Earth from the boiling core, the evidence of bygone rapturous relief.

We came across a small patch of pebbled beach in front of a hotel. There were a few swimmers and sunbathers, but overall, it was quiet. A few tanned figures rested on a floating platform, perhaps big enough for a dozen or so people to sit on comfortably. A chink of light reflected off a wet, bronzed shoulder.

"Let's rest here," Isabel said.

We slipped off our flip-flops. She took off her straw hat and tossed it on the pebble beach. I put the towel down, covering a corner of her abandoned hat, so that it would not get blown away. She looked at me and giggled, slipping out of her yellow dress in an instant, revealing her blue bikini. Her seventeen-year-old body was in bloom. The silhouette of her curves kissed by the Atlantic sun, and the smooth lines summarised her maturing figure – running from her pointy chin, down to her delicate neck, pronounced breasts, toned stomach and the profile of her long legs of silk and honey… I had to divert my attention from it all, to avoid any embarrassment.

"See who gets to the platform first!" she screamed and ran towards the waves.

Ouch, ouch, ouch! My feet hurt as I tried to catch up with her. It seemed that the pebbles did not bother her at all, as she raced ahead, and threw herself into the foamy sea. She swam. Front crawl.

By the time I awkwardly started my slow breaststroke, the only style I knew, she had already made it halfway to the platform. I tried hard to catch up with her, but the more I tried, the slower I seemed to go, as wave after wave tried to push me back to the shore, away from her.

She was treading water while pressing the hard plastic platform down with her hands. Then in a perfect jump, she lifted her body up onto the platform. She made herself comfortable and lay on her stomach, her legs casually dangling into the water. Her bottom faced me directly, covered only slightly by her narrow bikini bottoms. Sparkles reflected off the drips of water on her wet bottom and her thighs. I nearly sank to the bottom of the sea!

I struggled on, heart pounding like mad. The waves only got stronger. Were the waves being made larger by my increased heartbeat? She turned and sat up. She smiled, sitting on the edge of the white platform, with the sapphire sky behind her.

"Hey, come on!" She waved, one arm in the air, shaking her blossoming breasts under that blue fabric as she did so.

Finally, I made it. I was less than a proficient swimmer to put it lightly. Exhausted, I failed to get myself onto the platform on my first attempt.

"Come on!" She pulled me up.

My face burned with embarrassment.

She giggled, "Thank you for letting me win!"

Was that really what she thought? Was she saving me from the embarrassment of my deficiency? Was she mocking me?

We lay down. The warm sun caressed our teenage bodies.

"Hey! You from England?" A voice came from behind us. It belonged to a young man who was one of the original inhabitants of this platform.

"Yes, you?" She turned to face him, flipping onto her front, her pert bottom now in the air. I turned too, to see who the devil was disturbing my time with her.

The young man was deeply tanned, with a six-pack clearly showing despite his sitting position. He looked like one of those statues that aspiring students of classical art would sketch in a Greco-Roman museum. He had jet-black hair, slicked back by the seawater.

Me? I was not nearly as statuesque. Skinny. Pale. Curly brown hair. Large ears...

"I'm from Funchal," he smiled, lifting one corner of his mouth. "You staying in the hotel?"

"Your English is perfect," Isabel praised. (Well? Mine was even better!) "No, we're staying in Camara de Lobos. In my grandfather's cottage."

"Oh yeah? Good..." He looked at me through the corner of his eye, as if I was some fruit fly that should have flown off as soon as he'd started speaking to Isabel. "Hello," he said coldly. He was so fake. Did he think that just by saying hello to me, he could obtain a free licence to chat up Isabel? His eyes were all over her. It was disgusting. What should I do?

He turned to speak to his three male friends, all in their late teens perhaps. They giggled and laughed. I did not understand Portuguese, but I knew they were making fun of me, while perving on Isabel, as they turned to look at us occasionally through the corners of their eyes.

"Let's go," I murmured to Isabel.

"Hey! Don't go. Haha. Relax," the young man said to Isabel in his *yap-yap yalla-yalla yuk-yuk quack-quack* accent. Then he turned to me, "You go. You go…" That sick, slick, self-styled lothario casually pointed to the shore.

I jumped up and in one charge pushed him into the sea. I grabbed his hair and tried to push him down. However, the fish slipped away.

Suddenly, I felt his hands around my waist and then, in one stroke, he managed to untie the loose knot of my swimming trunks and took them off me. I tried to grab my trunks, but it was too late. He disappeared.

Splash. He emerged from the other side of the platform. Waving to me, tossing my trunks in the air, like some war trophy, and laughing wildly. His friends joined him, laughing at me.

I felt like either sinking him or myself to the bottom of the sea. Isabel looked at him, then at me. There could not have been a greater contrast – one tanned winner, one pale loser. She gave me a wink and smiled, looking at my bare bottom in the clear sea. I wanted to dive to the bottom of the sea, find some gap between the pebbles, and crawl in and stay there forever.

He swam back to me, that slimy eel, dangling my trunks in front of me. I tried to grab them, but he slipped away. I tried again. He slipped away again, laughing all along, as if it was a game of bear baiting.

After a while, the clumsy bear got tired. Isabel noticed it. "Okay, game over," she said to the baiter.

"Ah?" he winked at her, "for that, you have to kiss me!"

That is it! You rogue!

I did not know from where I found the strength and the swimming skills, but I quickly swam over to him, grabbed his hair and threw a punch at his jaw, as hard as I could.

In shock, he let go of my swimming trunks and I grabbed them.

"Okay, okay… my loverboy hero." He did not want to fight. "Calm down." He gave his friends, who were probably ready to sink me to the bottom of the sea, a little wave. His friends all jumped off the platform, laughing at me.

"Bye beautiful!" they chanted to Isabel.

"Bye loser!" they chanted to me.

I put my trunks on and got onto the platform. They swam away. I did not say anything to Isabel. I looked down at the waves, feeling my cheeks burning with shame.

Then, I felt a kiss on my cheek.

I turned to face Isabel, as if I had just got an electric shock. She smiled and then said, mimicking that rogue's accent, "My loverboy hero." She smiled and put her arm around my shoulders and shook me a little, planting another kiss on my cheek.

She was mocking me. She thought I was a fool. She would not accept me as her boyfriend… With those thoughts, I shook her off. I jumped into the sea and headed to the shore.

This was the end – my disastrous defeat on Day One of the holiday. If I had been an actor, the curtain was being drawn even before the completion of Act One Scene One, to protect me from the rotten tomatoes that were flying from the auditorium, ending this show, ending my career…

"Hey!" She followed me and quickly caught up. "Don't be like that. I was only teasing you! It was very brave of you to take him on like that – he was a lot older than you and there were four of them."

My shame was burning like fire, but her words instantly extinguished the flames. As for me being a stage actor, perhaps a heavyweight critic had spoken in favour of me amid the jeers. It was the audience who were the fools in misunderstanding the genius of this actor. The show would go on.

She smiled. I smiled. We swam towards the shore at my pace.

"I hated the way he had his eyes all over you," I muttered.

"Are you the jealous type?"

"I wouldn't say that. I just care…"

"Thank you for caring."

"Did you not care about the way he had his eyes all over you? Then speaking to you like that?"

"Umm… I didn't think much about it."

Didn't think much about it? Think? You didn't have to think! Just notice! Did she notice it at all? Why didn't she take offence? Don't tell me she enjoyed it! No, she didn't enjoy that sort of lewd behaviour. She simply did not notice it. She was unconscious of her own beauty. "Yes, that's right," I thought to myself, as we walked up the shore.

11

When we got back to the cottage, it was dinner time. We were both quite tired after our long walk back, during which my mental wrestling over the significance of everything that had happened had worn me out further. She made no mention of it, or anything else related to us. She just spoke of this and that, such as the stuff she had read in gossip magazines about dozens of celebrities I had never heard of, but obviously were of marked significance to her.

We went to a small restaurant. Black scabbard fish with bananas, a stew of clams and shrimps, a giant skewer of local beef... Isabel's grandpa ordered a bottle of wine and allowed us a sip each.

I thanked him for the generous order, then struggled to find something to say to him. Not wanting to be embarrassed by the silence, I asked him if he had eaten a lot of seafood when he was stationed in Hong Kong.

"Oh, yes, lots. Sometimes in the local style," he stated while stabbing at his fish. "It was usually okay. I went to the night markets on the odd occasion, mostly to satisfy the curiosity of visitors under my care... gosh, the stink!" His entire faced twisted into an expression of stupefying disgust. He then went on to explain how everything seemed to be so interesting to him at first, but things had started to bore and irritate him after a few months, and yet he was unable to secure a transfer to another place. My question prompted a long monologue from him. I listened at first, but my mind started to travel elsewhere.

I remembered talking to my grandfather about his time in Hong Kong. He too had mentioned the smell of the sea creatures at the markets. As he enthusiastically described crabs and fish of all shapes and sizes, his face lit up with excitement.

Through my grandfather's tales, I had constructed a picture of Hong Kong in my mind – busy streets, heavy downpours, shirt-drenching humidity, plus some grumpy officers who resented every minute they had to toil in this far-flung corner of the empire, but whose laughter echoed in the clubs where they sipped cold cocktails.

As Isabel's grandfather grumbled, I felt it was as if the empire was built on the suffering of people like him. How pitiful these officers were, so far away from their loved ones, enduring the heat and the subjects who sometimes became unruly.

"Ah, yes, it was 1967…" he recalled, "the workers took to the streets… the students as well. Oh my… so many of them…. It was quite frightful… But you must be tough… I told my men… They were trying to kick us out, you know… It was all those Leftists… Nasty sympathisers of Red China… Of course, most Hong Kong people loved us British… It was only a handful of anti-social elements… Oh yes, things got nasty… riots started, bombs went off, people got killed… Sometimes, even I thought this was the end… But I had to be there for the British Crown and the Free World…"

"The Free World?" I did not know what that meant.

"The Free World…" The old man answered, taking a rest from his battle with the fish, "ah, that's us. We represented the Free World, the democratic world…" He mumbled along, almost to himself, as he carried on eating, not looking at anyone while he talked. "Who was unfree? The Chinese, of course! No, no, not the Chinese in Hong Kong, young man – they were part of the Free World. I meant the Chinese in China," the ex-colonial officer explained, although perhaps the wine was affecting his sense of clarity.

"But at the end, we had to leave. I still can't quite believe it… Thatcher was meant to be the Iron Lady… Tut tut… Sold the empire… Then Chris Patten came, having lost his seat in Parliament… Yes, democracy was to be introduced… Yes, it was after Thatcher had agreed to surrender Hong Kong… Yes…" he mumbled along.

"Were you sad when you left?" I asked him.

"Sad? I suppose yes, but actually… no… I mean one can't help feeling attached to a place where you have spent so many years of your life… At the same time, it was not home, although the Yacht Club was pleasant… Sad, yes, very sad for those pitiful sods who had grown accustomed to their lives over there, getting married there, having children there, and getting bogged down there, now living under the red flag! Those Communists had it lucky, very lucky… Oh, and there was no need to hand over Hong Kong as the island was not leased… But off it went…"

While I tried to follow his mumbles, Isabel did not seem to listen at all. She looked at the sea, the hills and the setting sun. She played with her plaits, bit her nails and then played with her leftover food. She put her mouth to the straw in her Coke and sucked, making a cross-eyed funny face at me. It nearly made me laugh. I responded by a pulling a cross-eyed face too. Her grandfather was busy eating, drinking and moaning all at the same time, and so he did not notice our kids' play. A few more faces were pulled before her grandfather picked up his serviette and started to wipe his mouth, ending his mumble about the decline and fall of the empire.

After dinner, we strolled to the harbour. To the west, the sun was setting, a glow of red lavishly poured over the waves.

The old man took a deep breath. "So fresh," he remarked, "Didn't get this sense of freshness in Hong Kong – too many people running around." Perhaps he was depicting some ants busy moving home before the rain. I wondered if he had always felt he was the only creature that was not an ant in that part of the world, or any part of the world.

We reached an open-air bar and had a drink by the sea.

"How's your father doing these days?" the old man enquired. He was having a poncha – a strong liquor mixed with some yellow juice.

"Quite okay, thank you," I replied. "He's touring at the moment."

"When your grandfather told me his son wanted to become an actor, the old fruit looked a bit worried. Just a little bit," he recalled, "I suggested that the kid should be locked up for a few days to cool his head!" The ends of his thick moustache danced with laughter. Then he continued, "But your grandfather was soft at heart. Maybe it's because, unlike me, he had never been an officer in the navy. The Senior Service taught me many things." He was proud of his career path. The fading of the Imperial Pink on the map of the Empire probably challenged his own sense of self-worth; hence his increasing need to sound all important and all correct. After all, how significant could someone be if he was merely an officer on a small island, tucked away in the northwest corner of Eurasia?

"I don't think my grandfather was excited about my dad wanting to be an actor," I reassured him, "but he let his son get on with things," I added, recalling what my dad had told me.

"Yes, he did come to accept it, and his ongoing need to subsidise his son." Of course, Isabel's grandfather was always right.

A little bit later, the old man told us he was going back home to read a little, then go to bed. Oh, finally…

"We'd like to stay out a bit longer," Isabel spoke promptly and on my behalf too. Yes, to stay out a bit longer, a lot longer – forever – was just what I had wanted too.

12

We left the bar and wandered along the seafront. Darkness stretched from the black volcanic beach up to the sea, the sky and the hills. Yet, there were decorations too – twinkles of light from the boats, lamp posts, people's homes on the hills, and the crowds of stars in the sky.

The moon was so thin, a beautiful curve, glowing above the sea. It was freshly carved, just for us. Our moon. The beach had emptied for us, just us. I could hear nothing but the waves gently hitting the shore and each other.

I felt her hand on my arm, warm and soft. I wondered if she could feel my pulse racing.

Night was the time for dreaming. Being a teenager, I had many dreams. Life was full of them. It felt as if anything could happen – so much lay ahead.

"What do you want to be?" I asked her.

"Don't know," she shrugged.

"Oh?" I was surprised that she had not been inspired while sitting in the grand old hall of her boarding school, skiing down the Swiss Alps or horse riding in the Cotswolds.

"Are you surprised?" She looked at me.

"Well…" What should I say?

"Maybe one day I'll figure it out." She did not wait for my response, and looked away at the boundless ocean.

We sat down on a big rock – large enough to stop the waves from splattering us, and smooth and flat enough to easily sit or lie on, secluded enough from the street view by tall rocks and the dense coastal vegetation of the summer. It was like a private pavilion, with the star-studded sky being the roof.

"Maybe I don't want to be anything – just enjoy life," she continued, "You? What do you want to be?"

"I want to be a writer."

"Oh? What would you write about?"

"You and me..."

"That's sweet of you." She put her hand on my hand that was resting on my knee, "So, how would the story start?"

"As it has already started..."

"Then? How would the story end?"

"It'd never end..." From where did I get those cheesy words? Perhaps there was a lothario lying in wait underneath my awkwardness, who had been sleeping and in hiding for most of the time, waiting to leap out at the right moment, maybe to create the wrong effect...

"Haha. A story that'd never end? Sounds like... a long bore to me."

Oh dear... indeed, the wrong effect. "It wouldn't be boring." I tried to recover my poise. "It would be great, if we made it interesting."

"How so?"

I did not know. What could I do to unfold the story? I felt I was running out of tricks. I felt it was her turn now. What would she do? Did she have an end in mind so that she could unfurl the story towards it?

I stayed silent. Perhaps it was awkward that we were two writers pondering over the fate of the same two characters. The waves and crickets provided a welcome distraction from this otherwise painful silence.

Her hand moved, from my hand, to my arm, to my shoulder, to the back of my head. She pulled me towards her...

Her lips moist, warm.

My heart, pounding, racing.

Her hands, soft, exploring.

My hands, nervous, returning her touches...

The waves. The rocks. Rhythmic. Rocking...

One. Two. Three. Four...

Soft. Gentle. Tender. Beautiful.

The sea grew stronger, as if it had been held back all this time, waiting for its freedom to crash over the volcanic ashes and rocks that had been blasted out from the centre of the Earth millions of years ago in a moment of joyful liberation… The wind picked up. The waves grew stronger, hitting the rocks. Then, a strong wave came. Splash. The white foam splattered over us. We were all wet…

We rested on that rock as the sea became calmer and more subdued. The crickets serenaded us under a blanket of stars…

13

Our week in Madeira flew by all too quickly.

I then joined my cousins and uncles in the Welsh hills, but my mind was still in Madeira. Isabel was like a mighty invading army, crushing all the freedom I had for other thoughts.

Had *it* meant anything to her? Had *that* just been for fun?

I had no interest in walking across the bogland to reach the rocky hills or climbing to the top for the view of the green valley down below. I did not participate in card games in the evenings. Nothing was more boring than charades. My uncles asked if I was ill. My cousins probably did not think much about me, as they were happy enough messing about with each other.

One night, I walked out of the house, when everyone had gone to bed.

It was a cool evening. There were no fishing boats in the distance. No lights from houses in the hills. The moonlight illuminated over the valley, almost like a floodlight in the sky. I gazed at the moon. It had a face; a sort of sad face, a face of melancholy, of longing, of love…

14

Not long after our trip to Madeira, she was offered a place at Oxford. For her, it seemed all too simple. Even though she displayed little intellectual curiosity, it was clear from her description of her boarding school teachers and routines that the pupils there were destined for good grades.

Being a school year behind her, I wanted to follow her to Oxford, but knew my chances were limited. During my GCSE days, my teachers spent as much time taming the class as teaching. Very few pupils were interested in learning and even fewer, if any, thought about Oxford. As for our A-levels, some teachers were utterly useless and just copied stuff onto a blackboard for us to note down, day in day out. So, I worked hard at home, trying to make up for my school's deficiencies. However, self-teaching had its limits and my performance did not convince my teachers to predict a string of As for me. I begged them to reconsider, given that I had suffered from a high temperature during the mock exams and my knowledge was rapidly increasing given my hard work at home… No use. I simply had not impressed them enough. Oh well, such was life.

It was useless lamenting this, but I struggled to understand why, despite my intellectual curiosity, passion and hard work, I had failed. And I recalled that evening by the sea in Madeira, and how surprised I had been when Isabel told me she did not want to be anything. I wanted to be… but could not…

Perhaps if I had attended her school, it would have been all different, I thought, forgetting for a minute that she went to a girls-only school. Then, I realised how my mother, who was a hospital nurse, and father, a stage actor, could never have earned enough money to pay the fees, especially as there were four of us kids in the family. I sighed over my father's wrong choice of career, and wished that my grandfather had locked him in for a few days to clear his head, just as Isabel's grandfather would have done. Isabel's dad, you see, had chosen the right career in investment banking…

I felt angry at my dad for having ruined my happiness with Isabel. I knew that once at university, she'd forget about me and instead hang out with people who would inherit money, titles and perhaps princedoms. And then there was me… We were, after all, worlds apart.

I thought about applying to Oxford Brooks, the ex-polytechnic, but my predicted grades were so much higher than they required. So, I did not apply to any institution in the city of Oxford, but somewhere that my teacher thought was more befitting.

15

The summer after my final A-level exams, I met Isabel in London for a weekend to celebrate my completion of school. I tried to be as upbeat as possible, rather than lamenting over not following her to Oxford.

Isabel was happy to see me when we met up at Paddington. We embraced and she gave me a little kiss on the lips. I was glad that she had not grown tired of me; that more exciting people at Oxford had not managed to divert her affection.

We took the District Line to her father's flat in Earl's Court, where he lived during the week, and where we were staying for the weekend. To me, Earl's Court appeared very rich and his flat was luxurious with majestic high ceilings. To Isabel, this was just part of the ordinary fabrics of her life, but this apartment was almost as spacious as my home in the Cotswolds which housed six people.

We bought some ingredients for dinner from the local supermarket. I enjoyed cooking and preferred it to eating out, partly because I had very little money. Isabel would not have been impressed with my choice of affordable restaurants anyway, I thought, but if I cooked, that was something else entirely, and I could make up for my lack of money with my efforts and skills. Isabel did not like cooking, so she sat in the kitchen, on a tall stool, and sipped her wine.

Salmon wrapped in bacon with asparagus in a creamy sauce. Voila! I was quite impressed with myself, and Isabel said it looked amazing. She cut off a piece and put it into her mouth. She closed her eyes and let out a groan of satisfaction. It was quite loud, sexual even… or perhaps just fake?

She said she was having a good time at university, although the weekly essays were less enjoyable. Anyway, the people were fun enough.

"Who's the most interesting person you've met then?" I asked.

"Oh, interesting? Well, they are all quite different, yet similar at the same time, but towards the end of the last semester, I came across a Chinese guy who was a Masters student. He is friends with one of my friends – one of the very few Masters students I know. There are lots of friends and friends of friends, and loads of parties." She was happily telling me her life, while tucking into the food.

"Oh? What is this guy like?" I asked, not thinking much of it. Actually, I did. I recalled her grandfather's dismissive views of the Chinese. "Is he from Hong Kong?"

"No, he's from Beijing, which is quite rare. There are a lot of Hong Kong people at Oxford but I don't think there are many from Beijing. Then again, most Chinese students tend to be quite geeky and don't party with us. This guy's different."

"Sufficiently different that he would challenge your grandfather's views?"

"Ha! As if! Grandpa is probably the most stubborn old man on this planet! Actually, just imagine…"

"Yes?"

"Let's play it after dinner," she suggested.

"What game?"

"Our acting game."

By the time we had finished dinner, we had also finished a bottle of wine. Actually, we were nearly halfway through our second.

"Okay, okay, here's the scenario." She wiped her mouth. "Imagine you are my granddad, and I have come to you one day, let's say, for dinner or something, during the holidays. And I say, 'Grandpa, there's something I have to tell you.'"

"Oh? What is it, my dear child?" I said, quickly entering my role.

"I'm going to get married."

"Oh? Good news! But to whom?"

"This guy… I don't know how you'll take it."

Really? Someone controversial? Would I be that controversial?

"Come come, tell me dear." I carried on, waiting for her to spill the beans about marrying this guy she first met at cricket all those summers ago…

"He's a Chinese guy from Beijing from a Communist family…" she murmured.

Bash! Isabel's grandfather rose to his feet with a loud bang of his fist on the table, "WHAT?!" The old man was furious. I was furious. Heaven and Earth tumbled in rage!

"Hey, George. Don't overdo it. Careful with the table!" Isabel laughed.

I fell out of my role, but could not relieve myself of my own anger. Then again, this was just an acting game. But… what if it happened in real life? How would I take it? How *could* I take it? Forget about her grandfather – *I* mattered!

"So… you're not really saying that you want to marry this guy… in real life, I mean… I'm George now, not your grandfather. The game is over."

I must have appeared a bit too serious, as she laughed and reassured me, "Oh, dear George. It's just an idea I had for our acting game!" Then she kissed me.

I smiled. Gosh, that was frightful… but at the same time, was she testing the waters – both in terms of her grandfather's likely reaction and my own?

"I'd never marry him. It's an amusing thought, but I'm more of a realist than that. And the idea, in reality, is ludicrous! Don't you think?" She touched my cheek.

"Perhaps…"

"Why just perhaps?"

"Well… you know my feelings towards you. So, of course I'd like to say 'yes, it is ludicrous'. But at the same time, you are a free person and you can make your own choices, and you're free to love whoever you want. So, if you loved him, then I'd have to say, 'No, why would it be ludicrous?'"

"Well, it is ludicrous. For a start, I'm not in love with him." She smiled reassuringly, as if comforting me.

I smiled too, but awkwardly, wondering what her relationship with this guy was.

16

Our weekend was pleasant enough. We went to see a Noël Coward matinee, *Private Lives*. Given our money situation and the fact my mother found it tiring to manoeuvre four kids from the Cotswolds to London, I did not see many productions while growing up. I saw a few of my father's plays for free, but not many others.

Private Lives. Spoilt playboys and playgirls. Union and reunion. It was comical, as the characters fell in love and then out again, with tender words followed by bickering. I wondered if some people really lived like that. It was all so far removed from my own life. I thought it was fun but little else, but Isabel said it was her favourite play.

I wished I could be a bit less caring about things, just like some people were in that play, maybe just like Isabel. She appeared so at ease with the world. Which character was her favourite? Elyot, of course. He was such a cool guy! Full of panache!

We took a stroll in Hyde Park, then continued to Primrose Hill. We stood on the top of the hill, which was just a little mound, but tall enough to see London's skyline quite clearly. Then, we walked to Little Venice and on to Edgware Road for some Lebanese food. One waiter seemed overly attentive.

"Imagine if I were to say to my grandfather that his only child's only child wanted to marry an Arab!" she whispered, giggling.

It was almost disturbing that she found it so funny, although I did not know which element was more troubling – joking about marriage, joking about winding up her grandfather through marriage, or thinking political incorrectness was just a joke.

I did not answer, but Isabel seemed to be entertained by her own question. "He'd probably arrange for my assassination!" she whispered, as if already part of that exciting conspiracy.

I looked into her eyes. There was nothing but joviality. I came around to the idea that I should find it all terribly funny too, so I did a superhero gesture and declared, "I'd shield you from the bullet. Don't worry."

"What? So that I could be with another man?" Isabel was surprised.

Actually, why should one protect a girl so that she could marry someone else? Would I really do that? Yes, probably I would. But I did not admit that, as it would be just too... what was the word? Oh, whatever...

It was quite late by the time we had finished our food. Following my instinct, I headed to the Underground station.

"Let's take a cab," said Isabel, hailing one down. We hopped in. The meter seemed to tick away madly, but I was just happy that I was with Isabel. We held hands and looked at London at night, its lights, people, traffic...

"Do you want to live in London after university?" I asked.

"Yeah! Of course!" She sounded excited about her choice.

"Me too." I did not sound as excited. Of course, I wanted to live in London, if only to be with her, but I wondered what my prospects were; whether I would be able to secure a job here. London was not a city for the poor. Certainly, there were plenty of poor people, perhaps some of the poorest in the country. But to be one of the deprived would be so painful, as you'd be surrounded by so many rich people and things that only rich people could buy. Of course, I fancied a place like her father's flat in Earl's Court, but that was surely out of my reach. Why? Because I would not be able to secure a ludicrously well-paid job; because I could not go to the best university; because I could not get the grades; because my efforts were held back by my school; because my dad could not afford to send me to a posh school; because he chose the wrong career; because my grandfather did not do as Isabel's grandfather would have done... "Oh stop it, George!" I screamed at myself in my head.

We did not make love that night, although I could feel Isabel was in a playful mood. Soon, she was sleeping like a log.

I got out of bed and took out a cigarette. I had started smoking, but was not a regular smoker. I lit up and sat naked next to the tall window in the dark living room. The curtain was open. I gazed at the stars – it was not a blanket of Madeiran stars, just a few were visible here. The other lights were too bright. Man had dimmed nature. The pure light was being suppressed by the artificial. Smoke rose from my cigarette. Higher. Higher. Then, vanished into the dark night.

17

I enjoyed my three years in Bath where I ended up going to university. I spent a lot of time exploring the city and its surrounding countryside. The classical architecture there reminded me of Oxford where I had wanted to go, to be with Isabel. The rolling hills and fields of wheat and barley reminded me of my time in the Cotswolds with Isabel. I went to Mole's for its indie rock a few times, and was once kicked out for smoking my tobacco pipe. They obviously thought I was enjoying something more potent. I had a better experience at the Hat and Feather, with bearded male punters snorting some stuff, while stylish women wearing net-like veils and feathers in their hats smoked cigarettes through long holders, enjoying the jazz jam sessions.

Whenever I had drunk a bit too much, I would recover the next morning by strolling to Café Solé, where I sat with friends sipping homemade milkshakes with chunks of strawberry and other fruit. Sometimes, I would wonder about what Isabel was up to on those sunny Sunday mornings.

Isabel and I continued to exchange e-mails but they became irregular. Maybe she was terribly busy with her essays. After all, Oxford's academic routine sounded a lot more demanding than Bath's. I did not find my academic work particularly hard, so I had a lot of free time – time to think about Isabel, time to think about what I might do after university, time to think about how our relationship would develop.

Some bankers in the United States had lent money to those who could not afford to borrow, and then packaged up these toxic loans into financial products that lacked transparency. Eventually, the bubble burst. The bullish UK economic upturn that had lasted for several years could not escape the ripple effect and nose-dived. This was the great recession of 2008/09 and, upon graduation, my friends and I found that most doors were closed to us. It was disappointing, yes, very much so, but since everyone was in the same sinking boat, it felt okay at times.

I moved back home to my parents' place and looked for jobs. I submitted lots of applications for professional positions in London, but few even bothered to reply to me beyond the automatically generated acknowledgement of receipt. I started to lose hope. So, when Isabel asked me whether I wanted to move in with her in London, the decision was easy.

After her time at Oxford, Isabel did not seek a professional job. She made no attempt to get one during the big firms' recruitment rounds and her father's connections in the world of high finance were of little interest to her. She wanted a care-free life, and her grandfather was only too happy to indulge her. He rented a flat near to Clapham Junction station for her, as she'd wanted him to, where her nearest supermarket was Waitrose. It was a two-bedroom Victorian conversion.

The flat was decorated with her things. A few photos had been Blu-Tacked onto the fridge door – photos of her getting drunk with her friends at university, including a Chinese guy. I guessed that must have been the "interesting guy" she had joked about marrying when we'd staged our mini-play in that flat in Earl's Court. In the photo they looked nothing more than two drunken friends. I guessed that if he had meant something to her, then out of decency to me, she would not have displayed the photo, however nonchalant she was about everything in the world. On the mantelpiece above the fireplace, there were a few framed photographs of her and her family.

The rest of the flat was furnished with bits of random stuff. She did not seem bothered by the eclectic mix – an elegant two-seater Chesterfield sofa that had been picked up from her grandfather's was placed alongside a non-descript coffee table from IKEA.

Isabel and I shared the master bedroom. She used the other room as a study. Well, it was initially more of a storage room, where she piled her bills and bits of paperwork on a large desk. I helped to tidy up the mess there, and turned it into my study. I put my laptop on the desk and thought I would start a novel or something. I would now work towards my goal of becoming a writer.

Apart from the study, I did not change the other rooms too much. In the bedroom, I had a few bits of clothing, which I managed to squeeze in amid Isabel's stuff. In the bathroom, my washbag fitted into the cupboard. Only my toothbrush was on display. I brought in no additional furniture into the living room. The only thing of mine on display in this room was the little statue of the red-faced Chinese warrior that my grandfather had randomly given me all those years ago. I did not know why I had brought it here to this flat. Maybe it had found its own way into my bag amid the chaos while I was packing.

Looking at Isabel's family photos, I often wondered what her family thought of me. Isabel's grandfather sort of liked me, I guessed, and her father did not mind me either. I wondered how her father felt about it all, whether he thought our tender age meant that one day she would grow out of her childhood romance and come to her senses, and settle down with someone with clear prospects, money and prestige. I did not know for sure, and sometimes, I frankly did not care what they thought. As long as Isabel loved me, I was happy.

Did Isabel love me? I should think that she did, otherwise she would not have invited me to move in with her and would have ended this relationship a long time ago. However, every now and then, I did wonder what she saw in me. Perhaps she saw a young man who cared about her and who loved her madly. Perhaps she simply enjoyed my love. Anyway...

Isabel certainly loved her drink. She got a job at a wine shop near Clapham Junction. The work was not terribly hard and she enjoyed learning more about wine. She had some good workmates, who were also fond of a drink or ten. Given that I was unemployed and needed something to do, she introduced me to this world of easy work and drunken play, and I eventually got a job in another wine shop not too far from our home. While the pay was not exactly high, the work was enjoyable enough, and often, when there were no customers, I would sketch out a few ideas for my novel or novels.

I grew more and more comfortable in this lifestyle of idle bliss. We would have a bottle of wine, on the cheap, from one of our shops almost every night. Quite often, we had guests over or we went to theirs. Weekends were usually spent drinking, strolling, sitting in the parks and drinking. Isabel enjoyed smoking cannabis, and so did all her friends. I smoked some when I was at school, but my friends at university were mostly non-smokers. Besides, I did not really like cannabis as it tended to give me stomach ache. Nevertheless, when a joint was passed to me, I rarely said no.

Soon enough, I had forgotten all about wanting to write novels, or wanting to do anything. Isabel and I were just happily drinking and partying with our group of equally chilled out friends. Aspiration? That was a negative word among this crowd. Enjoyment? That's better. Cheers.

Our friends were a mixed bag of people from Western Europe – a few French guys and girls, a Spaniard, two Italians and quite a few more English youngsters. No one came from a poor background, and at least half of the group were subsidised by their parents or grandparents. My parents could not afford to subsidise me. I had never approached my grandparents for any money. I had enough money to live on from my job at the wine shop, especially as I lived rent-free.

My mother hoped a career in the alcohol business would turn out wonderfully for me. I fed her hope by citing success stories of wine dealers, some entirely based on my imagination, not admitting that I had neither the talent nor genuine enthusiasm for the trade.

My father was less optimistic, as he could see through me. "I don't mind what you do, but you should have dreams and pursue them. Unless you put your heart in it, whatever you do will be a waste of your life, whether you work as a writer, actor, wine dealer or banker," he often reminded me. Fortunately, we never fell out over this. At least he was not in a strong position to lecture me about the importance of earning large amounts of money. Had my grandfather locked him in for a few days and cooled his head, so that he became an investment banker like Isabel's dad, rather than an actor, then things might have turned out differently. How lucky I was, in that respect, not to have to argue with him over work or life choices.

My grandfather was not best pleased, knowing that his beloved grandson was not pursuing any dreams, but he probably felt that it was not his job to tell me how to live my life. Such talks were best left to my parents.

Life was one big jolly, but…

18

I was summoned to my grandfather's death-bed. He rested there. My grandma, parents, an uncle and an aunt, as well as two of my cousins, plus my brothers and sister, were all there. Some people could not make it, as they were far away in South Africa and Australia.

I called out to him. He opened his eyes, perhaps with a great effort. He held my hand. His voice was weak, trembling.

"George…" he murmured, "I hope you are well…"

I said gently that I was well, as gently as I held his hand. I told him that I was very happy and the people around me were as well as they could be, and that we all looked forward to him recovering. I said that next year's cricket match had already been arranged, and we were all looking forward to seeing him score many sixes…

He looked at me with half-closed eyes. His face was expressionless. He was so weak that each movement, however minute, seemed to demand so much energy. However, I could see through his eyes that he was smiling sadly at me, and looked almost disappointed in me, somehow. He wanted to speak, but his whispered words were so quiet, they amounted to little more than a feeble breath from his lips. I put my ear to his mouth, wanting to hear his words. But I could hear almost nothing, except perhaps, "Do… something…"

I could not be sure of his exact words, as his barely moving lips had now stopped moving all together. His eyelids dropped…

I cried.

His eyes opened, ever so slightly, as if my crying had woken him. His lips started to move again, ever so slightly. I listened to him as best as I could, and again put my ear close to his mouth.

"Live… only… once…" I think he said, as his light grip on my hand loosened. His eyes did not close. Perhaps he wanted to see something…

His world ended. Tears. I knelt down by his bed, holding his hand, kissing it. I did not want to let go, but let go I must… His time had come, and he'd gone…

19

On the way back to London, I thought about his final words, which were all said to me, not to anyone else in the room. He loved me. I would never forget his hand holding mine, the loosening of his grip, and his eyes that remained open when he departed. It was as if he desperately wanted to see me becoming someone – someone who had dreams and pursued them, whatever they were – a writer, an actor, a wine dealer or a banker.

Do something. You only live once.

Perhaps it was only through death that life could become meaningful. Perhaps when I told Isabel that I wanted to write a novel about us, a story that would never end, she was right to say that it sounded like a long bore. Perhaps only the end can drive on the whole story and make it exciting, interesting and meaningful…

When I got back to our flat, I talked to Isabel about it all. She shared my grief, but she did not think much about my thoughts on what it meant to lead a meaningful life. To be honest, at that time, I had not yet come to realise what it meant either.

The next day, I returned to my wine shop and the same routine kicked in. I tried to take an interest in the trade, but my mind travelled elsewhere. Then came the weekend, and we drank more than we usually did during the week.

I woke up on Sunday with a massive hangover after trying to have a good night with all our friends. I had drunk too much, trying to forget my grandfather and my grief. Suddenly, I jumped out of bed and ran into the living room, stark naked. I always slept naked.

"What is it? Are you all right?" Isabel asked, thinking I was about to throw up. She had come after me, also naked. She always slept naked too.

I was sitting on her grandfather's Chesterfield. I did not answer her but turned and looked at her. She stood by the door, her right hand on the door-frame, her left arm dangling by the side of her body. Through the crescent gap between her straight left arm and her curved waistline, I gazed at the light that came in through the window of the study, for however long, then I looked at her.

She was beautiful. Her eyebrows arched, as if she was puzzled by the world's business and intrigued by what the fuss was all about. Her thin nose and slight freckles had not changed since I first saw her on that summer's day at the cricket. Her hairstyle had changed, her cute plaits were long gone, and her bosom had matured since our first meeting. I gazed at her. She gazed at me. Two naked bodies, in the same state as Adam and Eve when they were first created.

It had been a year since I'd graduated. It was the summer again. A year ago, I was just moving in here, penniless and purposeless. Now, I was still penniless and purposeless.

"I'm sorry Isabel," I murmured.

"About what?"

"I have to go..."

Isabel did not get upset. She did not say anything. We were fixed there, in our individual spots in the living room. Silence. Just naked silence. No ticking of the clocks. No creaking of the floorboards. No birds singing outside the windows. Suddenly, the fridge started up its usual hum.

She walked towards me on the sofa, bent forward and kissed me lightly on my lips, then my forehead.

"Best of luck," she murmured, in a soft passionless voice.

She then straightened her body and pressed my head onto her stomach, with her breasts resting on my head. How long did we stay in that pose for? Minutes? Hours? Days? Years? Enough time for the sea to be drained and the mountains to collapse through old age. Silence. Apart from the occasional humming noise from the fridge.

"I'd rather you stayed," she whispered.

Stay for what? More years of the same? More years of drinking every night, and drinking even more at the weekends? More years of smoking joints? More years of living under her roof, courtesy of grandfather's subsidies? More years of just letting life pass by?

"Okay, George, if you want to live a different life, then go for it. The life you want to live isn't exactly what I want." Isabel was calm. We were still fixed in that pose. "But where are you going to find this life that you want?"

"Maybe I should leave England."

"And go where?" She sat down next to me, skin to skin.

I did not know. All I knew was that I stood at a crossroads in my life. I could continue the way that I had been travelling purposelessly, or I could cross the road onto a different, more promising path. Yet, where in the world was that new path? I looked around the living room, as if trying to find some inspiration…

IKEA furniture. Scandinavia? To do what?

Old-school furniture? Stay in England? And do what?

Persian rugs. Iran? It'd be a miracle if I could find anything there given the hostile relationship between the Islamic Republic and the UK.

My eyes moved around and finally settled on the little wooden statue of that Chinese warrior. He was looking at me too. His eyebrows were knotted as if he was deep in thought. His glaive, although in a resting position, could be used to deadly effect in a flash. Who was he? What did he do? Hadn't I seen similar statues in Chinese restaurants? Was he a real person or a god?

"China," I said.

"Oh?" Isabel seemed surprised. Our voices were quiet. Still murmuring. "And what would you do there?"

Well, for a start, it was pretty far away, so that I could forget about my wasted time here. But I could not say that to her. It was different. Yes, I said that. Its economy was growing close to double digits even in this deep recession. Yes, I said that. It wanted plenty of English teachers. Yes, I said that. There may be something there for me, and I might write something there. Yes, I said that…

After a while, she did not seem to listen to my reasons. Perhaps, in reality, she was not after any justification for my departure – she just wanted to know there was a reason.

"Are you sure, George?" She started smoking.

"Yes." I picked up a cigarette too.

We sat there, in silence, and just smoked, side by side, skin to skin, facing the mantelpiece on which the little statue stood.

When she finished her cigarette, she stubbed it out, stood up and walked away.

I was a slow smoker, unlike her. Just as I was stubbing it out, she came back and handed me a small piece of paper.

"If you are ever in trouble in China, call on this guy. He's very helpful. Actually, call on him anyway, even if you're not in trouble," she instructed.

I looked at it. A Chinese name. A telephone number.

"Is this…?" I wondered if this was some contact of her grandfather's.

"Yes, it's the guy I told you about from Oxford." She walked away. Where to? I did not know. I sat there, gazing at the piece of paper that she had found so easily, despite her usual disorganisation.

20

Isabel did not see me off to the airport. In all the years I had known her, she was quiet for the first time, a far cry from her usual light-hearted self. We did not kiss each other when I exited the flat's front door carrying my large backpack. This was my first step crossing that road, down a different path. "Let fate come," I thought to myself.

I did not look at her, as I walked down the stairs. My footsteps were heavy, but I could hear her faint steps behind me. I opened the front door of the house and stopped. Her faint steps behind me stopped. I knew that she was just a few steps behind me. I stood there, frozen. Then…

I pulled my backpack up.

I walked out.

I did not say anything.

I did not look back.

She did not call my name.

We did not say goodbye.

Was that the end of us? Was that how my novel about us would end? The story that I said would never end? Had she enjoyed this novel, which now had an ending? To her, a book without an ending was a long bore, as she had told me when we were in Madeira. How did she want this novel to end? Did I really mean to end this book this way? A flight of fantasy, a stream of consciousness, could carry the author to unintended destinations. Destinations? Or intermediate stops?

21

The airport lounge was filled with people of all shapes and sizes, colours and voices. I stood by the window, my face was almost touching it. Raindrops ran down the glass, blurring my vision.

I tried to sleep as soon as I got on the plane. But I ended up watching the darkness that was the back of my eyelids for what seemed like hours, days, years…

I walked to the back of the plane for a few cans of beer and mini bottles of wine from the air stewardess, who looked concerned about the amount I had requested. That was it. I was going to drink so much that I would knock myself out.

One can. Two cans. Three cans. One bottle. Two bottles. Three bottles… This variant of "counting sheep" did not lead me to the blissful land of Nod. Instead, a fire wolf was trying to burst out from within my soul, break free from its chains, and leap out towards the nearest emergency exit to let some air into this super dry environment. After that, it would leap off the plane and fly at supersonic speed back to Isabel, scorching the whole of Siberia. Although made of fire, the fire wolf would not leave a single burn mark on Isabel's slender figure. It would carry her and fly to Madeira, under crowds of stars…

I had to stop my fire wolf, so I threw myself in between him and the emergency exit. We stood there, man to man, and I felt his burning breath on my face. Suddenly, he let out a deafening cry, as if to frighten me off. I hit him with my bare fists. He scratched me with his iron claws. I kicked him in the stomach. He whacked me with his tail. I pushed him. We wrestled. I rolled over him. He rolled over me. We rolled over each other. The Ural's peaks and the Mongol Steppes, the rocks and the dust, the pines and the birches, the rivers and the streams – they bore witness to our struggle…

Morning broke. A ray shone through the window. The Great Wall emerged under the sunrise, stretching for thousands of miles, east and west. I gazed at the ruins. I had left him north of the Wall…

PART TWO

22

Capital International Airport. I had entered another world with a different sense of dimension, where the term 'grandeur' was too insignificant a word. Instead of crowds, there were just a few dots, littering the floor that was so polished I could see my own face in it when I bent down to tie my shoelaces. A planeload of people counted for nothing under such a huge ceiling spanning thousands of feet, arching high above me. If there had been stars on it, it might as well be the heavens. People talked to each other as they walked, but there was hardly any noise. Their speech, like their physical presence, was swallowed up by the sheer magnitude of this building. Here, we were all insignificant grains of sand, as if our existence mattered little and this giant structure existed for its own sake.

I followed the other passengers and got on a monorail train. I was in the last carriage and saw the building behind me as the train travelled soundlessly. Giant columns of red, hundreds of feet tall. A roof of gold, thousands of feet across. Everything was laid out with a clear sense of order, as if the heavens had planned this huge structure, exalting its dimensions to awe new entrants, making sure that these little people kowtowed to the Celestial Kingdom.

Compared to the airport's grand structure – so vast it seemed inhuman – Mr Lu was a compact man, with a broad smile. Had it not been for his ears, the corners of his mouth would have met at the back of his head. He led me to the waiting Volkswagen.

"Welcome to Beijing!" Mr Lu said in his thick Chinese accent.

"Thank you," I replied in my tired voice, having hardly slept on the plane.

He must have picked up hundreds of people before me. Hundreds of English teachers who just came and went, doing their time, having their fun, and returning to Britain or elsewhere. Could I make a proper career out of teaching English in China? My contract was for a one-year fixed term. If it worked out well, maybe it could be extended. Alternatively, I could start teaching English and then broadening my horizons and taking on something else. I did not despise teaching. In fact, I felt almost proud that I was here to teach. Through it, I thought I could spread a little bit of British culture. What that amounted to beyond afternoon tea and the summer cricket, I was not sure. Perhaps the culture was so rich, it was hard to pinpoint to anything in particular, and could not be defined in a few words. Perhaps I could teach my students about the urban jungle of the East End, of Jameel and that girl in her colourful dress, of the gentle hills of the Cotswolds, of the drunken nights in London, all of which formed a sense of what Britain was to me. Perhaps I could become a cultural ambassador in a somewhat minuscule sense. But miniscule or not, I felt I could build some sense of purpose to my existence, which would benefit some people.

"You from England?"

"Yes."

"London?"

"Well..." I thought about telling Mr Lu about my early childhood in London's East End, followed by my formative years spent in the Cotswolds, my time at university in Bath, and my return to London again... hence, it was difficult to say exactly where I was from. But I was tired and said, "Yes, from London."

"London... England... First World! Beijing... China... Third World!" Mr Lu stated.

What imagery would 'the Third World' conjure up for you? Hungry children too tired to cry, with flies circling above their heads. Barefooted women carrying water pots on their heads, walking for miles on dirt tracks under the blazing heat of the sun. Little huts washed away by floods. Such imagery could not be associated with what I saw, as we travelled on the motorway – high-rises, giant shopping centres, billboards, flashy cars... There was no sign of poverty, of people in need, of children hungry for food or opportunities. Everything seemed fine, just fine. Everyone was well-catered for.

I wanted to tell Mr Lu about my first impression of his country, the awe-inspiring airport, comparing it to the chaotic and crowded Heathrow, but I was so tired that I stayed silent. As if being rocked in a cradle, I fell asleep to the gentle noise of the car and the occasional word from Mr Lu. Perhaps I was the most boring passenger he had ever encountered.

I felt the car stop and heard Mr Lu say something to me. I opened my eyes. He was already at the back of the car, opening the boot and getting my backpack out. He insisted on carrying it for me, as if I was his guest simply by virtue of him being in his native country, receiving this tired person who had travelled over thousands of miles to be here. We entered an ordinary looking residential tower and took the lift to the tenth floor.

"Your flat." Mr Lu turned the key and pushed opened the door. We entered a one-bedroom flat. "Not far from school." Then, he explained the relative locations, including a series of hand gestures for left, right and straight ahead, as if my jet-lagged self could grasp all this complicated geography.

The flat was not big. The late summer sun lit up the whole place, streaming through the large south-facing windows. Unlike the wall-to-wall carpet in my English homes, the floor here was covered by cream-coloured tiles, as if the whole place was meant to be a bathroom.

Mr Lu showed me how the boiler worked. "Remember, this switch first, cold water, then boiler on." This line from him came out almost effortlessly. He must have had to say this to many people before.

He turned the air-con on for me, which seemed straightforward enough, so he did not bother to explain the buttons. He pointed to the TV and handed me the remote control. Then, he pointed at the landline, lifted the receiver, heard the tone and then smiled, saying, "Okay!"

Before he left, he repeated the thing about the boiler and said, "I will come here tomorrow, eight thirty. We go to the school. Have breakfast."

I opened my backpack and let everything fall onto the floor. I looked at the mess and picked up various items, as if I was looking at them for the first time. I picked up each thing, one at a time, and put it away in the right place. I even placed my small collection of CDs on the shelf in alphabetical order, then wondered why I had bothered to bring them here in their cases, rather than putting them all in a small folder.

Among the stuff I had brought over from England was the little Chinese statue – the inspiration behind my trip here. I put him on top of the TV. There he stood, proudly looking at me, as if wanting to praise me for having made it this far and about to start a new life.

I walked to the window and looked out. The roads were laid out in neat grids. The cars crawled. Tall poplars lined the streets. Behind them stood the other high-rises. Everything seemed so quiet down there, as I gazed on it from up here.

I opened the fridge. To my surprise, someone had left some food in there. One aubergine. One carrot. One cabbage. A few eggs. A carton of milk. I say! Two bottles of beer! What a pleasant surprise! I wondered if it was Mr Lu who had left the beers there. Whoever you are, thank you very much! I opened a bottle and lit up a cigarette. "Any staples?" I wondered, opening the cupboard, and there it was – a bag of rice staring back at me. Excellent!

I went back to my living room, turned the CD player on and took out my David Bowie CD. The stereo was quite an old machine, but I was thankful it was here in my flat.

"*Ooh, ooh, ooh, ooh, little China girl...*" I turned the volume up.

I stood there, slightly rocking side to side, almost dancing, drinking my beer and smoking my cigarette.

Was there someone at my door? Oh, yes... Oh no, was my music too loud? As part of my pre-departure research, I read that many Chinese people, especially the elderly, took a nap in the afternoon, especially on Sundays.

I was all ready to say sorry, which I had learnt was "*dui bu qi*". I opened the door. Nope. No old Chinese man wanting to tell me off, but a chap with curly blond hair.

"Hiya! How's it going? I'm Charlie. I was wondering when someone might move into this flat."

"I'm George. I just landed today." I informed my fellow Englishman. "Come in."

"Cheers, freshie." He swaggered in. He was not exactly slim, but I wouldn't say he was fat either. Just well-built, without being particularly muscular.

"Freshie?" I was puzzled by this strange term.

"Ah, you've just arrived, so you are very fresh. So you're a freshie."

I laughed slightly, out of courtesy. Charlie threw himself on the sofa.

"Did Mr Lu leave you two bottles of beer?"

"Yes. Did you find two when you arrived too?"

"Yeah. Enjoy. That's all you're gonna get," he laughed. "Let's have one mate."

"Of course."

Charlie put his feet on the coffee table as he spread himself on the sofa, looking very much at home in my flat, perhaps too comfortably so. I had not developed any real attachment to this flat, so it did not feel like he was invading my space. However, at the same time, I felt his behaviour was… how could I put it? Un-English? Where was that sense of genteel courtesy, of personal space? But I was not in the mood for turning on my own countryman on Day One of my life in a new country. I opened a bottle of beer for him.

We sat there and chatted. Charlie had been teaching for a year now at the same school I was about to start at. Was he enjoying it? Absolutely. The pay was good. The kids were nice, and the supervisors were easy-going. Beer in Beijing was cheap, and sometimes, if you went to the right places, girls were ready too.

I confessed that I did not have a teaching qualification, and that I had not taught anything to anyone at all.

"That's no problem at all. They've hired you and that's enough. Mate, I don't have a qualification. In fact, I think only a handful of English teachers are qualified. You don't need it," Charlie assured me.

He talked as if he was an Old China Hand. Compared to me, of course he was, but there was something that I did not like about the way he talked. What was it? Perhaps he made it sound all too easy.

Charlie had no plans to go back to rainy England. He could not find a job when he'd left university, which was at the same time as me. So instead of getting wasted and staying at home, he packed his bags and came here straightaway. It was the best decision he had ever made.

"It's a great laugh," he said. "You won't feel bored here. There's a big group of us lads, and a few girls too, teaching at this and other schools. We have some really good fun in Beijing during the term, and in other places during the holidays. I'll call them over and let's party!"

So he did, before I could tell him that I actually felt really tired. But hey, let's party!

Before I knew it, Tom, Phil and Gav had arrived, with plenty of booze. How did they manage to arrive so quickly? Well, they lived in the same building. What a party block!

Tom was a lanky guy with quite a posh voice, although he mumbled a bit. He worked briefly as an estate agent in London but was laid off at the start of the recession. He was the only qualified person here, having done a Teaching English as a Foreign Language – TEFL – crash course.

Phil was a bit scatty and mumbled far more than Tom. I wondered if they both mumbled this much in class, and whether their students mumbled like them, so that the whole class just produced some sort of humming noise… Phil had worked for British Telecom for a little while, before becoming mind-numbingly bored by his nine-to-five job, and so left Hemel Hempstead, a satellite town just outside London.

Gav began dancing to my *China Girl* tune as soon as he arrived. Fortunately, he was not completely mad and stopped as soon as he realised that no one was paying him any attention. He did a variety of odd jobs before coming to Beijing, including timing traffic lights and counting people crossing the streets.

"CDs!" Gav exclaimed. "You are old school."

I was puzzled.

"Look here dude! This is called an MP4!" He took out a tiny little gadget from his pocket and handed it to me. He then went on to explain that this little thing could store hundreds and thousands of songs, and it had cost him only a couple of hundred yuan, about twenty quid, in one of those big indoor markets.

A few minutes later, there were more knocks on my door. Before I could get up from my chair, Charlie had already launched himself to the door and opened it. A girl walked in. Her blonde hair was in a short pony tail. She was quite pale and did not wear much make-up. The plainness of her face only made her large blue eyes look more alluring. She gave me a little smile – the sort that was befitting for a stranger. I returned the same smile and she walked towards me, her hips gently swaying from side to side as she walked. It was not as exaggerated as the catwalk, but a sense of femininity oozed out from her every step, even though she was wearing just an ordinary T-shirt and blue jeans, plus a pair of nondescript trainers.

"Hello, I'm Jillian," she said, introduced herself in a relatively high-pitched girlie voice. I sensed a slight twang of Essex in her speech.

I stood up and we exchanged a "hello" kiss, smacking our lips in thin air, while touching each other's cheeks for a couple of milliseconds.

Jillian kept the volume of her voice modestly down, in contrast to the lads' roaring laughter. They were practically screaming like children, mucking about and pushing and shoving each other as they all tried to fit on the sofa at the same time. They had spread themselves in all sorts of relaxed ways, with their legs and feet in various places, some distance off the floor. At first sight, an average Englishman would have said these people had been my friends since we were toddlers. Perhaps my male visitors did not think this was my flat, and thought it was merely one room in our collective barracks – that I was here temporarily, then someone else would take my place.

"We'll go out and show you the highlights some other time. Got to go to work tomorrow," Charlie winked.

So… that meant that no one left my place until two in the morning. Boy, was I tired…

23

The next morning, I found that Mr Lu was already waiting for me as I stepped out of the lift. As soon as he saw me, he chucked away his cigarette.

"Good morning. Did you sleep well?" This line was said smoothly. It must have been one of his standard lines.

"Yes. Thank you."

"You tired?"

"Yes. It's the jet lag…" Well, a bit of a hangover too, but let's forget about that.

The school, as it turned out, was just around the corner. He pointed to the signs along the way for me to remember. We had a pancake on the way. Boy, that tasted so good. I was hungover and starving. During last night's mad, jet-lagged drinking session, I had forgotten to eat.

The school was in a commercial building. I was presented to the director of studies, who was a mild-looking woman. Her English was not particularly good, but better than Mr Lu's. After a cordial, yet contentless chat, she led me to my classroom.

The kids were of kindergarten age. Nowhere in the document they had sent me, did it say I was going to be teaching toddlers. Although I did not think that I'd be lecturing university students, when I faced a group of chubby-cheeked little ones, I felt… somewhat lost.

"Where is the teaching assistant, please?" I asked my director. Their brochure stated that all foreign teachers would be supported by Chinese assistants during the first month, to help ease them in.

"You will be fine. You are very good. No need for assistant." She smiled and left me to it. I looked at her as she closed the door on her way out.

"Well, George, you are on your own now. Anyway, just remember, you are very good!" I thought to myself, as I cleared my throat and tried not to let the kids' age distract me. I introduced myself, and wrote my name on the blackboard.

"George," I said to them, pointing at the letters.

No response. Blank faces.

So, I pointed to the letters and said my name again, pointing to myself. After a few attempts, they finally repeated "George" after me.

"Good!" I almost cried.

"What's your name?" I walked to one chubby cherub of a boy. He did not understand my question perhaps. So, I pointed to myself and said "George", and then pointed at him.

"George."

Oh dear…

I tried the same thing with another kid, this time a girl. Yep, her name was George too. The entire class consisted of kids who were all called George!

"George! George!" The kids all cried out aloud, and they laughed. It was if the name 'George' was a hilarious joke. Did it sound like something rude in Chinese? I asked the director of studies later, and she confirmed that it did not.

I gave up on finding out their names. I thought I would do it some other time, once they had got over the 'George' joke. So, I opened the textbook.

"A."

"A." They responded in unison.

"B."

"B."

They were good at letters of the alphabet. So, I thought I would test them. I wrote on the blackboard a big "M", and asked, "What is this?" pointing to the letter.

Silence. Did they not know? Or were they too shy?

So, I tried "P", pointing to the letter.

Silence. Did they not know? Or were they too shy?

Finally, a boy with ultra-thick glasses put his hand up.

I was delighted.

"Blackboard," he answered with considerable pride and confidence…

To say it was teaching was over-glorification. It was more like babysitting, as the kids giggled away every now and then. They could not really speak English. A few words perhaps, but barely a sentence, let alone a conversation. Then again, had I expected them to be able to hold a profound conversation in Chinese?

The lesson did not go as well as I had hoped. Perhaps their age counted against them. Maybe my expectations were wrong, or I was not ready to teach kindergarten kids. Had the information pack from the school told me that the pupils were toddlers, I probably would not have accepted this job, or I would have at least prepared more. I felt that I had failed them in some way and was ashamed that I had not managed to teach them anything during the lesson. Oh well, at least they had fun, giggling over my name.

The kids politely stood up when the lesson was over and said, "Goodbye teacher," in unison, somewhat mechanically churning out a phrase that they had often repeated to my predecessors.

I had no lessons in the afternoon, so I thought I'd go home and prepare for next day's lessons. My key question was how to engage with a bunch of four-year olds. That seemed like a good challenge. What did four-year olds like? I thought I'd go to the shopping mall and have a look at what toys there were, and maybe I'd be inspired.

"Hey George!" a voice came behind me. It was Charlie.

"Hello," I smiled.

"Where are you off to?"

"Umm, I thought I'd get some food and go and have a look at toys."

"What?"

"It's lunchtime…"

"Yes yes, but toys?" His face was twisted into a weird expression of surprise which words could not describe. Was he thinking of sex toys?

I explained my motive and he slapped me so hard on my shoulder that I nearly collapsed. He laughed wholeheartedly and exclaimed, "Oh George… You *are* a freshie."

I was not sure if I liked that label, but I did not argue with him. We had some meat-stuffed buns from a street vendor and he categorically stated that I should not go to look for toys, but instead come with the crew to the bar.

"But it's only lunchtime…" I protested good-naturedly.

"Oh George… You *are* a freshie…" Charlie laughed, pushing me along.

24

My grandfather had been to China about two decades ago and taken photos of an austere country, with sombre-looking people whose clothes were black, blue, green or grey. His description of China was a country of bicycles and no bars. However, as Charlie and I sat in the taxi, I saw a few bicycles and plenty of cars. And when we arrived at our destination, there were plenty of bars.

Charlie led me into one. It was in one of the old two-storey houses. We sat upstairs, facing the lake. The windows were open as it was quite hot. We spread ourselves on the balcony. We were the only customers here, on this quiet midweek afternoon. In front of us was a tranquil lake with weeping willows on the banks, and sparkles of light were reflecting off its waters.

"This area is called '*hou hai*', literally meaning 'Back Sea'," Charlie explained. "Sometimes, lakes are called 'sea' in Beijing, because back in the ancient days, people from around here didn't have different words for 'lake' or 'sea'... something like that. I think Danny once told me something along those lines..."

"Who's Danny?" I asked.

"Ah, Danny! You'll meet him. Danny is a great lad. Compared to me, he's a real Old China Hand. Been here for years. Maybe four? Or five? We all like him."

Charlie pointed at a tower with a sloping roof in the slight distance. "That's the drum tower. In the olden days, that's how the people here knew what time it was."

"Beijing's summers are really hot. But it's okay here. There's a bit of a breeze from the lake," Charlie commented. And I did feel a light breeze.

Hot or not, the lager was cold, although at thirty yuan, or about two pounds, I thought it was a touch extravagant – our taxi fare cost less than this. Anyway, I justified my spending by telling myself that drinking with Charlie and learning about Beijing in the old quarters was a good thing, a cultural experience, and hence money well spent.

I asked Charlie if he had asked anyone else to come along. Although Charlie was a welcoming guy, I thought I'd feel more comfortable if there were more than the two of us. Charlie spread himself on the chair – feet on the coffee table, with one hand holding his beer and one arm dangling over the back of the chair. He looked as if he was the princeling of Beijing, or at least of this bar.

Charlie said he had not asked anyone, as over here, people in our crowd rarely organised anything – we just contacted each other naturally and got together impromptu. No one had a busy diary to keep.

I secretly wished that Jillian would turn up. I did not have a mobile phone; otherwise I would have contacted her. But would I have contacted her really, given that we had just met?

Charlie's phone rang.

"Yo, Danny," he shouted, "How's it going?

"Yeah, I'm just having a beer with George. He's a freshie, just arrived yesterday… Yeah, yeah… come come…"

"Is he a teacher also?" I asked.

"Used to be. Then he jacked it all in. The beauty of Beijing is that it's not an expensive place, and once you've built some good contacts, you can survive pretty nicely without doing a great deal. Danny does a bit of on-call teaching here and there, proofreading students' writing every now and then."

"Sounds comfortable."

Charlie and I exchanged background information ourselves, and just chit-chatted.

"Hello." A northern voice came from behind us, and there he was, Danny. He was a blond fellow with a slim face. As he walked towards us, I noticed his walk was a bit funny, as if every step he took was a considerable effort, as if he simply wanted to rely on nature's momentum to drag himself along.

"All right George. Just landed, have you?" He shook my hand. "Welcome to Beijing." He mimicked some Chinese accent, which together with his northern accent sounded quite funny.

Danny was born in Bolton. He was put through a private school, like a lot of kids from up north whose parents weren't exactly poor. He went to Birmingham University, and then tried his hand at something called work. He saved a bit of money from his fraudulent expenses and left the company in good time. He loved his life in Beijing, surviving on his savings, interests, and a bit of work.

"Well, I try to do as little as possible." He was proud of his inactivity.

"Yeah, that's right. While everyone here is on speed, chasing after skirts, Danny can't be bothered!" Charlie mocked.

"You what? Na… I don't need to bother. Only looooooooozas bother…" He made an 'L' sign with his fingers. "They just flock to me mate!"

"And when did that last happen?" Charlie challenged him.

"Well… Not that long ago!"

"About…. Ummm… four months ago?" Charlie reminded him. "She was wasted…"

Wasted… I did get wasted, as the rest of the crew joined us later on, plus some other people who were not from our school. While most of the people there were around my age, there was one bespectacled guy who was perhaps in his forties. Where was he from? Some place in the Midlands? He was quiet, in contrast to the rest. For most of the time, he chain-smoked and drank beer. When he went to the loo, Danny told me that this guy was from this other school, a bit of a weirdo, a hanger-on with the lads. Meanwhile, the other lads saw Danny's little smile and guessed what he was talking to me about. They all had a little mischievous laugh. I was puzzled. Why, if hardly anyone liked him, was he still included in the gang?

"You'll understand one day, George, about life in Beijing," Danny patronised.

I shrugged my shoulders, puffed and drank away, wondering if Jillian would turn up. Unfortunately, she did not. Why? She did not feel well. The best cure for any illness, according to the crew, was alcohol. But apparently Jillian was not convinced. I was a little disappointed by her no-show, but I was not sure why. Maybe her sense of distance made me feel comfortable in contrast to the rest of the crew, who somehow took it upon themselves to bring me under their wings as the little freshie. I was the novice, they were the self-appointed veterans in charge of my training.

Jillian-less, we drank and did a little bar crawl of the area, then went on to another area. I can't remember what it was like, but I seem to remember there was a Chinese girl hitting on me. What happened? The next thing I knew, I woke up in my room, seeing the ceiling spinning.

Crumbs! It was eight o'clock. I jumped out of bed, frantically got ready and went to school. The day passed painfully slowly as my head was spinning all the time. It was good that I did not chance across anyone important that day and the kids couldn't tell that I was hungover.

"What is your name?" I asked one cherub.

"What is your name?" he answered.

"My name is George," I answered

"My name is George," he answered.

I stopped that particular dialogue, if one could call it a dialogue, in case we went back to giggling over 'George'.

My greatest achievement that day was to learn that the whole class was not filled with kids called George. A few of the kids finally realised what I was after and told me their names. I wrote them all down.

Again, there were no lessons in the afternoon, so I went back to my flat. There I rested in bed, nursing my hangover. My eyelids felt heavy and my mind drifted. My thoughts flitted from the sound of the kids' giggles to the sight of the weeping willows by the lake, to the drum tower behind the lake, then the treetops, the rolling hills of the Cotswolds, the fields of wheat and barley, the cricket pitch, that summer's day, Isabel walking towards me... Isabel....

The thought of Isabel woke me up a little. I rubbed my eyes and stared at the ceiling. I wondered how she was, whether she was mad at me for leaving, whether she was sorry to see me go, whether she was having fun without me…

I had wanted to get in touch with her a few times since arriving in Beijing, but you see, my soft-hearted reader, whenever I wanted to write to her, I became lost for words. I did not know what to say to her or whether an e-mail from me would make her happy or sad.

I sat up, with my head in my hands, and asked myself if I understood who Isabel was at all. Maybe I didn't, otherwise I would have written to her. Maybe I had never truly understood her, and all I had of Isabel was a person that I had constructed, based on my own imagination and my flights of fantasies… Maybe now that I had taken a new path, over the crossroads, I would look back and understand things more clearly. Maybe this was true, but perhaps nothing would ever be totally clear to me. I wondered whether I ought to feel ashamed about not having understood Isabel. I did not know. Maybe all these thoughts were just random flashes caused by the alcohol still in my system. I started to question myself, whether I knew who I was, where I was and what I was doing here in Beijing. Or what I had done since childhood, and whether my actions were all the results of my intention or merely the twists and turns of fate…

Knock knock.

I dragged my sorry self to the door, and put on a brave and happy face.

It was Charlie.

"Yo! How's it going?" He gave me a big grin as if he knew something that I didn't, then threw himself on the sofa and started to give me an account of the events last night. I didn't really want to listen to him, but was polite enough to stand there, leaning against the wall, with my arms folded.

It turned out that this girl and I were snogging like mad, then I tried to show her my Michael Jackson move, only to fall on my backside. There, on the floor, I rested, and had to be carried home. That explained why I'd woken up still wearing the same clothes.

"Don't worry mate. You'll get used to it," Charlie encouraged.

I thought I could handle my drink, as I was not exactly teetotal back in London. Clearly, that was just child's play compared to these guys…

Wait a minute. What did I come here for? To get pissed every night? I could have done precisely that without having made it all the way here!

"Na, I don't fancy going out tonight," I explained.

"Don't be a party pooper!" Charlie mocked. "Won't be a big night tonight. Just something to eat in the open-air market. You must see it! It's what Beijing in the summer is all about. The summer's almost over. So you'd better catch it!"

Well, it sounded cultural. I was in.

Not far from the school was a square full of food stalls. Smoke and steam rose from various places. Everything you cared to eat was on sticks. It was like some crazy shish kebab place but with vegetables and tofu too. As for the meat, there was lamb, chicken, whole small birds… No insects.

"They eat insects down south. Not here in Beijing. We'll go to the south at some point. There, wow, crazy! Snakes, grasshoppers, maggots, you name it, they've got it!" Charlie knew a lot.

"But," Danny added, "if you want the best shish kebab, or shashlik, you've got to go to Kashgar! Man, it's good. And the naan too. Fresh out of the tandoor. Well, China's a big place and in the northwest, they're like Turks or something. Eurasian. The girls there are pretty hot, but I didn't try, as the men looked a bit scary."

We had a few beers with our food. Danny and Charlie told me loads of things about Beijing and China. The dos and the don'ts.

Do shout out to the waitress if you want something in an ordinary eatery, otherwise you'll be there forever.

Don't shout at people in an argument. No one speaks English here.

Don't get into an argument in the first place.

Don't be afraid though, as people aren't violent here.

See any bobbies on the beat here? There's a reason why police patrols aren't needed here. But hey, that does mean that if something kicks off, however unlikely, there won't be any passing police to help. Don't worry, George. Don't get scared. The likelihood of you getting involved in some big trouble is… zero point zero zero… zero one percent.

Do try to chat up girls using your broken Chinese, as they think it's cute.

Don't bother chatting up girls if they look at all the homely type, as nine out of ten times you'll be banging your head against a brick wall. Go for those in short skirts and plenty of make-up. But don't go for the ones who just sit at the bar, as they're probably prostitutes.

Do talk to your fellow foreigner girls, as we are all in the same boat, surrounded by Chinese people. The girls can be easy too, as nine out of ten times they're in holiday mode, even though they might be working here. At any rate, Chinese blokes don't typically chat-up girls, foreign girls especially. Well, unless you're Jillian, in which case you do attract some attention with your blonde hair and big knockers. But hey, nothing came out of all that attention, did it? Anyway, those Chinese blokes who do try chatting-up foreign girls tend to be retards anyway and don't get anywhere. It's proven.

Jillian was absent again, so she could not talk for herself on this matter.

Don't bother entering a conversation with old expat men. I'm telling you, they can be the most boring people on Earth. Before you know it, somehow, they are part of your gang and you can't get rid of them…

So, my survival guide to Beijing was pretty informative – practical at least, if not highbrow.

"Culture?" Danny seemed to find the concept weird. "See what we are eating? How we are eating? This is culture, isn't it… Ah, you mean 'high' culture… Na, unless you've been here for twenty years and you're fluent in Chinese, you won't get it. Don't bother, I say… Peking Opera? Gosh, I'll find you a cat and torture it in front of you – it's the same thing."

25

It only took me a week or so to realise why Charlie felt so comfortable in my flat. I started to feel equally comfortable just barging into a fellow English teacher's place, asking for a beer upon entrance. In Beijing, it was rather easy to form bonds with our fellow foreigners, as we were living in our little enclave, tied together by our sense of being aliens. The locals were removed from our lives, as if it did not matter whether they existed or not. Well, it did matter, of course, as without them we would be without our comfortable livelihood. I wondered if I would ever feel and live like a local. Well, to do that, I would have to learn Chinese.

"You what? Learn Chinese?" Danny seemed surprised. "Mate, I've been there... umm... how many years now..." He did not seem to be able to remember, then he continued, "Na... You don't need to learn Chinese. Just a few words to get by. It's such a difficult language... I did try... Ugghh." He let out a rather prolonged groan of displeasure. "Na... Gave up after three months..."

"I tried too," Charlie added, as we sat comfortably in my flat, drinking beer. It was autumn and the night stalls, with their range of meat and vegetables on sticks, had packed away after a few evenings of heavy rain.

"Did you? Did you find it difficult too?" I asked. "I bought a book..." I walked to my bookshelf and picked out a thick volume.

"A waste of time, mate," Danny insisted.

Charlie took the book out of my hands and flicked casually through its pages. "It's damn hard. Well, you can just go in, do a bit of teaching, then get out and enjoy life. You've got us."

Yes, that was right. It would be difficult, of course, because none of us really interacted with any local people, but just got drunk among ourselves.

"I'll give it a go," I said.

"Get yourself a Chinese girlfriend or something, that might provide you with some motivation," Danny chuckled, "Then you'd get bogged down here. Before you know it, you've somehow got yourself married, had a kid, and you're going to her parents more than once a month… Ugh." Danny had that unique way of letting out a prolonged groan of displeasure, as if he had just been released after years in the gulags.

"Well, I'm not sure about that," I replied.

"Which part? The getting a girlfriend part or getting bogged down here?" Charlie asked. "If you want a Chinese girlfriend, I'll take you to hang out at the (so and so, I cannot remember the exact name) foreign language institute."

"Why?" I asked.

Danny laughed uncontrollably. "Yeah, ace!"

Charlie informed me that the institute was filled with underachieving, but fashionable youngsters from relatively well-to-do backgrounds. Most of the students were pretty girls and the only reason they wanted to learn a foreign language was to marry a foreign husband and then move abroad, often falsely believing that the moon was brighter abroad – that was the Chinese way of saying "the grass is greener on the other side".

"Did you try it yourself Danny?" I wondered if his laughter came from personal experience, as he was the Oldest China Hand in the room.

"Yeah, only for a while, before I realised that she was a complete retard."

"Or maybe she realised you were the complete retard!" Charlie mocked.

These two lads loved winding each other up, although they never managed to do it properly. At most, one would pretend to be angry, only to see if the other would believe he was truly angry, leading to wind-ups and counter wind-ups.

26

I enjoyed my time with the rest of the crew. Well, mostly, or at least sometimes. I felt I'd learnt some things from them and they were good people who had welcomed me with open arms. At the same time, I quite often felt tired of being with them. I just wanted some quiet company, but they did not seem to know what that meant; all they seemed to know was drinking, banter and wind-ups. I thought that Jillian felt the same as me, as she was often absent when they gathered. So, I told her how I felt one day, when we were walking back to our flats from school in the early afternoon.

"Yes, don't you feel how we live is a bit surreal?" Jillian agreed.

"It is quite bizarre. Each time Charlie or someone asks me to join them, I always struggle to say 'no'. I feel obliged, somehow. They are English teachers and so am I, so it's like some sort of unwritten rule that we must stick together, always. Don't get me wrong. I do enjoy being with them most of the time, but sometimes, I just feel that I need a break from it all. Do something else."

"You know, that's exactly how I feel! I've slowly built up this picture of a group of ants living in a little sandcastle – I know this sounds weird, but that's just me – and we all arrive here one by one, and we are meant to live in our little castle, with a moat and a drawbridge." She started to laugh, as she put her hands underneath her chin, fingers moving like ants' legs, with her eyes squeezed shut and her mouth protruding, pretending she was an ant. She continued, "We lower the drawbridge to crawl out to gather some food, as in teaching to earn our money, and as soon as that's done, we have to run back into our safe world of familiarities and pull up the drawbridge!" Jillian made lots of hand gestures as she spoke. She was clearly enjoying herself, as she burst out laughing.

I knew then that Jillian had not talked about this to anyone else, yet had longed to tell someone about it, and now she felt a sense of relief having done so. So did I. We laughed together, almost in tears.

We carried on exchanging views on our own situations, and joked about each of the crew members, impersonating their drunken laddish ways. Soon, we had arrived at our block of flats.

"Want to come in?" Jillian said as we reached her door.

"Sure." I was delighted to have found someone to open up to, who understood me.

Jillian's flat was just like mine. The biggest difference was that she had a laptop linked up to the internet. Oh, my tech-savvy reader, can you remember the days when Wi-Fi broadband was not available everywhere? Back then, nearly a decade before publishing this story, in Beijing, the most hi-tech equipment I had in my flat was a CD player that had been there before I'd arrived. Whenever I needed to use the internet, I went to an internet café. How different our lives were, before the days of widespread smartphone usage and 'all you can eat' data! Back then, I did not even bother getting a simple mobile phone, as I had no need to call anyone.

Jillian could not survive without the internet, and to go to an internet café every day was too much work for her. So, she asked for connections to be set up in her flat. The school duly obliged, after taking some money from her.

We had some tea together that afternoon, and carried on chatting about how we felt. I enjoyed Jillian's company. I felt comfortable there with her, as if finally, I had found a sense of home.

Ever since that early autumn afternoon, Jillian and I became true friends. Although I did not go to her flat every day, my visits were frequent. I would bring something occasionally, such as vegetables I had bought from the local market. The beef tomatoes in China were big and juicy. Jillian would cook for me sometimes in the evenings. Her signature dish was instant noodles with beef tomatoes and eggs, plus a few bits of spring onions to top it all off. The instant noodles in China usually had three sachets – soup powder, oil, and dried bits of vegetables. Every now and then, I would find myself having my noodles with her, sitting on the sofa watching yet another episode of Travelogue on CCTV 9 – China Central Television and not Closed-Circuit Television. That was the only English channel on TV. The programme was not bad, although I preferred to watch documentaries about old scholars, their intellectual pursuits, the harsh conditions they faced during the Cultural Revolution and their tormented love-lives. Jillian occasionally shared an interest in these documentaries, but we mainly just read after supper and talked about what we had just read.

I enjoyed reading about Chinese history on the internet, and through my research, I managed to establish a loose understanding of the country's peaks and troughs over the course of thousands of years. If my knowledge was incomplete it sparked more questions that were satisfied by further browsing and reading. The facts were not dry at all – in my mind, they emerged either as a whole or as miniature paintings. Facts? I recalled my history teacher from my old school repeatedly stressing that history was not about the past, but interpretations of the past. Whatever, I found that facts, stories, myths, legends and folklore, all had their place in my mind, satisfying my curiosity…

Did the Shang charioteers arrive in China from the west over three thousand years ago or were they native to the land of central China? How did the army of the Martial Emperor of the Han Dynasty manage to march all the way to modern day Uzbekistan to secure the heavenly horses that sweated blood? Once the Xiongnu were defeated by the Hans, did they travel west and became known as the Huns? Were there really Roman soldiers in the Han army? Born in modern-day Kyrgyzstan, could the Tang poet Li Bai have spoken any of the languages of Central Asia, and what were those languages? Did Marco Polo bring noodles from China to Italy, which then became spaghetti?

Jillian would sometimes listen to my reading of various things I had found on the internet. Sometimes, I knew she was not listening, but reading her magazines – sometimes the same ones, for there were hardly any English publications in the city. At times, I wondered if I was intruding on her life. However, overall, I believed that she enjoyed my company, even though for a good proportion of the time, I was physically closer to the computer screen than to her. Sometimes, I felt we just enjoyed being in the company of someone we were comfortable with – nothing loud or wild, just a peaceful, almost quiet life with a hint of normality, whatever normality was meant to be here in Beijing.

We usually did not have any alcohol when we were together, so it was almost like a detox after the nights out I'd had with the crew. I never left her place late; usually saying bye before ten in the evening, and she was always courteous when seeing me off.

Occasionally, when I was at Jillian's, I had flashbacks of my time with Isabel, not that they were in any way similar. Jillian was taller and paler, both physically and emotionally. There was no infatuation here. Everything seemed so plain, real, and ordinary. Yes, Jillian was pretty but my heart simply did not race when I looked at her. Maybe that was fate.

Sometimes, when I got back to my flat at night, I thought about Isabel. It would be the late morning or early afternoon in London and I wondered how she was getting on at the wine shop. Maybe she was explaining a vintage to a customer. Maybe she was having a cigarette break. Maybe she was chatting to a new member of staff, perhaps a young lad who was dark and slick from Madeira, an excellent swimmer and a great tease. Maybe she was getting on well with this new guy. Maybe they had started dating. Perhaps he had already moved in with her and taken his place in the bed I used to sleep in… My thoughts ran on and on. I started to depict all the tiny little details… It hurt. However, I somehow enjoyed this pain, just as I had enjoyed tormenting myself when I first met Isabel. No, it was not enjoyment. How could torment ever be enjoyable? And yet why was I continuing like this, hurting myself, as if I was my own blood sport… What was going on?! Was this all my subconscious way of pushing myself along? To let go? To go? Move on? Maybe I had not yet put Isabel finally behind me, in the past. Maybe. Maybe…

27

Although I spent more and more time with Jillian, I still enjoyed drinking with the crew occasionally. I guessed I needed a mixture of both quiet and wild times. Meanwhile, my Chinese book rested on the shelf, gathering some dust. I looked at it a few times from a distance, but never bothered picking it up after Lesson Three. Yep, there was no need to learn. I was getting by just fine.

I was fine. I had a reasonably-paid job, work was mega easy, once I had stopped trying my best and realised that everyone was just cruising along like me. I no longer went to see the director of studies for advice and she never bothered to ask me how I was getting on either.

Sometimes, I thought about why they had not employed a couple of people working full-time rather than a whole bunch of us working pretty much on a part-time basis. Then I guessed that it made the school's brochure look better if it said there were dozens of foreign experts working here, rather than a small handful.

If you bought your beer from a local shop, it was only a tiny bit more expensive than bottled water. No wonder the builders working down the road had bottles of beer over lunch and you'd often see people enjoying a beer as if they were having a soft drink. The locals didn't really misbehave after binges – sure, they binged like we did – but would head home instead of singing football songs with their fingers in the air. I had never seen a drunken brawl here, which was good, as I was not the fighting type anyway.

Yep, I was just fine. I didn't miss home at all.

28

Shit! Shit! Shit!!

I woke up with yet another hangover after a night out with the crew. Thank God it was Saturday! Okay, it was midday and the sun was practically shining on my backside. What was the plan for today? Yep, I was meeting up with Danny and Charlie. Well, Tom, Phil, Gav and Jillian as well perhaps. Activity? Sod all. We might go to Xidan, the shopping area, even though I could not think of anything I needed to buy. After that, the Back Sea area for drinks. Then, maybe some karaoke at Party World. Man, Party World was fantastic! Decorated like some five-star hotel, it had comfortable private booths, real music videos on the screens, rather than the usual random stuff or no pictures at all, plus the complementary all-you-can-eat buffet, which was really quite nice.

I got up, thinking over the plans for the day.

Shit! Shit! Shit!!

My head went wooooosh. I dragged myself to the kitchen and turned on the boiler. I was a pro by then, following Mr Lu's instructions, which I vividly remembered from Day One.

Uuuugh… As the warm water hit me, I let out a prolonged groan… People always say that a hot shower sobers you up. Sober…

Shit! Shit! Shit!!

I slapped my face. Ouch! That hurt.

What was I doing? Why was I here? Who was I with? Hell! I didn't come all this way to repeat the life I had wanted to leave behind in London!

After my shower, I sat down on the sofa and shook my head like a wet dog. There, on top of the TV, stood my little statue. He was looking at me. I looked at him. I saw his disappointment. He was screaming at me about why I had let myself down. I pictured him standing on the mantelpiece at Isabel's flat. I remembered how I had looked at him back then and decided to come to China. How would Isabel feel if she knew that I had left the boozy London life only to repeat it here? If I were her, I would be disappointed. No, more than that, if Isabel had left me, saying that she was going to change her life, but had ended up not doing so, I would have felt she had lied to me, and that the only reason she wanted to leave was to leave me, rather than to pursue some great ambition. If that was the case, I would have preferred she had just told me, simply, without all this lying. In my mind, I was kicking and screaming at myself, saying, "See? In front of you, George, there is the crossroads. Cross it! And take the right path!"

I called Charlie to say I would not be coming today and I just wanted to spend the day alone. He thought I had gone mad, and wondered if I was turning into a sad loser.

No, it was they who were mad, sad losers…

I opened my drawer, and pulled out a box file containing all sorts of random things I had brought over from England. Among the bits of paperwork, certificates, photos, I found that little piece of paper Isabel gave me just before I left London.

I went and sat on the sofa and looked at it. A Chinese name. A telephone number…

29

In imperial times, there were two main markets in the city, east and west of the palace. Linking the two markets and the Gate of Heavenly Peace was the Avenue of Eternal Peace. In the 1960s, during the People's Republic, Line One of the Beijing Metro was built underneath the avenue. I travelled on the underground train and got off at the West Market – Xidan. Although it was December and most of the trees had shed their leaves, the sun warmed me as I surfaced. I headed east.

I was happy, and at the same time, slightly nervous. I smoked, marching along, in my grandfather's greatcoat. My grandfather was in the army, briefly, and he managed to keep his green military greatcoat, with the Queen's Coat of Arms proudly displayed on the buttons. I wondered whether I had chosen the right attire – whether a display of British military association was appropriate for this meeting with a Chinese person who could help me, given the British military's past, which could be perceived as one of imperialism. But then again, I did not bring with me another greatcoat. To cope with the winter in Beijing, one had to wear a greatcoat. Was I overthinking? Probably.

I arrived at Beijing Hotel, situated between the West Market and the Gate of Heavenly Peace. The hotel's magnificent columns stood proudly at the entrance, greeting me. They were decorated with Communist symbols – flags, wheat sheaves, sickles, gears and hammers… It was quite an awe-inspiring sight, as if this grand entrance was built to cow any visitors and ward off the evil ones who dared to challenge the might of the red flag…

I straightened my coat and assured myself that although I was the grandson of a colonial officer, I was a good person and the red flag should look kindly on me.

I walked in. The footman gave me a polite nod. The lobby was grand, with large Art Deco chandeliers hanging from the ceiling. Through the tall windows – as tall as those in a cathedral – everything was bright, with a tinge of gold. It was the work of the soft sunlight on this winter afternoon. It was warm inside, so I started to unbutton my coat, while looking around for the café.

And there it was. I sat down.

A waiter floated over.

"A cup of coffee, please."

The waiter returned. Real coffee, the aroma of which I had not smelt since arriving in China, where coffee was rare.

Quarter to four. I was slightly early. I took off my coat and tossed it on the sofa. I found some English magazines and flicked through them, just to pass some time, and enjoyed a smoke. It was a Chinese brand that I had randomly bought in a shop. Chinese cigarettes were different. They were… how could I describe them? They tended to be higher on the tar level, but tasted smoother and were full of aroma, with more 'body', like some wine. I liked these cigarettes. Charlie did not. He and the rest of the crew stuck to the Western brands, like Marlboro Lights.

A man about my height entered the lobby. He was wearing a dark blue blazer, a garment rarely seen in China, especially one with polished brass buttons. He wore a pink shirt, open collar, two buttons undone. He also had a medium brown belt, grey chinos and medium brown brogues. He gave the waiter a gentle nod, who then followed him. He did not have a coat with him, so I guessed he must have arrived here in a warm car, rather than by public transport.

He walked towards me. Some signs of chest hair, rare among Chinese men. Were those dark pink socks? Radical. Unseen in China. He had hair with a side-parting that was neatly trimmed, thick eyebrows, tall nose, sideburns and angular jaw. He looked a bit older than he did in the photo I saw of him and Isabel on the fridge in Clapham. Overall, quite a dashing man still, a Westernised playboy. I noticed that he wore no jewellery, neck chains or rings, which was not surprising as I had never seen any Chinese men wearing them.

"You must be George!" His English was almost perfect, with the flair of a bygone aristocratic era, filled with a sense of nonchalance, warmth and self-belief.

I stood up and we shook my hands, his eyes looking sharply into mine; they looked a lot sharper than those of the average Chinese man I'd shaken hands with. He smiled, displaying a few quiet wrinkles around the corners of his mouth.

"I hope I haven't disturbed your afternoon." My opening gambit was delivered as calmly as I could.

"Not at all, old bean! Not at all. I'm free now. Well, I have to make a dash at five, however." He then spoke to the waiter, as we sat down. The waiter floated away.

Old bean? A Chinese man speaking English so perfectly, using phrases like 'old bean'. Okay, he did go to Oxford, but there were a few Chinese students at my university too, and all of them spoke with thick Chinese accents, and of course, there were no words like 'old bean'.

"Did Isabel mention to you that I was…?"

"Nope. I haven't been in touch with her for quite a while now. Have you been enjoying your time in Beijing?" Before I could answer, I saw him looking at my coat. He stepped over, asking, "May I?"

"Of course." I handed him my coat.

As he stretched out his arms, the blazer's gold buttons reflected in the sunlight.

"Fine, very fine. The British had some fine buttons. Very fine coat," he said, expressing his admiration for my imperialist garment. "A family heirloom? Seen any action?"

"Yes, it's my grandfather's. Um… No, he didn't see any action…" I did not think the old man's participation in the Korean War, on the side of the imperialist aggressors, would put me at an advantage here. I took a sip of my coffee.

He asked about me and I told him a bit about my background, an abridged version of my past.

"George is a powerful name," Mr Na commented. He then explained his name to me – Bohan. 'Bo' meant 'broad', which was typically used when talking about one's collection of books, and 'han' was a literary Chinese term for writing or painting brushes, associated with the imperial academy. Then, he laughed at himself, "Well, I wouldn't say I've lived up to the great expectations of my parents who gave me such a scholarly name!"

I laughed at myself and explained how I was hardly the epitome of a dragon slayer.

The waiter floated over to us, then poured Mr Na's tea. Wearing white gloves, he rested the little white porcelain pot on the table and then floated away again.

Mr Na put my coat back on the sofa, then took out a packet of cigarettes from his blazer pocket. He gestured if I wanted one. I politely declined. He took one out and lit it with a match. "How's your stay in Beijing so far?" We resumed our conversation from earlier.

He sat back down in the large armchair, cross-legged, with one arm flat on the armrest and another standing up, his other hand holding the cigarette, while the smoke rose gently. He looked so at ease here, as if he owned this café, this hotel, this city, this world.

"It's been very good," I explained, starting with my first impression at the airport, my flat, my friends from the school, and then naturally moved onto my problem. Having told him how I felt here, that I was wasting my life with a bunch of drunken fellow Brits, I was amazed by how the conversation progressed, as if he had set up some steps for me to climb so that I could get to the point where I wanted to be, but was worried that I would be too shy to take the steps myself, uninvited.

"Good." He stubbed out his cigarette.

Good? Did he derive some morbid pleasure out of my difficult situation?

"I like what I'm hearing. I know what you mean," he smiled. "If you don't mind, we could explore the idea of you coming to help me," he said gently, as if he was asking me a favour.

"Of course!" I leapt at this opportunity, although I did not know what it was – whatever it was, it would be better than getting drunk every night and teaching a few kindergarten kids from rich families who probably just wanted some extravagant babysitting service.

"Very good of you!" He looked at his watch. "It's five o'clock. I guess our chit-chat has taken up too much time. But hey, it isn't a business meeting. I'm afraid I must dash." He stood up.

Oh? But he had not told me what I could do for him. I wanted to ask, but held myself back, trusting that he was not just saying it to make the situation amicable. I stood up too.

"Well, we haven't gone into any detail about how you could help me, but I'm sure you will be able to, if you so wish. Haven't got enough time now, old fruit. Got to go. But why don't you come over to mine… um… on Friday. Dinner. Seven o'clock, okay with you? Here is my address." He took out a pen and scribbled on the serviette.

"Of course." I was delighted to have been invited over for dinner.

"Cheerio!" He dashed off. Handing the waiter some money on his way out.

I threw myself back into my chair and lit a cigarette. I smoked in self-congratulation.

30

"Hey George!" A voice came from behind me as I walked back from the school on a Friday afternoon. It was Charlie. He excitedly explained his plan for a pub crawl that evening, this time in an area that meant 'five level crossings' when translated into English.

"You're not coming?!"

"I'm meeting a friend of a friend," I explained.

"Who's this?"

"No one that you know."

Charlie looked puzzled. Maybe he thought he knew everyone I knew, and vice versa, so where this new friend of a friend had jumped out from perplexed him.

"Long story," I said, trying to brush it away.

Charlie looked at me. His lips parted as if wanting to ask me about this long story, but perhaps realised that had I wanted to explain things to him, I would have. His lips closed again. He nodded slightly and we carried on walking, in total silence. Our block of flats had never felt so far away from the school. Thankfully, we did not walk the whole way together.

"I'm off to the shops," Charlie muttered. "See you around." He patted me on my back and walked off.

I stood there for a little while and watched him crossing the wide road. Shops? I could not see any.

Knock, knock.

It was Jillian. She asked me if I fancied coming to the park for a stroll. Anyone else coming? Nope. Fine.

The park was just one of those nondescript places, like the commons in London, or the village green in the Cotswolds. The wintry air cut like little knives into my nostrils as I breathed. I loved it all. It made me feel conscious of being alive. No smell of booze anywhere. Refreshing. I smiled.

"Do you feel odd? I mean, about the situation we are in?" Jillian asked.

I did not know how to respond. I was not sure what she meant, whether she was referring to our alien status in this land, how we were different to our drunken fellow Britishers, or the two of us. Surely not the last.

My hesitation and silence led her to elaborate, "I haven't been here long – a few months longer than you, but still, not long. I have been enjoying myself, but I knew that something wasn't quite right."

Sure, there had been some changes. She was glad that I had arrived. At first, she had felt she'd been thrown into the deep end with the veterans, those battle-hardened tough nuts, who appeared to have no idea what sympathy or empathy meant. I was glad that she shared the same feelings as me.

While the crew was a tight-knit mini-community, somehow neither Jillian nor I felt comfortable in confiding in the rest of the gang. Yes, it was okay to muck about with them and share the good times, but anything profound, sad or downbeat would be met with indifference or even despised.

"But now, I can see my life changing, and I so want to tell someone about it, and you are the closest person I have here... I have met someone," Jillian confided.

It turned out that she had met a Chinese guy online who wrote beautiful poetry in English. Very rare. So, she was captivated by all this. She then met him a couple of days ago, face-to-face for the first time, for a simple supper. Where? In a little eatery not far from West Market. He studied in England and spoke good English, and hence the poetry. He mostly wrote poems in Chinese, but he was familiar with the works of Auden, Shelley and Byron.

"Well... that's good news." Perhaps I did not say it with great passion.

"Don't worry, George. We will always be good friends." She tried to comfort me. "Anyway, it's very early days. Let's see how it goes. You know, I need a new life. I need it. This place is suffocating."

"I might be about to start a new life too," I smiled. Jillian was intrigued. I told her about my meeting a couple of days ago at Beijing Hotel.

"I have no idea what Mr Na meant when he said he'd be able to help me. We didn't get to talk about anything in detail as he had to shoot off," I explained, "I guess everything will become clear tonight, when I go to his for dinner. Anyway, what's your man's name?"

"His name? Guangxuan."

"What does it mean?" I asked, still struggling with local names.

"Guang means wide," she explained. "Xuan is something to do with the paper that a calligrapher uses."

We laughed about how Chinese people bestowed their children with such ambitious literary names.

31

That evening, the taxi driver took my little piece of paper and looked slightly puzzled, as if he had never seen an address before, and everyone else travelled with references to local landmarks instead. He made a phone call and after a few *hao*s and *aye*s, he pulled away from the curb.

It was already quite dark as we travelled along Beijing's poplar-lined boulevards. Then, the streets narrowed and the buildings shrank as we entered central Beijing, inside the Second Ring Road that's built on the ruins of the city wall.

I was not sure that he knew exactly where we were going. I thought I saw the same place twice, and the driver made more calls. Then, he stopped. No, we had not arrived. He went to an old man who was walking by. He came back after a few nods and we continued on our journey. Meanwhile, I looked at the bottle of Shiraz I had bought from a shop specialising in imported luxury food and drink, and wondered if this was a good choice. Sure, it was expensive enough.

Finally, as the meter ticked towards forty yuan, we arrived at my destination. I handed over the money and got out.

I stood in front of the entrance and straightened my greatcoat. Like many entrances to courtyard homes in the old quarters of Beijing, the entrance here was almost like a little house in its own right, with a sloping roof to shelter the visitor as he waited for someone to open the door. Two drum-shaped stones stood, one on each side of the large red double doors. The red paint had faded a little. The door knobs were two stylised lion heads, each holding a mental ring between its teeth. I knocked using one of the metal door knockers and stood there for a little while, before knocking again. Still no answer. Then I noticed the electric door bell. Doh. I rang the bell.

A girl opened the door. She was plain looking, slightly peasant-like. I could not say what made me think that she was a peasant. Perhaps it was her slightly weatherbeaten face, although she looked just eighteen or nineteen. Perhaps it was her plain jumper.

"I'm here to see Mr Na." In China, many people simply referred to themselves only by their surnames, and it was impolite to use unfamiliar people's given names.

She said "yes" in English, and then some words in Chinese as she led me in through the little gatehouse. We turned left, passing a row of bungalows in the outer courtyard, and then to our right there was another gatehouse. It was much more ornate than the one that faced the street, with carved wooden beams, some painted. She opened the door and led me in. In contrast to the passageway we had just come through, which looked nothing special, here the view was more impressive. This was the inner courtyard, the main part of Mr Na's residence.

Arranged around the square courtyard were three bungalows with sloping roofs and red pillars. The largest one faced me with its roofline higher than the two smaller ones on the left and right edge of the courtyard. The three houses were all connected by pavilion-like passageways, with ornate paintings on the beams. In the middle of the courtyard, there was a fishpond.

I turned and looked at the gatehouse behind me, and it looked just as ornate on this side as it had on the other. On the walls, a few lantern-like lamps lit up this courtyard. I looked at the lamp nearest to me, which appeared to be made of bronze. The girl led me to the middle of the courtyard, by the pond. There were four koi swimming idly, sometimes apart, sometimes close together, then parting again. There was some vegetation in the pond, but had become sparse in the winter.

The door of the bungalow on the right opened. My host emerged looking much less Western than when I had last seen him. He was wearing a long, dark blue robe with Mandarin collars. I saw two knotted cloth buttons, fastened; one at his neck and one halfway towards his right shoulder. His hair was slicked back neatly. Mr Na closed the door behind him gently, and walked down the little steps onto the square towards me.

"Glad you could come," he spoke softly and gestured a "please". Gently, he insisted that I walked into the main house first, then closed the door behind him. There was a slight squeak. Mr Na's gentle words and gestures somehow negated the need for shaking hands. The fact that we did not, as per Western norms, did not jolt me at all. It felt natural to me, strangely perhaps. The girl who had led me here had disappeared.

The hall, or living room, or whatever it should be called, was quite large with a Chinese ink painting in the middle. This depicted a river flowing in a gorge, with a little boat floating on the river and a little pavilion standing on top of one of the mountain peaks. There were two scrolls of calligraphy, one on each side of the painting. Of course, I had no idea what they said, but the writing looked beautiful in its flowing style. Under the painting, there were two wooden chairs facing me, of the sort I had seen in films about China in the olden days. Between the chairs, there was a teak table.

Mr Na turned left and led me to the dining area, with a round table surrounded by four stools. On the table, two bowls and two pairs of chopsticks were already laid out.

I felt as if I had stepped back into the imperial China of centuries ago. Without his sharp blazer, Mr Na appeared to have become a different person in this setting. Which Mr Na did Isabel see?

"Please," he said, inviting me to sit down. His gestures were flowing and subtle, as if to move more would have compromised the elegance of this setting. "Many people are not used to having dinner sitting on these stools. I could give you a chair should you wish." He spoke softly and calmly, with words that rolled off his tongue gently, without being animated. His manner made me feel that all the world's affairs, however dramatic they were – wars, famines, earthquakes, floods and forest fires – would be like floating leaves on a trickling stream to him – merely passing by, without troubling his philosophical mind.

"No, it's fine. Thank you." I took the bottle of Shiraz out from the plastic bag. "I hope it's okay."

"Too kind," he smiled a little. "If you were Chinese, I'd say, no, there's no need. Then you'd counter argue, then we'd spend a minute or so in this ritual of 'no' followed by 'please'. Would you like to try it?" Despite the jovial nature of his suggestion, his expression was still calm and gentle, as if it would have been uncouth to laugh out loud.

I thought it was quite a fun idea, so we went through this act, with me the foreign devil aping the elegance and grace of the Celestial Kingdom. We both laughed a little over this piece of theatre.

"Times have changed, George," Mr Na quietly explained. "People are more direct with each other these days, even in China. Old rituals are dying. Some say it's a good thing, as there is no need for pretence. Others say it's a terrible thing, for such rituals have been part of our culture. Perhaps it is good that we, in the East, do some things differently from you in the West. The world would be a rather boring place if everyone was the same, don't you think?" He smiled a little and found a corkscrew in the sideboard. I handed him the bottle and he popped it open effortlessly. He took out two wine glasses and placed them down on the table.

"Shall we air it?"

"Let's not. I can't wait to have a sip," I spoke directly, without ritual.

He smiled, pouring some for me first, then for himself. The glasses stood on the marble table, with natural patterns that looked like they had been pasted from a traditional Chinese ink painting of mountains and rivers.

He raised his glass, "To your good health."

"To yours too!" I exclaimed, then suddenly thought that I had spoken too loudly, so uncouth. Before I could adjust my tone to suit the environment and my host's demeanour, I had already taken a large gulp of my wine.

Mr Na flicked the back of his long robe then sat down. Compared to his all-at-ease posture in the armchair at Beijing Hotel, he was now, at home, sitting perfectly straight on the hard stool. At the same time, he was not stiff, but comfortable in his old-world Eastern posture.

Mr Na sipped, then looked at the wine and said, "Very good, George. I haven't had Shiraz for quite a while. Shiraz, the city of Persia, where poets sat in the shade, drinking this fine wine and exchanging words of wisdom." He sipped again, then reflected, "How interesting the world has changed. You know, wine was part of society before Islam became strict with people's habits in more recent times. That has been true for Persia, also true for the northwestern region of China. There are many poems and songs from that part of the country, mentioning wine as part of the celebration of harvest and laments over lost love, even after most people there had converted to Islam about a thousand years ago." He spoke with his eyes half closed, almost dreamily.

At the end of the hall, there was a little door. It opened. The girl who first led me in, came through with a tray. She laid out the dishes from the tray onto the table, and then went away.

"A few humble dishes. Hope you like them." He gestured for me to start.

"I wouldn't say they are humble!" My mouth was watering. There was lamb fried with leeks, aubergine with bits of chillies and garlic, and meatballs in a red sauce.

As we ate, I provided a quick recap of our conversation in Beijing Hotel about how I felt I was wasting my time at the kindergarten, and that I wanted to live a more meaningful life. He listened to me without interruption, then as I finished, he smiled and put his chopsticks down.

"I understand what you mean. To find your purpose in life is the start of the ultimate fulfilment. In that search, you have to try out different things."

"True. I'd love to try something else now."

"What do you think about the migrant workers in Beijing?" he asked.

I did not know what to say at first. I was not expecting this question. I mumbled along, explaining that I had noticed them, as they were everywhere – building houses, cleaning the streets, running small eateries, working as waiters and waitresses.

Mr Na explained to me that since the economic reforms that had started in the late 1970s and picked up pace in the 1980s, people were allowed to move in search of work. When they relocated from the countryside to the cities, many people left their kids behind with the grandparents in the villages, so that the kids could continue to go to school. But others did not want to live away from their children and see them only three times a year, during the May Day holidays, National Day holidays and Chinese New Year. So they brought their kids to Beijing. However, they were not registered residents, so they were not entitled to schooling here.

Some migrant workers tried to educate their kids at home, but some found it too difficult to find a balance between work and teaching their kids. Facing financial pressures, some sent their kids out to work. But, being kids, they could not find real work. So, they did random little things, like selling roses at night to lovers walking down the street. Sadder still, some sent their kids out to steal. Being kids, they could not be persecuted. The parents could be fined, but the kids would often just receive a warning from the police and were let off. Sometimes, they would be ordered to leave Beijing and go back to their registered homeland. Given that there was little to do at home, as it did not require five brothers to look after a single herd of goats, some would simply return and do exactly what they had done before. China was going through a massive change, from the planned economy to a market-orientated one, and social services had not caught up.

"It's a great shame that these kids can't go to school," I empathised.

He smiled, "Very good of you to feel this way. This is a good start."

At this point, we had finished the dishes. The girl came and brought dessert – little yellow cones.

"Try," he gestured.

"Very nice. Not very sweet, but so fine in texture. What is this made of?"

"Chestnuts and maize."

"Chestnuts and maize?" I was quite surprised, as it was so finely ground, with such a smooth, almost silky texture.

"Chun'er bought these from *fang shan*. *Fang* means to imitate, and *Shan* means meal, but more specifically, Palace meal. When the last emperor was driven out from the Forbidden City in the early twentieth century, his cooks became unemployed. So, they opened a teahouse and brought Palace cuisine to the wider public."

"Chun'er?" I wanted to ask Mr Na who she was, and before I could string together a full sentence, he was ready to explain. Meanwhile, Chun'er topped up our glasses. She smiled and exited.

"She's my helper here. My grandfather still knows a lot of people from his olden days when he fought the Japanese and the Nationalists. That was in the countryside. Every now and then, an old acquaintance would ask him for help, to get a son or a daughter moved to Beijing. So, he takes on the youngsters, first as domestic helpers, then later, they find other things to do. Chun'er has been here for a couple of years now. She says she's okay working here. I pay her a bit, as well as providing food and accommodation. My last helper worked here for a just a year, and then became acquainted with the publishing world. She became an entrepreneur, buying and selling children's books. I wonder when Chun'er might leave me for better things." Mr Na paused a little, then continued without haste, "Talking about better things… where were we? Yes, schooling for migrant workers' children…"

"Yes, you were talking about the lack of schools for these kids."

"That's right. Before dessert arrived, I was about to tell you about my work in this area. I run a little school for these children. So, when you said you wanted to find some meaningful work, I wondered whether you'd entertain the idea of teaching at my school," Mr Na smiled.

"Oh, yes, I'd be delighted to help!" I said, feeling excited.

Mr Na looked less overtly excited. His face was not animated like mine. Perhaps that was his Eastern calmness, refinement and elegance. He just smiled a little and explained that he had set up this school a couple of years ago, with a few paid staff but mostly volunteers. They had turned a brownfield site and converted workshops and warehouses into a makeshift school. His speech was all matter of fact, as if it was all part of an ordinary act of kindness, as ordinary as saying 'please' or 'thank you'.

"We only have one English teacher at our school, and I don't know how long she'll stay on for. She's rather old. She's a volunteer. There is someone else who teaches English occasionally. However, we don't have many teachers. The teachers who are not volunteers are paid one thousand five hundred yuan a month. Don't laugh at this sum, which I know is only equivalent to about one hundred and fifty pounds. I know it's not a lot, but it's more than what many of the kids' parents are paid. People do live off such money in Beijing. As you'll have noticed, it is a lot cheaper here than in the UK. Unless, of course, you want to drink at bars in *hou hai* every night."

"It's a decent amount," I assured him, even though the amount he offered was about a sixth of my wages at the kindergarten.

"As for welfare, we all help each other. As for the school's coffers, I have established some steady sources of income, so paying wages shouldn't be a problem. We're a charity, not a business, so we do have to go cap in hand and rely on donations. So, there is some risk and perhaps one day, the funding will dry up. But so far so good." Mr Na picked up his glass. "So, what do you say?"

"I say, yes! I'm in." I lifted my glass with enthusiasm.

"Cheers," Mr Na smiled.

"Cheers!"

We finished our wine and I thanked him for the superb dinner.

"It's nothing, just our humble homely dishes. I'm glad you liked them. I look forward to sharing more of our country's cuisine with you in the future." Mr Na nodded, as we stood up.

Mr Na walked with me, out of the inner courtyard and through the outer courtyard. We agreed that I would come to visit the school. He opened the front door for me and we nodded to each other, and bid goodbye. I exited from the Na residence, that film set, got back on to the main road and flagged down a taxi. As I sat in the cab, I felt very merry. At the same time, I struggled to piece together this Mr Na. Was he the dashing Western playboy I had met at the hotel or the old-world Eastern gentleman in his traditional long robe that I had met tonight? However, my mind did not dwell on him for too long. Instead, I dreamt about starting a new life…

32

"I know, the best cure for any illness is alcohol," Danny exclaimed, "but there's an even better cure – well, it goes hand-in-hand with alcohol – quick-boiled lamb – *shuan yang rou!*"

Jillian had often said she was ill to excuse herself from the rest of crew, as a cover for her dates. I had also been telling the crew that I was not feeling well to excuse myself too. Yet, we both knew that the rest of the crew knew that we were not really ill, and they all knew that we knew that they knew. Did they drop in on us only to find out that we were not there? At least we had not been ill and absent at the same time, so that they would not think we were forming a splinter group, breaking away from them. What had life come to?

Given I had not had quick-boiled lamb before, I was ready for this new experience. Jillian was happy to go as well.

Midday. Taxi. Restaurant.

"Quick-boiled lamb – *shuan yang rou*. Yeah! Bring it on!" Danny was delighted as he threw himself onto a chair. "You know this stuff – invented by the Mongols. Yeah! That's how they conquered half of the world! This place is pretty authentic. It uses traditional charcoal pots – none of that electric cooker nonsense."

The waiter set up the table. A large brass pot sat in the middle, with charcoal burning beneath, and the smoke rising through the pot's chimney. Dishes were brought to our table and surrounded the pot. The meat was sliced as thin as paper. The pot contained a broth with ginger and various other flavoursome roots, as well as plenty of chillies.

"This is how you do it," Danny demonstrated. He dipped in the meat, which cooked instantly in the boiling broth. He then dipped this cooked meat in his bowl of sesame sauce, which also had chilli oils, fermented tofu, plus a sprinkle of spring onion and coriander. He then went on to quick-boil other things too, like tofu, glass noodles, spinach, Chinese cabbage, bean sprouts and enoki mushrooms.

I followed, together with Jillian. The other members of the crew were too busy downing glasses of lager.

"How did they invent this?" I asked Danny.

Danny gave us a little lecture. Legend had it, the dish was invented by Kublai Khan, during the fifty-year war between the Mongols and the Southern Song Dynasty. One day, the Mongols suddenly found themselves facing an approaching Song army and there was no time to roast whole lambs. No soldier could not fight well on an empty stomach. To make things worse, it was wintertime, and the meat was all frozen solid. Suddenly, Kublai Khan came up with a great idea. He asked the cooks to slice the frozen lamb as thinly as paper and put the pots on, filled with hot water. Dip, quick-boil, eat. The soldiers were soon well fed and managed to repel the enemy. Some say that battle was an important turning point in the war, and all thanks to quick-boiled lamb.

Danny was proud of his knowledge. I was proud of him too. It seemed almost strange that this knowledgeable Old China Hand should enjoy mucking about with the crew so much, mostly talking nonsense. It seemed to be the done thing for him, and everyone else to appear almost stupid. Maybe it was a sense of reverse snobbery.

We conquered a few kilos of lamb between us, plus a case of beer. No one asked me or Jillian about our recent illnesses. Instead, after Danny's lecture, people talked about other things. What did people talk about? My memory fails me. But I do remember that throughout lunch, my thoughts were elsewhere, away from the crew.

I looked at Jillian as she half-heartedly engaged in the conversation. She saw me looking at her, and looked into my eyes. We looked into each other's eyes, and understood that we were both at our crossroads, waiting to take our step across, down our new paths.

As the charcoal burnt underneath the pot, and the broth boiled in the pot, I gazed at the flames. I burnt...

33

I arranged with Mr Na to visit his school in south Beijing on Tuesday morning. He told me how to get there by bus. It was quite a long journey, involving an interchange. Mr Na could not be there, so Teacher Zhou would meet me at the bus stop. She was the current English teacher, the retired volunteer. As for her title, I had gathered that in China, teachers were not referred to as Mr or Mrs or Miss or Ms, but as Teacher. In any case, I knew that in China, no woman would change her surname upon marriage, so all females were Ms.

An elderly lady in a greatcoat greeted me at the bus stop with a smile. Her hair was short, completely white, slicked back. "Glad to meet you, George." She had that typical Beijing accent. Not very smooth.

"Nice to meet you too, Teacher Zhou."

"Our school is a little walk away from here, but I'm sure you're warm enough under your greatcoat."

We started walking. Here, in southern Beijing, things looked different. There were not many people, hardly any smart high-rises. There were some old brick bungalows. Some looked inhabited, others derelict, with smashed windows. The roads were not busy with traffic. In the distance, a man was peddling a tricycle, with a large board at the back on which a giant box was tied down. A group of shabbily-dressed young men cycled past us, slowly and silently. There was no pavement on this road we were walking on, just compact earth, frozen. In the distance, I saw dust rising as a lorry crossed a junction. The trees were leafless, standing there quietly, together with old industrial chimneys, smokeless.

"Why is this area of Beijing so different?" I asked.

Teacher Zhou explained, "It is less developed. Since hundreds of years ago, the rich and the noble people lived in the northern parts of Beijing, while poor people doing low grade jobs lived in south Beijing. Things are changing, but not over night. Has Mr Na told you a lot about our school?"

I informed her that I knew a little bit about the school thanks to Mr Na, and that I had been looking forward to this visit ever since my dinner at Mr Na's residence.

"Yes, Mr Na has a very nice place."

"You've been?"

"Yes, every year, just before the Chinese New Year, Mr Na hosts a party for all of us teachers from the school, plus some of his contacts in high places. It's almost Chinese New Year now."

"I was amazed by Mr Na's place. It was like a film set, very different from the sort of places normal Beijingers live in. How come he has got such a place?"

"Oh… you will have to ask him," she smiled.

Our conversation moved on, away from Mr Na and onto me. I summarised my life so far, and she was pleased that I wanted to do something with my life now. She told me about her own life, which was a whole load more exciting than mine.

Teacher Zhou grew up in a palatial courtyard in central Beijing, similar to Mr Na's. At the turn of the twentieth century, as the Manchu Qing Dynasty fell and gave way to the Republic of China, many noblemen struggled to make ends meet. Teacher Zhou's father had owned a successful textile business and grown rich. So, he bought the courtyard from a fallen Manchu nobleman. The business survived the upheavals of the warlords, the Japanese invasion, and then the civil war. Soon after the Liberation, when the Communists won the civil war and established the People's Republic of China in 1949, her father's business was brought under private-public joint ownership, and then was nationalised all together. The family moved out of their 'palace', which was then redistributed to house several proletariat families, and moved into a normal apartment. She had been just a child back then.

Child Zhou went to an ordinary local school in Beijing, in the New China. At first, everything was okay. She had some good friends at school. However, when she became a bit older, her friends became more distant from her. Eventually, she was heartbroken as even some of her best friends refused to play with her, and worse still they started to call her names. Why? Because she was the daughter of a bourgeoisie. A bourgeoisie? But had not her father handed over his business to the state willingly? Yes, but the political tide had turned from relatively gentle social reforms to violent political struggle.

How did the kids become so politically aware? It was simple. Every day, in almost every lesson, the kids would be told about the bad old days, when labourers toiled under the whips of their employers, and peasants rarely had enough to eat as all their produce went to pay for rent or high-interest loans, and that those bad old days should never return. She laughed at the ignorance, as her father was a kind businessman, who had treated his staff well. But when the Cultural Revolution started, even the most faithful of her father's ex-employees denounced him, as a result of the pressure exerted by the Red Guards, who wanted people to denounce everyone. Those who did not comply with the madness were themselves denounced as Enemies of the People. Her father died of a broken heart during that era, when the world was turned upside down. Fortunately for her, all the madness ended in the late 1970s and she had the opportunity to be a proper member of society again.

"Sorry, if I'm boring you, after all, you do not share our collective memory."

I assured her that I found it all very interesting. Perhaps old people like her felt the need to tell younger people about their lives, so that their experiences would not be wasted, and their past could live in the memories of future generations. Maybe that was immortality to them, as they got closer to facing their own mortality.

"Here is our school," she said and pointed.

Compared to the smart commercial building where I taught, this school looked makeshift. If it was not for the children's voices reading in unison, one could have mistaken this place to be a disused industrial site. There were a few rows of old redbrick bungalows. Some of the buildings used to be warehouses, so many of the windows looked newer than the walls. Around the windows, I could see newer bricks. The builders must have knocked through some walls to create these windows. Pale smoke rose from the chimneys, telling me that these bungalows had no central heating. Everything was low-tech. There was no gatekeeper, unlike almost everywhere else in Beijing. Teacher Zhou pushed the heavy metal gate open. I felt a bit sorry for the kids and teachers here, as it felt like I had stepped back in time, or into another country. I recalled Mr Lu, the kindergarten's driver who picked me up from the airport, saying how China was a Third World country. "Well, look at this school," I thought to myself. "This is pretty Third World. Okay, here I come." I took a deep breath.

She led me to the staffroom. There was a stove in the middle of the room, coal inside and a kettle on top. A makeshift pipe formed a chimney, which rose to the roof and beyond. There were also a few desks and chairs. No one was in.

"Everyone's teaching. Unlike teachers at normal schools, we don't have the luxury of lots of preparation time during the day. People come here after school to do their lesson plans and mark homework. But for most of the day, it's just a little room for teachers to have tea during breaks. If you join us, we'll find a desk and a chair for you."

It was cold here. I put my hands close to the stove. It did help, but the stove was just too small.

"Come and see the kids." She led me out of that staffroom. We walked across the open wasteland. No grass. No concrete. Just the frozen earth. She pushed open the door of another bungalow.

All the kids turned to look at us as we entered. Some whispered to each other. Some laughed. Some just stared at me blankly. Most of them looked a little bit shabby, just like this school.

A teacher stood in front of a blackboard, on which were rows and rows of calculations written in chalk. He said something in Chinese to the kids, then all the kids stood up and said in unison, *"lao shi hao"*, which meant 'hello teacher.' I waved to them. In their eyes, I saw sparks of joy. From their nostrils, I saw their warm breath, condensing in this cold room. A few kids had runny noses. All of them had chubby red cheeks, like little cherubs, little scruffy angels.

"Look at our kids. Different ages, different heights, different levels of knowledge. But they have the same spirit – they want to learn and want to shoulder the responsibilities of being the next generation of masters of this country," Teacher Zhou reflected.

We left the class and went through a few more wooden doors, one nearly fell off its hinges. Behind every door, were kids, who looked almost identical, all with chubby red cheeks and half-dirty clothes, short hair, runny noses, with smiles of surprise upon seeing the foreigner.

The last place Teacher Zhou showed me was the school canteen. It was, again, in a bungalow. A fat man shook my hand. His once white chef's uniform was now quite yellow. The kitchen consisted of two super-sized woks, resting on the cooker which used wood and coal. Teacher Zhou suggested that I stay for lunch, as Master Zhang was a brilliant cook, even when working in such basic conditions. I politely declined, as I had lessons to teach that afternoon. Master? Yes, in Beijing, anyone who had a particular trade was referred to as Master, including taxi drivers, car mechanics, barbers and chefs.

"So, you have seen our school now. It's very basic. But it's better than nothing. The kids can learn here and be fed by Master Zhang. It's better than them not learning but doing bad things. I hope you can come and teach here. You will help them with their listening and speaking. The kids will benefit from just talking to a native speaker. I know foreign teachers often have classroom assistants, but we don't have the luxury. I will concentrate on their reading and writing, getting them to pass their exams. Does that sound okay?" Teacher Zhou looked at me. She was a tiny woman, looking up. Yet, I felt she was a giant and I was merely a humble sinner looking for redemption through good deeds.

"Yes, sure," I agreed, "but I will need to sort out my current employment first. To be honest, I have not even read the contract yet. So, there may be some complications, but I'm sure it'll be all right."

Of course, it would be all right! So, I tried to reassure myself. What was the difference to that kindergarten if I was not there? Who would lose out? The kids there? No! They would not lose anything, as they had so much anyway.

I nodded goodbye to Teacher Zhou, for in China, physical contact was limited in social interactions, even though at heart, I felt like giving her a big bear hug.

I headed to my bus stop, first walking, then I picked up a little speed and ran…

<h1 style="text-align:center">34</h1>

"Yes, I do feel that this is it – the start of a new life for me," Jillian said. We were at my place, just the two of us, that very evening after my visit to Mr Na's school. She had no lessons that day and had met up with her newly acquainted man for lunch.

"He's so gentle and learned. He makes me feel that I am becoming part of his life." She took a sip of her wine.

For some reason, since meeting Mr Na at Beijing Hotel, I thought something was going to happen, something good. So, I splashed out and bought two bottles of Shiraz, waiting to celebrate. Of course, one of the bottles had already gone – I took that to Mr Na's when I went over for dinner. As Jillian called on me, saying she had something fantastic to tell me, I opened the other bottle. For her? Yes, but also for myself.

"You know, hanging out with the crew is okay up to a point, but it… it feels a bit suffocating. Danny knows quite a bit, and it's great when he talks about his experiences and tells us about the stuff he has learnt, but most of the time, everyone just behaves like… like mindless drunks… well, most of the time they are drunk, actually. Sometimes, it just feels like living in a ghetto or something. Now, I feel so much better. It's like becoming free, becoming my own person! I'm so happy I've found someone!" Jillian's voice became louder and her pitch higher as she spoke, getting increasingly excited.

"I'm very glad. I wish you two all the very best!" I raised my glass. "To you two."

I told her about my visit to the school. Although it had been a few hours since I had got back from my visit, it felt as if I had just walked out through the gates seconds ago. I told her that I was very much looking forward to starting my new job. I asked her if she had read her teacher contract, and she said yes.

"You'll have to pay a break-off fee. I can't remember how much it was. Maybe as much as five thousand?" She tried to recall.

"What?! Five thousand?!" Oh, dear... I did not have the money! I rushed to the shelf and brought my folder of paperwork to the sofa. I flicked and flicked... No, she was wrong. It was ten thousand.

My heart sank like a lead balloon. No, she did not have any money to lend me. I could ask my parents, but I did not want to trouble them. Although ten thousand yuan was perhaps not much more than eight hundred pounds back then, I would feel too much shame if I were to ask them for help, as they were supporting my youngest brother and sister through university. I didn't think my other brother would have any money to lend me either.

But it would not take me long to save up ten thousand. Perhaps a few months? A few months too long.

Jillian said that she could save with me and lend me some money. That was extraordinarily nice of her. However, I could not accept.

That bottle of Shiraz did not taste all that nice after all...

35

I called Mr Na to explain my situation. But before I could bring up the topic, he said he could not talk then, as he was in the middle of something, but I should come to a kids' performance at the school on Friday, and whatever it was, we could discuss it after the show.

Even though I could have explained to him my situation in a matter of seconds, I felt my words were somehow being shoved back down my throat, and that I could not insist on letting my words pop out against his wishes.

Friday later afternoon, I headed to the school for the show. The wind of the Mongol hordes charged down from the steppes, over the Great Wall, over the mountains, breaking into Beijing, running wild, ransacking the tall buildings – the naked poplar branches were useless in the city's defence. Heavy snowflakes were fired by the crazed raiders, piercing through every poor soul's armour, mine too. I walked from the bus stop, in my greatcoat and under my fur hat, head-on against the blizzard. By the time I arrived at the school, my grey fur hat was white, and the entire front of my greatcoat was frozen solid with a shield of snow.

I pushed the metal gate open and walked through. There was a red banner above a bungalow. I pushed the door open.

Everyone turned. The eyes of the little kids, their parents, the teachers and Mr Na. He was in a dark blue Mao suit, as if he was at a state function, buttoned up to the top, not a single crease in sight, rather militaristic.

"How was Stalingrad?" Mr Na welcomed me, jokingly, and extended his hand.

"The battle was won, comrade." I shook his hand, looking into his eyes.

He looked at me and smiled, "Come, let me present you to everyone here!" Instead of the softly spoken gentleman with an old-world calmness, Mr Na was now clearly excited. He led me to the front, and said something in Chinese, projecting his voice. He applauded first, then looked at me, and then everyone else applauded and smiled at me. I smiled back, then looked at him puzzled.

"Don't worry, Comrade George," he whispered to me. "I just said that we have an English teacher visiting us and he's a friend of mine."

Perhaps the only foreigners the parents had seen before me were distant tourists. Their eyes dwelt on me. Their gaze was warm. Perhaps the snow on my coat and my frozen red cheeks had reassured them that I was not a distant foreigner who had no interest in the ordinary people of China, but just an ordinary person, who had, like everyone else, endured the harsh beating of the Beijing winter.

Teacher Zhou was there too. She waved me over to her. I gave Mr Na a little nod, then gave the audience a nod too, then went over and sat down next to Teacher Zhou. Like all the chairs, mine was made of wood with a metal frame. I shook off the snow from my coat and took off my fur hat.

"I'm glad you could come to our show. It's for the Chinese New Year. Soon, most of the kids will go back to the countryside with their parents for the holiday season," Teacher Zhou explained quietly.

Mr Na struck a gong. It wasn't a real gong but one of the supersized woks from the kitchen. He cleared his throat and made an announcement. I guessed it was to say thanks for coming and that the show was about to begin.

He pressed a button on an old stereo. A detachment of kids emerged from the back of the room and moved to the front. There was no stage. They danced, with their quick steps representing those of horsemen. Mongol horsemen? Perhaps. Quite suitable given the wind from Mongolia that was blowing outside, which occasionally whistled through the building. It was reasonably warm in this bungalow, with all the people here and the stove burning in the corner.

Then, another detachment of kids emerged. The two columns crossed, then joined. They faced the audience, with their chubby red cheeks, and some with half-runny noses too. Soon, their parents were applauding in unison, providing a background beat to the music.

The first piece ended with loud applause from the audience.

Then a little girl stepped up. She bowed to the audience and started singing. No music accompanied her, just her clear voice of purity and innocence. Untrained. From the heart. Her song touched me, even though I had no idea what it was about. Then I saw a teardrop fall from the corner of her eye. Teacher Zhou whispered to me, explaining that the song was about her being a little blade of grass, who was not as fragrant as the flowers, nor as tall as the trees. Perhaps in this city of riches, these kids had developed a sense of social awareness from an early age, realising that they were not like the children whose parents were registered residents. They could not go to a real school, despite their parents building the new China, working on construction sites or serving in restaurants. They were just transitory figures that many of the 'real' locals had cared little about.

An upbeat song followed, with a Central Asian twist to it, sung by a group of boys and girls. Teacher Zhou informed me that it was about how the motherland was like a garden and how happy the people were. The boys and girls shook their heads from side to side, and clapped their little hands to the music. Teacher Zhou told me it was a Uyghur song, and the Uyghurs were one of the largest ethnic groups in northwest China. There were no Uyghurs at this school. In fact, there weren't many Uyghur migrant workers in Beijing. Watching their sweet smiles, and listening to their cute song, I wondered if they lived in two worlds – one in which they were mere little blades of grass, and another in which they were the flowers of the motherland. Were the two necessarily contradictory? Perhaps not, for while the country was being transformed, lives too could be transformed, and that was the purpose of this school.

Apart from songs and dances, there was a reading by a small boy, followed by a very short play involving a few kids helping an old woman with her luggage, with the old woman played by a girl with chalk dust in her hair and wrinkles drawn on her face with a black marker.

Mr Na cleared his throat and made an announcement. Adults now walked onto the stage, including Teacher Zhou. I guessed they were the staff. They stood in a row. Mr Na turned and faced them, and they sang. Mr Na conducted a stern-sounding song, resolute in its harmony. There was optimism in people's voices and it was all powerfully delivered. Then it stopped. Mr Na turned to the audience and took a bow, followed by the singers, to wild applause from the kids and their parents.

After the show, people went their different ways. Teacher Zhou asked me when I would start, as if my mere presence at the show confirmed my sign up. I could not answer and perhaps looked a little awkward. She did not persist and walked away quietly, nodding me goodbye.

"Hope you enjoyed that!" said Mr Na, who came up to me once he had shaken the hands of the departing parents. "Not quite the Royal Opera House or Sadler's Wells!"

I assured him that it was one of the best shows I had ever attended, not in terms of artistic prowess, but just… I struggled for words. Was it warmth? Sincerity? Comfort? Faith? Or just being human. Anyway, Mr Na understood.

He put on an old army greatcoat and fur hat, and gestured for us to head out.

"Look, my coat is similar to yours!" he commented. "Come on, Comrade George, let's find something to eat. Have you eaten?"

"No."

We walked out into the cold night. The snow and wind had stopped.

This part of the city had gone to sleep. It was peaceful, a far cry from the noisy night life of central Beijing. We both lit up a cigarette and our smoke rose into the dark sky as we walked, side by side, with the fresh snow under our feet.

He led me to a small restaurant around the corner, down an alleyway. It was a shabby little place, with just six tables inside, four stools per table, and a nondescript waitress who was watching TV when we entered.

We ordered a couple of simple dishes – stripy pork and egg-fried tomatoes. Egg-fried tomatoes? Yes, this was a typical dish in China, very mundane. So much so that Mr Na explained it was only served in very low-key eateries. He went on to explain what he thought constituted the best egg-fried tomatoes – that the eggs must be fried first, on their own, on a medium-high heat, with just a tiny bit of spring onion, and a touch of salt and sugar sprinkled on top. Then it is all removed from the wok, and you get the heat as high as possible for the chopped beef tomatoes to be chucked in. Then reduce the heat to medium to allow the tomatoes to stew a bit, with the fried eggs put back in again at the end… Well, something to that effect, if I remember correctly. I did not know there was so much art in just frying some eggs and tomatoes.

When our dishes arrived, I asked Mr Na whether the dish was cooked to his standard, and he said it was okay – it was a shame that the eggs had been fried for too long with the tomatoes at the end, and hence the eggs looked a bit red and tasted too soggy, rather than distinctively yellow and firm. Mr Na explained that each time he ate here, the same egg fried tomatoes tasted different. Sometimes perfect, other times dreadful, as if this place constantly changed chefs.

I asked Mr Na if he had ever wanted to become a chef, as he seemed quite a connoisseur, even when it came to something as simple as fried eggs and tomatoes.

"A connoisseur? A chef?" Mr Na laughed a little. "I know a bit about food. True. Well, I also know a bit about gymnastics, but I could hardly do the Thomas salto!"

"You could be a head chef, just boss people around a bit."

"Well, maybe you haven't been into a busy restaurant kitchen. I have. A friend of mine opened a restaurant some time ago and business was good. The kitchen was like a warzone between seven and ten every night! I would rather be a café owner." Then Mr Na started humming the theme tune from the old British comedy *'Allo 'Allo*. He put on his French accent for René, then his German accent for Lieutenant Gruber.

"Very good!" I said.

"I loved that show when I was in England." Mr Na almost looked melancholic when recalling the pantomimic sit-com series. "The idea of opening a café appeals to me. Not in Beijing. The cafés in this city are all kitsch – overpriced, poor quality, no soul. Could I open one that's reasonably priced, good quality, with soul? I wonder if your average café goer here cares about price, quality or soul. But London is different. Cafés are part of the culture there. Yes, in London, on a quiet little street, yet close enough to the hustle and bustle. A few different types of coffee and tea, maybe a few types of Chinese tea too. Food? Maybe just some sandwiches and salads, plus a small selection of cakes. Cooked food? Maybe not... Actually, I shall serve just one cooked dish – fried eggs and tomatoes!"

I thought about where in London he could open his café, then said, "I used to live in an area that might be good for you to open your café, where it'd be quiet, yet close to business. It's an area called Clapham Junction..." I was going to explain further, when I was interrupted by the waitress who brought us our beers.

"Cheers!" Mr Na exclaimed, and our conversation about Clapham Junction and the café ended. Instead, we chatted about the kids at the school and other things related to China in transition. Mr Na enthusiastically interpreted things through various social and philosophical lenses, especially Marxism. I think our conversation went something along the lines of this, a bit like an interview...

George: Did this move from a command economy to market economy constitute a reversal of progress or a failure of socialism, and had real socialism died in China and indeed in most parts of the world?

Comrade Na: No, socialism was not set in stone, and Marxism was not a religion set in an unchangeable holy book. In order to progress, people had to try different approaches to see what would work, and if people solely dwelt on the works of Marx, Lenin and Mao, without any intelligent reinterpretation, then that'd be dogmatic or fundamentalist.

George: However, was it right that the workers of today's China appeared to be living in the same condition as those in England during the Industrial Revolution, as depicted by the likes of Dickens?

Comrade Na: Again, no. On the one hand, it'd be wrong to think that Chinese workers were suffering the same fate as the unfortunate poor during the Victorian age in England, and on the other, it was right to think that working conditions in China were far from good. The trade-off between workers' rights and the need to accumulate capital was a delicate one. While during the late 1980s and early 1990s, the latter need was more emphasised, there had been good progress to readdress such a trade-off in recent years.

George: What was the future for the kids of migrant workers?

Comrade Na: Their future's bright; things were improving.

George: Were charity schools the answer to these kids' education?

Comrade Na: Yes, in the short term, but ultimately no; the state would need to take on the role of the educator for these kids, just like it had done so for the kids of permanent residents.

George: So, how long did he reckon his school would need to last?

Comrade Na: A few years, hopefully not too long.

George: How could people be confident that tomorrow would be better than today? Most British people did not have such a general assumption.

Comrade Na: China had been on the rise for the last several decades. It was inconceivable when he was young that there'd be things like private cars. Now there were perhaps too many private cars. A couple of decades ago everything, from rice to bicycles, was rationed, and where the possession of money in itself was insufficient to acquire goods. Now, people ate too much and bought useless things almost just for the sake of consumption. Tracing it back a bit further, half a century ago, ordinary people survived on mostly grain, occasionally supplemented by vegetables. Back then, people generally only had meat a few times a year, if at all. Going back even further, a hundred years ago, to live beyond sixty years of age was rare and considered fortunate. Despite the turmoil that had plagued China since the mid-nineteenth century, marked by the Opium War against Britain – China's first major defeat at the hands of a Western power – things had been improving. So drawing on past experiences, people thought things would get better still. Besides, Chinese Communists had always possessed a spirit of revolutionary optimism.

We did not rush to leave the eatery. Having finished the food and the beers, Comrade Na spoke to the waitress, who then brought a bottle to us.

"Two Pot Heads!" Comrade Na explained. "This stuff is very popular in Beijing, especially among the working men. It's only five yuan, or about fifty pence in sterling terms." He showed me the bottle. Seventy-five centilitres. He opened it and poured some for us both. In his haste, quite a bit spilt onto the table. He did not seem to mind. "Cheers!" He raised his glass and exclaimed wholeheartedly.

"You look so happy."

"Why not?! It's nearly the New Year, and I'm optimistic about the future, you know."

We talked about being optimistic and on that theme, Comrade Na emphasised the importance of being positive. "Here's to revolutionary optimism!" He toasted, then went on to explain the term's historical importance.

Having cooperated with the Nationalists during the Northern Expedition in the late 1920s, and helping to unite a China that had for decades been in the hands of various warlords, the Communists found themselves being hunted down and purged. Thousands were killed. Many fled to the countryside. Without revolutionary optimism, the cause would have died in 1927 or 1928.

Later, having learnt through bloodshed that a Soviet model of city-based industrial worker-led revolution could not succeed, the Communists established bases in the hills of southern China. After five major attacks by the Nationalists, the Communists had to give up their base – and hence, the Long March. They trekked some eight thousand miles, fighting hunger, thirst, cold, fatigue, disease and the encircling enemy soldiers along the way. Only a small fraction of the original marchers made it to Yan'an in north central China, their new base. At Yan'an, they faced food shortages, the Japanese invasion and Nationalist blockades. After the Second World War, the Communists faced a Nationalist army that was nearly four times its size, and with many divisions equipped with the most advanced American hardware. The spirit of revolutionary optimism helped to support those in the darkest hours. The same spirit lived during the Korean War as well, when the one-year-old People's Republic, which had barely risen out of the ashes of a century of war and turmoil, took on the might of America, the world's superpower.

Comrade Na was so full of passion, and this grew as the bottle of Two Pot Heads was close to being halved. My mind travelled with the speed of light as I tried to keep up with him. I loved it all, the stimulation. I felt I had not been so stimulated since I arrived in China, since I graduated, since being with Isabel...

He looked like a true Communist in his Mao suit. Although he had unbuttoned it, loosening the stiff collars and front, he still looked very smart. I wondered if many girls fell for his suave oratory and handsome looks. Maybe it was not inconceivable that Isabel had... but I didn't let my mind wander off too much.

Having passed the halfway mark of the firewater, I finally picked up the courage to inform him of the complication there was with my lock-in fee.

"How much?" he asked, lighting up a cigarette and handing me the packet.

I did not take one out. I placed it on the table. "Ten thousand."

He did not seem at all surprised, or worried. He took a long drag. "I'll bail you out..."

"No, no, no…" It was too kind of him to do so.

He laughed. "There's no need to play the Chinese game of yes and no, for the sake of appearing courteous. Between us, we can be direct with each other."

I recalled the time when he first invited me over for dinner, when we jovially practised the Chinese art of declining a present before accepting it. I smiled. "Okay, I'll be a barbarian with you – what's the catch?" I lit up a cigarette and took a drag like a baddy from a Spaghetti Western film.

"You'll work for me for free."

"How would I live?"

"Don't eat too much."

I smiled at his simple suggestion, "Where would I live?"

"At mine."

I nearly choked on my cigarette. Me? Living at his? But…

"I trust that that you will not eat too much. There is a small room at the back. I won't charge you rent and you can eat for free too. The school will give you money, maybe a hundred or so yuan a week. I'll arrange this, but you will need to promise me, on your honour, that you will work here for a year. I hope this is agreeable to you."

A teacher's wage at his school was one thousand and five hundred yuan. Ten thousand yuan bail out… I quickly did the maths in my head and thought it was a good deal. Although it could become awkward to live under my boss's roof, it was time to adjust to new conditions, I thought.

"This is my crossroads. I have to take that step! Go George! Take it!" I encouraged myself. I stood up and picked up the bottle of Two Pot Heads. I poured us both some, and plenty got splattered onto the table.

I extended my hand to him, over the little dinner table. He stood up too. We shook hands firmly, then raised our glasses.

"Cheers!" We downed our drinks.

A toast to the start of a new chapter in my life…

PART THREE

36

It was a Saturday when I left the crew. Everyone was calm, as if somehow the veterans had known that one day I would desert them. They wished me luck, but for some reason, I felt that their words of lukewarm compassion were just rolled out for the sake of courtesy to a compatriot, and they would have said nothing at all if we were in England. Jillian was the only person who was genuinely happy for me. She could not hide her excitement for me, as she kissed me goodbye on the cheek. I looked back at them as I jumped into a taxi. The men disappeared back into the block of flats. Jillian stood there on her own, waving me goodbye. I waved back at her.

My room was behind the main hall where I first dined with Mr Na. It was a small room in a terraced row of bungalows at the back of the courtyard. But that was only relative to the size of the flat the kindergarten had provided me. It was sufficient.

Conveniently, the room had its own bathroom and shower. Maybe someone had lived here once upon a time, or perhaps it had been a guest room. Compared to the modern feel of my previous flat, this room seemed to have been left behind by the march of time. There was an old wardrobe, perhaps from the 1960s, with faded paintwork, a metal framed single bed with bits of dark blue paint chipped off, a bedside table, an old desk that had perhaps once been painted white but now was a shade of greyish cream, and a wooden chair. That was it. There was no decoration in this dark room. As the room was located behind the main building, little light came through the windows, although the cast-iron radiators did keep the place warm. Overall, it felt somewhat unloved, although Chun'er had already cleaned the place, as everything was dust-free.

I dropped my backpack onto the slate floor, tipping everything out. I looked at each item in turn and placed it in the right place. I put my little wooden statue of the Chinese warrior at the centre of the desk. He still looked just as fearsome. There was a sense of dignity in the way he stood upright, with his chest puffed out.

I threw myself onto the bed. Ouch! It was very hard. I jumped down to investigate, and discovered that it did not have a sprung mattress. Instead, there were just layers of duvets on top of a solid wooden board. Good for my back, I comforted myself.

Knock, knock.

I opened the door. It was Gentleman Na in his long robe with its Mandarin collars and knotted buttons. I gestured for him to come in.

"How are you settling in?" he asked softly.

I said everything was okay and that I was happy with my room. I thanked him.

He nodded slightly and looked around. Spotting my little Chinese warrior on the desk, he picked it up. "Do you know who this is?"

No, I was ignorant.

Gentleman Na sat down on the chair next to the desk. I sat down on the bed. He explained, "This is Guan Yu. He lived during the fall of the Han Dynasty in the third century. He had two blood brothers, one of whom was said to have been of royal descendent and hence was also Guan Yu's lord. He fought for his lord. But he was captured by the villainous prime minister who had hijacked the emperor. The prime minister lavished him with honour and riches. Still, he dreamt of returning to his lord, who by then was suffering defeat after defeat and faced an uncertain fate. Eventually, he returned to his lord, helping him to establish one of the three kingdoms of that period. He was a man of dignity, bravery, strategy and above all, loyalty. Ever since his death, he has been revered as the god of war and loyalty. He is worshiped in temples. Loyalty is perhaps the most important virtue of a true gentleman." My educator smiled. He put the statue down, stood up and walked towards the door.

I stood up too, to see him out. But he turned.

"You know, George, in China there are many ethnicities, and we all value loyalty above everything else. Guan Yu was from the central plains. On the grassland, there was a story about Genghis Khan. He was battling against Jamukha. Two of Jamukha's men betrayed him and took his severed head to Genghis Khan. Do you know how these two were rewarded by the great Khan?" he asked me softly, looking into my eyes.

No, I was ignorant.

"Genghis Khan said the two men had betrayed their lord and that betrayal was the greatest sin. Therefore, their only reward was death." He smiled at me slightly, then nodded goodbye. He pushed the door open and left.

I looked at my little warrior of great stature and imagined how Guan Yu had fought for his lord and kingdom, and how Genghis Khan had punished the two men who had betrayed their lord, even though their betrayal was to his own advantage. I felt Mr Na was not quite the person I had talked with at length at that low-key eatery. Somehow, I felt he had become a different man, a much colder man. Was I overthinking about it all? Maybe.

I was now, of course, under my employer's roof. He was to provide me with shelter, food, work, and maybe a sense of purpose. I tried not to feel uncomfortable that perhaps he was more like a master to me, under some old feudal set-up. It felt a little strange. Although we had talked many times and got on well, he was more or less a stranger to me.

Did he live here with just Chun'er? Somehow, I felt there were more than just the three of us in this courtyard. I sensed that things were not so simple; that there was someone else in the picture. Mrs Na? I had not met her, and did not know what she thought of me, this stranger, living in her home. But then, again, wife was perhaps just a member of the household in this feudal set-up, whose views were not important, and whose life was determined by the master, who was herself tucked away hidden from view. At any rate, unlike an English home, with all the rooms in one building, this Chinese set-up of different rooms in different buildings was more convenient for strangers like me to set up camp in. The interconnecting passageways were outdoors, creating that sense of distance and otherness. Apart from my room and the main hall, I was not shown any of the other rooms. So, there was a gentle separation between me and my hosts. Nevertheless, it was still strange to be living in someone's home without having met them. I wondered if my acceptance of Mr Na's offer had been made too hastily. Then again, I guessed he was the host and since he had made the offer, why would I hesitate? But *should* I have hesitated? Should I have asked Isabel? Maybe she could have advised me one way or another. Maybe.

I went to an internet café. Beijing was full of these places before Wi-Fi and smartphones became widespread. Some had perhaps a hundred computers, with kids screaming at each other as they played network games, while others had just a handful of machines crammed into a little hole. The one I found was the latter.

Dear Isabel,

I hope you are well. I'm sorry that I have not contacted you sooner, but given that we had said our goodbyes (or rather, not said them) I thought that perhaps you would not want to be disturbed by me. Also, I wanted to make a fresh start, and so did not want to contact you. I don't know if I have been selfish by not contacting you, even as a matter of courtesy to tell you how I was getting on.

Maybe you were upset by my leaving. I was upset, even though it was my own choice to leave, but I guess you understood why I felt I had to go. Anyway, I hope you're well and having fun.

You see, thanks to your piece of paper, I am now about to start working for Mr Na. I wonder what sort of a person he is. After all, you know him much better than me. I hope he's a good guy – he certainly appears to be. The thing is, I have moved into his place...

I typed and typed. Okay, finished. I stared at the screen for a while…

I logged off but did not press 'send'. I wanted to ask her about Mr Na, but then that would lead to other questions...

I paid and walked out.

Let the future come – come what may. I had crossed the junction in life, down a new path and I would to find out by myself where it was leading to. I returned to my room.

Knock, knock. It was Chun'er. She gestured for me to come with her, then led me to the main hall. It was time for dinner.

"How was your first day here?" Gentleman Na was in his long robe of the old world. He gestured for me to sit down. He was already seated on a hard stool, in his perfectly upright posture.

"Fine, just a bit of *me* time."

There was just Mr Na and me at the dinner table. No sign of Mrs Na. I could not help enquiring and the answer was that she was at her parents' place. The master of this house did not look at me when he responded. He spoke coldly. I took the hint, and did not ask anything else. He gestured for me to start eating. On the table were three dishes. He explained that Chun'er had cooked a spicy pork and vinegar-sauced cabbage, but he had cooked the egg and tomatoes himself. "See how it compares to the eatery's version," he requested without excitement.

I assured him that it tasted great, better than the eatery's, as the tomatoes were not over-infused with the egg.

Instead of probing about Mrs Na, I asked what he had got up to during the day. He explained that he had gone to do some business.

Business on a Saturday?

Well, a man like Mr Na did not confine his business only to weekdays. He knew two people – one managed a company that wanted to secure a loan and another person who worked at a bank as an investment manager. So, he bridged the connection. Since both parties knew him well, he provided some sort of proof that they could trust each other simply based on his reputation as someone who knew good people and whose friends could be trusted. And what did he get out of this matchmaking exercise? A good amount of money, some of which he was going to put aside for his own maintenance, and some as funds for the school. What an easy bit of money-making! I was amazed.

How did he come to be in such a good position? He said we would perhaps save that conversation to some other occasion, as he had a private appointment after dinner. He had a certain way of speaking when he did not want to dive into the details about some things. He brushed them aside and pulled up the drawbridge.

After dinner, Chun'er cleared up. Since I was living here I felt it would be good manners to offer to help. Chun'er looked puzzled as I started to clear up with her. Mr Na said something to Chun'er and she smiled. Then he bid me good evening and went off back to his room. Perhaps he was getting changed to go out for his private appointment.

Chun'er gestured for me to come with her to the kitchen. There she washed up, and I helped to put things away. The kitchen seemed rather small and plain. The ceiling was low and the distance between the walls only allowed a couple of people, at most, to move around.

In that small space, she washed up quickly, stopping every now and then, pointing out where to put the plates, pots, bowls and chopsticks. Most of the stuff went into a unit near the sink. There were a few other units, and out of curiosity, I opened one.

I was not an expert in antiques, but my untrained eyes told me that the plates, bowls and little tea cups I was staring at were no ordinary china, but exquisite porcelain. Chun'er said something, perhaps telling me to be careful. I took a bowl out. It did not seem new at all, but there was a sense of youthful grace that emanated from it. The border was painted gold and there were four Chinese characters that were evenly distributed along the border. Chun'er gestured for me to put it back. I joked that I was going to drop it. She did not think it was funny and tried to grab it, saying something in a stern manner. In that instant, she transformed from a little servant girl to the boss, and I was merely her assistant. So, obediently, I put the bowl back.

Chun'er did not look at me again while we were in the kitchen. After finishing the washing up, she walked to her room at the back of the kitchen. I followed her, to apologise, but she did not look at me at all. She closed her door on me.

I felt embarrassed and went back to my room. Was that bowl really a priceless antique? But if it were, then why was it in the kitchen, rather than stored away somewhere safer, or displayed somewhere in the living room? Was Mr Na a collector of fine antiques? Or did he inherit them? Did he not like them? Why else would those beautiful works of art be kept in the kitchen, hidden from guests' eyes?

37

My host gave me an old, fixed-geared town bike to ride. All the bits worked, just about.

Sunday afternoon was sunny and windless when I set off to the Purple Bamboo Park, northwest from the courtyard. Beijing was incredibly easy to navigate, with as almost all the streets arranged in grids, north-south, east-west. Mr Na told me that all imperial cities in China were laid out in such an orderly manner.

I had cycled a few times in London, and found that the battles against the pedestrians, other cyclists, buses, cars and taxis were an adrenaline rush. However, in Beijing, cycling was a sedate experience with most of the cycle lanes as wide as car lanes, and segregated from motorised traffic by rows of poplars. I rode slowly, wearing my greatcoat, fur hat and leather gloves. Every now and then, I'd come to a section where half of the cycle lane had been taken over by parked cars in clearly marked bays. I guessed that this was a recent development. There were not many fellow cyclists and those that used the road, rode almost as leisurely as me.

Most people in Beijing were quite accustomed to the sight of foreigners by the time I had arrived here, a year after the 2008 Summer Olympic Games, when the world descended on this city. Even so, when I walked around, people would sometimes look at me out of curiosity. Now, on a bicycle, I was practically invisible – no one looked at me at all, apart from the drivers at a junction when I accidentally jumped a red light. Fortunately, there was no accident.

I rode on, smoking as I went, slowly taking in the sights. There were old men with their caged birds, perhaps exchanging tips on birdsong training, and old women with their shopping baskets full of fresh vegetables, perhaps exchanging recipes. A group of men surrounded two men playing Chinese chess, with the strategists airing their views on what the next moves should be, saying, "If you had listened to me…"

My ride had been so pleasant, I was almost disappointed when I arrived at the southern gate of the Purple Bamboo Park. There I waited. And waited. I did not have a mobile phone. At a time like this, I wished I had one to find out where on earth Jillian was.

However, the only thing I could do then, was just wait, and wait, and wait…

Wrong! It was not the southern gate but the eastern gate, I suddenly remembered. So, I jumped on my bicycle and rushed to the correct gate.

There, Jillian stood. She was wearing a long puffa jacket with the hood pulled up. I had not seen her wearing it before. I thought she was a bit more style conscious than that and would not wear such an item of utilitarian vulgarity.

We hugged and air-kissed.

"Gosh, George. Get a phone!" Jillian was not best pleased about having waited for me all this time. I nodded and parked my bicycle to the side of the entrance, where the other cycles were. No bicycle was chained to anything, just freestanding.

We strolled in the park. The lakes were frozen over. Adults were skating and kids were dashing around on their sledges. Jillian thought the kids were cute, as they were all wrapped in layers and layers of jumpers and coats. They looked like little sugar balls. She took a photo using her smartphone.

"So, how are things?" I asked.

"Fine, my beloved came over to mine last night." Then, she showed me her smartphone and explained he had given it to her as a gift. Not many people had that sort of phones back then. Although she had never seemed like an overtly materialistic girl, she was clearly pleased.

"Well, look at that! It sure looks good!" I was pleased for her. "I won't ask what you got up to last night, or shall I?" I winked.

Jillian laughed a little with a sparkle in her eyes, somewhat telling.

"Anyway, how are you getting on with your man, generally?" I asked.

"I think we are getting on really well. We are thinking about going on a little getaway together."

"Where to?"

"The Mogao Caves in the northwest." Jillian explained that her boyfriend had suggested a trip away and that he was a lover of mural art. She simply wanted to have a break from Beijing for a little while.

"A little getaway? The Mogao Caves are over a thousand miles away from Beijing!" I was surprised.

She said even if they just spent a long weekend there, it was still worth travelling all those thousands of miles there and back, for she just wanted to be with him, in the caves, or on the sleeper trains.

"What about you, George? How are you getting on at Mr Na's?"

"Erm… Good."

"You don't sound too sure there."

"How should I explain?" I muttered to myself. Eventually, I gave her a mumbled jumbled rambling outpouring of my confusion over who this Mr Na was and what our relationship was. First, there was Mr Na the lighthearted playboy in a blazer, then there was Gentleman Na in his Manchu robe with his old-world manners, and then there was the passionate Comrade Na who ran this school for migrant workers' children. First, there was the friendly chat at Beijing Hotel, then there was the cordial dinner at his palatial courtyard home, followed by a warm-hearted supper and drinks at the low-key eatery near school. Now, that I had moved into his home, I somehow felt he was colder towards me.

"Am I overthinking, Jillian?"

"Erm… Probably." She then comforted me by saying that because I was a thoughtful person, I overanalysed people and situations; instead, I should chill out a bit and go with the flow more, especially now that I had achieved what I had wanted and was leading a new life.

"Thanks Jillian." I smiled at her and she smiled back. It was just nice to be with her again. I recalled how comfortable we were with each other when I used to visit her in her flat in the evenings. Then, I thought about her new boyfriend visiting her in the same flat.

I lit a cigarette, trying to depict this dashing young man at Jillian's. Often, to imagine something, I relied on my recollection of film reels, as they provided me with the most visual stock of life-like images. The first person that surfaced to my mind was Fu Manchu. *Oh dear. Change!* Bruce Lee and Jackie Chan came up next. But even their characters were not just cool and sexy; they were also a bit comical, even trivial – certainly less serious than the typical Denzel Washington, Marlon Brando, Elvis Presley, George Clooney or Sean Connery characters. While I was busy sifting through my film reels, I realised that perhaps my lack of words had killed that conversation, right from the start. If it was strange for an Englishwoman to be dating a Chinaman, it was also quite strange for an Englishman to live under the roof of a Chinaman, with everything provided by his Chinese master. How bizarre.

I thought about Isabel's grandfather and his English friends arriving at Hong Kong's Royal Yacht Club when the British flag was still flying high, wearing fine white linen whilst being served gin and tonics by humble Chinese and Indian waiters. The sunlight meandered through the gaps of the shutters, pouring onto the marble floor. I had no idea whether the interior was exactly like this, but it seemed fine in my film, with the tune of Noël Coward's *Mad Dogs and Englishmen* echoing from a distant gramophone. While the men were sipping and yachting, their good ladies gathered for tea, fanning themselves, wondering when their husbands would finish their tours of civilising missions in this corner of the empire…

I smiled. Then, that smile developed into a laugh. Jillian was shocked by my sudden burst of laughter. I explained through my giggles. She found it amusing too.

We spent a whole afternoon in the park, and took a break from our stroll at a teahouse built on stilts above the frozen lake. It was warm indoors and the hot tea melted me into a puddle. It was a struggle to get up. The tea girl reminded me of Chun'er, so I told Jillian about my kitchen incident.

"You fancy her, don't you?" Jillian teased.

"No! Come on, I barely know her! I have just moved in. Besides, she doesn't speak English," I protested. But then again, the idea of me and Chun'er tickled something in me. The imagery of me and her.... Two servants falling in love at the master's house. So, I started to talk about this romantic fantasy with Jillian.

"Imagine, if you marry this Chun'er and settle down living at Mr Na's for the rest of your life!" Jillian mused.

"That'll be an interesting set-up for a novel. Let's call it *The English Servant*!" I laughed. Then, that smile disappeared from my face – not so much about the daunting prospect of marrying Chun'er, but more about being a servant. "Am I a servant now?" I asked Jillian.

"Come on George! I thought we had gone over this – stop overthinking!" We laughed with over my own neuroticism.

I really enjoyed my afternoon with Jillian. It was so nice to catch up with her. Apart from her boyfriend and my situation, we also talked about the crew briefly. She was still involved with them every now and then, but was growing more distant from everyone. Danny had stopped bothering with her, after she had declined a few pub crawls. Charlie and the other teachers were still friendly, as they lived in the same block of flats. No one had contacted me, of course, as I did not have a phone. No one had e-mailed me either. I was fine with that.

"Really?" Jillian did not believe me.

I shrugged my shoulders. "Oh well…" I looked down. I took out a cigarette.

"Maybe you should cut down on the smoking, George."

"Oh… yes… maybe."

The sun was setting over the mountain ranges to the west. The clouds were all dyed crimson red, like wild fire raging in the sky. It was time to say goodbye.

We arranged to meet up again soon. Yes, I'd have a mobile phone then. I joked that perhaps Mr Na would give me a smartphone, rewarding me for my loyal service.

I cycled back. After quite a while, a fog developed and I could not quite see clearly into the distance. The only thing I could see was what was immediately in front of me. I just had to go forward. What was behind me, I knew.

38

Monday. I fed the koi in the pond. Although they still swam slowly, as they surfaced, they looked happy to see me, happy to be fed, happy with their idyllic and satisfying lives.

I set off from the courtyard and headed south to the school. Unlike my ride on Sunday, when it was windless, the mighty Mongol horde of a wind was charging down from Siberia. With this gale force behind me, my cycle ride would be a breeze, I thought. As I got on my bicycle, I was proved wrong. It was so windy that I found it difficult to control the bicycle. I was thankful that the bike was a big heavy beast, rather than a light road racer. If I had strapped a kite to my back, I would have lifted off! All the while, my hands were clutching the brakes with various strengths. I wondered if I would need to replace the brake pads after this ride. Anyway, I thanked the wide segregated cycle lanes – if this was in London, I'd probably have crashed into several buses.

I arrived at the school safely, but was quite tired from the struggle. The thought of cycling against the same wind on the way home was not exactly comforting. Still, I was excited by my first day at this school.

The kids were walking in through the gates. They saw me. Some waved. Some screamed. Some waved while screaming. Some screamed while waving. I waved back. I thought it would have been funny if I screamed too.

I reported at the staffroom. Teacher Zhou was already there.

"Good to see you, George."

"Glad to be here."

"The other teachers have already gone to their classrooms. Here is a textbook for you. Like I said to you before, you should focus on talking to the kids, helping them with their listening and speaking. You can use the textbook if you want to, but you don't have to. I will follow the textbook and teach them to pass their reading and writing exams."

I took the book and it looked like a dog had been playing with it. It was yellow edged and the pages were bound together by thick threads.

"Okay, let's go!" I smiled.

We walked out on to the frozen ground. Teacher Zhou took out a piece of paper, with a timetable detailing when I was due to be in which classroom. She said, "We have five classes in total for English. The kids are graded by ability. You see that room? That's where Class One will be. There's the room for Class Two…" She went on to explain where the five classrooms were, pointing to the piece of paper for me to understand my rota. I nodded.

"Class One is the best," Teacher Zhou explained, "then Class Two, then Three, and so on. See how you get on. Once you have understood the kids' abilities for yourself, you can think about how best to plan lessons for them. So, today, just start to build up your relationship with them, start to understand them."

She led to me to Class One.

The kids all stood up upon seeing me entering. "*Lao shi hao*," they said in unison. It was not quite a shout, but certainly louder than ordinary speech.

Teacher Zhou introduced me to the kids, and then said something to them. She then turned to me and smiled, "Here you are, these are the kids who are the best at listening and speaking, I think. See what you think." I thanked her and she left me to it.

I looked at the kids, who were all still standing. They were of different heights and complexions. I guessed their ages probably ranged from ten to fifteen. I gestured for them to sit down and they did so.

I did not know what to say. They were all staring at me with the utmost attention, unlike the kindergarten kids from my previous school who were quiet, but did not seem bothered whether I was there or not.

I took off my greatcoat. Then the gale force wind blew the door open. Ouch! It was so cold that it hurt! I pushed the door shut and wedged a chair against it. It was still cold. So, I put my greatcoat back on. All the while, I felt the eyes of the kids on me, who stared at me almost unblinkingly.

I felt that all these eyes spoke to me, asking me what I could do for them to give them a better future. I felt as if their parents too were asking the same, through the eyes of these children, with their cheeks rosy from the cold. Then, through the kids' eyes, I felt as though Mr Na was looking at me too, asking what I could do, now that he had invited me to his home and paid for my bailout.

"Good morning!" I finally pronounced my first words.

"Good morning!" they replied.

"How are you?"

"Fine, thank you, and you?"

"I'm fine too, although I'm very tired from my cycling. It's very windy out there!" I spoke slowly, and finished the sentence with an impression of cycling in the wind.

The kids laughed. I laughed too. A few of them had runny noses with snot nearly reaching their lips!

"Why are you here?" I asked.

Silence.

One girl finally put her hand up.

"Yes?"

"I am here to study," she stood up and said.

"Why do you study?"

A boy put his hand up.

"Yes?"

He stood up and wiped his nose with his sleeve, "I am here to study for my country's rise."

His words were like thunder to me. "For my country's rise?" I had expected something along the lines of "so I can get a job" or "so I can make money" or "so my parents will be proud of me". No, instead of the self-focus, which I thought would be prevalent among Chinese youngsters that were under an environment of market-driven reforms, this boy, perhaps eleven or twelve, certainly not tall enough to be older than fifteen, was telling me that he, the son of poor migrant workers, was here to study so that he could help his country to be better. The Middle Kingdom… For so many centuries, even millennia, it had been the most powerful country on Earth, and only been surpassed by the Western powers since the mid-eighteenth century. Now, it was growing again, economically and in terms of its self-confidence…. My mind began to wander a little.

We talked about where their parents were from. I had not heard of some of the places, so they walked to the map on the wall and pointed them out – hundreds and thousands of miles from Beijing. What did their parents do here in Beijing? Builders, waiters, cooks, street cleaners, housekeepers… What did the children want to be when they grew up? Doctors, soldiers, scientists, teachers, businessmen, officials…

Did anyone want to become a celebrity? Okay, they did not understand the word. I tried to explain what a 'celebrity' meant, but my explanations by way of a 'singer' or 'dancer' were all inadequate. Singer? They told me who their favourite singers were – names I could not grasp. Dancer? Not as enthusiastic. Ah, I found an alternative to the word for 'celebrity' – 'socialite'! Blank faces all around. Okay, so, no one there wanted to become a celebrity or a socialite.

Where were their grandparents? Back in the villages. Did they miss their grandparents? Yes. Did they want to live in the countryside like their grandparents? Most of them said no. Why not? There was not much to do in the countryside? Why?

"We have small land. Grow vegetables. Land. No more. People. More, more, more. One people, one land. Okay. Two people, one land. Okay. Ten people, one land. Too many!" one boy explained animatedly, waving his arms to represent the size of his land and his people. "City. Not same. One people, one job. Two people, two job. Ten people, ten job. Not too many!"

We talked about a lot of things. Although the kids' English was not perfect, and in some cases only just comprehensible despite them being in the advanced class, their enthusiasm impressed me. Instead of being timid in front of their new teacher, they wanted to tell me all about their lives and their dreams. I tried to share some of my life stories and some of my dreams, but I wondered if they understood what I was telling them. Anyway, it was a pleasant first lesson for me, and I hoped they had found it useful.

After the forty-five minute lesson, I went back to the staffroom to get something to drink. Teacher Zhou was there, getting ready to go to her class. I told her what the kid during my lesson had said about studying for the country's rise. I explained that I was very pleasantly surprised by such ambition. Teacher Zhou smiled a little.

"I think that boy must have picked that notion up during their Chinese lesson."

"Oh?"

"There is one piece of text about when the young Zhou Enlai was studying. Do you know Zhou? He was a great revolutionary. Very handsome too. He was our first Premier after the People's Republic was founded in 1949. When he was a student, he was asked the same question you asked the kids, and his reply was what that boy said to you."

It was no bad thing to have such a role model. I hoped the boy meant what he had said, even if he was just copying his answer. Maybe that boy could do something profound, although somehow I could not imagine that snotty kid as the leader of this country.

I went to my second class. It consisted of kids of different ages who looked similar to the ones in the first class, with snotty noses. As the kids of Class Two had less ability, we didn't talk about what they wanted to be when they grew up and why. Instead, we focused on food. Noodles. Buns. Rice. Pork. Lamb. Stir-fry. Some of the less shy kids came to the blackboard and drew their favourite dishes and tried to explain how they were cooked, through mostly a series of hand gestures. Here was the air wok. There was the air pot. And this was how things were chopped. It was great fun! I laughed with them, and thought how much I was enjoying teaching these kids, who were so much more animated, keen, curious and engaging than the rich kindergarten kids that I had sort of taught, although I had really been more of a childminder.

As my classes were arranged in descending order of ability, by the time I reached Class Five, I found a group of kids who were barely able to speak English. Like all classes, the kids were of different ages. After a little while, I understood that in order to communicate with them, I needed more than just words. So, I drew on the blackboard various sports – football, basketball, table tennis… I asked them what they liked. Almost everyone pointed to the picture of the football.

"Football," I said.

"Football," they repeated after me.

Then, a little boy took out a ball from under his desk. "Football!" he screamed.

All the other kids screamed, "Football! Football!"

I walked over to the kid and took the ball from him. I kicked it gently. I pointed to my foot and said, "Foot!"

They pointed to their feet and repeated, "Foot!"

I pointed to the ball, "Ball!"

They pointed to the ball, "Ball!"

I linked the words together, "Foot – ball!"

They looked at each other. Some spoke excitedly while others nodded.

"Yes!" I thought to myself, "they have understood why it's called 'football'!"

At this moment, the wind suddenly blew open the door. The ball rolled to me. I kicked it and it flew out through the open door.

"Come on!" I waved to the kids.

It took them a couple of seconds to realise what I meant, then they all jumped up and we charged onto the ground of frozen earth and played football.

"Football! Football!" they exclaimed and played.

I explained the rules in English and pretended to be a coach and a referee.

"Man on!" I exclaimed.

"Wide!"

"Offside!"

Gradually, fewer and fewer kids paid attention to my instructions, as they were all playing enthusiastically.

After the game, some of them gave me the thumbs up. I was delighted that they liked me and understood the word 'football' down to the root words.

I felt my day went quickly. I cycled home in the dark. The wind was as strong as I had feared, charging straight at me. I pedalled and wished that my bicycle had gears. My heavy tank of a bicycle moved slowly, as I struggled, leaning forward. At times I lifted my bottom up, pressing the pedals with my entire body weight. Red light. Stop. Green light. Restart. My legs grew stiff from the exertion. The wind felt like a thousand knives cutting into my face, despite the scarf that I had wrapped around me.

Onwards! Onwards! In my head, I heard my own voice, calling me, telling me to struggle on, against the wind. Then, the voice became deeper like that of an old man. My grandfather's voice. Then it became sharper, breaking into a few dozen voices in unison, the kids' voices.

The children did not have gear changes. The bicycles of their lives were old fixed-speed tanks, like the one I was riding. Born to peasant families, they did not have the best start in life, unlike so many kids in Beijing who were on racing bikes, motorbikes, in cars – kids fortunate through birth. But my kids were pedalling hard in their lives to make something of themselves, against the odds, in this society where the workers no longer had the prestige of their forefathers in more conventionally Communist times.

Onwards! Onwards! Their voices pushed me home…

When I got home that evening, after my first day at school, Mr Na was coming out of the main hall. He was in his smart Mao suit, the one he wore while presenting at the school performance.

"Hello George. How was your first day?"

"Very good!" I explained how encouraged I felt about teaching there, giving him a summary of my day. "Where are you off to?" I enquired.

"I'm off to a reunion dinner, with some of my old school friends. I'll see you when I get back, yeah?"

"Sure."

I had a simple supper with Chun'er that evening, then retired to my room. I picked up my old Chinese book and tried to learn again. I sat in my chair, then took myself to bed and read the book there. I fell asleep, even though I had agreed to see Mr Na when he returned from his reunion dinner.

Knock knock.

I rubbed my eyes and jumped out of bed.

"Did you have a good evening?" I asked, as Mr Na came in. He was still in his Mao suit.

"Very good, thank you." Comrade Na threw himself onto the chair and put a bottle of Two Pot Heads on the desk. He saw my empty mug on the desk and poured me some, and drank from the bottle himself. "Cheers!" he said, handing me the mug.

"Cheers!" I raised the mug, which had plenty of fifty-six percent firewater in there.

"Good news!" he said. "I managed to get some funding for the school!" Comrade Na explained that at the reunion dinner, he managed to persuade a successful entrepreneur friend to give him some money.

"How did you manage that?"

"Ah ha, that's magic!" He was proud of it all. "Well, some people I know have more money than they know what to do with. Some buy properties in London, you know, while others buy huge farms in Australia. This guy bought a farm so large over there, that he had to fly around in a helicopter to see all of it. This is socialism with Chinese characteristics! We grew up together, you know, and we were both from communist families. So, I appealed to his communist conscience. 'Look at you, Mr Rich,' I said to him, 'and think about the poor migrant workers and their kids.' Anyway, after a chat, he agreed to hand some money over!"

Comrade Na drank from his bottle, then sighed about what a shame it was, that this paradise of the workers, which was originally meant to be the People's Republic, had done so much to turn itself into a workhouse for the poor. Take the mining industry, for example. Before, the miners were championed as a key proletariat group, and China was to be led by the alliance of the proletariat workers and peasants. Now, however, it was more dangerous being a miner in China than a soldier in Afghanistan.

"And look at how the middle classes in Beijing treat the migrant workers. The migrant workers build their flats, clean their streets, serve them at restaurants, yet so many Beijingers have such contempt for these hardworking compatriots. Sometimes I wonder if your average Beijinger views these people as fully human. Look at the way they talk to them," Comrade Na raged.

We chatted into the night. Comrade Na flipped from rage to joy, then back again in quick succession, as he drank from the bottle. I wondered how he truly felt about himself, living here in this palatial home, while many migrant workers lived in shacks. I guessed he was doing his own bit, answering his own set of values, through his work for the school. I wondered if he felt he could have become one of those rich guys at his reunion, so I asked him.

"Rich? To be rich is glorious. You know, Deng Xiaoping launched the reforms in the early 1980s saying, 'Let some be rich first, then let them help others to get rich.' I suppose, as a whole, we have managed to get richer. You Westerners love talking about human rights. Yes, rights. But what does the right and freedom to write anything you want mean if you don't know how to write? The right and freedom for self-fulfilment means nothing if you are hungry and cold. You have to the get the basics right first... That's right... Those basics are your first rights. Starvation is not anyone's right... We don't talk about highbrow theoretical rights much here. Instead, we have increased literacy and lifted tens of millions out of poverty within a couple of decades. China's contribution to mankind? This alone should count for a lot! Get warm, get fed first, talk about the other stuff later… Ah, yes, we are talking about the 'other stuff' now… You see, those kids at the school? They will be in a better position than their parents…" Comrade Na's speech became increasingly incoherent, as he drank from the bottle. "Oh dear…" he rubbed his temples. "Drank too much, I think… Gosh, that reunion banquet was quite a heavy session. Well, alcohol helped to secure the funds… Damn, these banquets are surely blocking my arteries… but there are things I have to do – to secure relationships, George, to secure them. My livelihood depends on these relationships – setting up relationships, nurturing relationships, closing relationships when necessary but in an agreeable manner so that in time those closed relationships could reopen. Relationships between me and the others, as well as to support relationship between others. That's how I earn my own money, as well as securing donations for the school. I'm such a hero!" he mocked himself, "I'm selflessly sacrificing my heart, arteries, and liver for the kids of the school!"

How long did our drinking session go on for? Not sure. Eventually, he shook his head and muttered, "Right, enough. My bed is calling me." He stood up and stumbled along to the door. "Good night, George!"

I saw him off to the door.

I enjoyed our drinking sessions, and learning about China according to Comrade Na. He showed passion and I liked that. He was warm towards me, almost a far cry from the cold demeanour when he first came into my room, on the day when I moved in. "Strange guy," I thought to myself.

39

Saturday afternoon. I was at home in the courtyard with Chun'er. We watered the potted flowers and the shrubs. Chun'er went back to her room and I sat at the edge of the fishpond. The four koi were swimming idly, sometimes coming together, sometimes apart, then back together again, circling each other. I wondered whether they understood each other and how they felt about their lot. They were calm creatures, so calm it was difficult to tell whether they were happy or sad, or even whether they were aware of me watching them. Maybe they did not care about anything and just existed in their own world, which was this pond. To me, the pond was quite simple with a few water lilies dotted across the surface. However, maybe for the koi who lived here, their world was highly complex, full of stories and intricacies. I was the fool for not being able to understand their world.

The door of the main hall opened and Gentleman Na stepped out in his long traditional robe.

"Would you like to have some tea, George?" he asked me, speaking in his soft tone, smiling a little.

I put the watering can down and walked into the hall with him. He laid out a tea set, and performed a ritual. He warmed the little pot and the cups with hot water, then put some tea leaves in the pot. He filled the pot with hot water, then poured it out over the cups, then from the cups back onto the pot, as if washing the kit. The tea flowed into the tray.

He explained how the first pot was not for us to drink. It was for the gods. Also, washing the pot and cups with the tea meant everything would become warm and start to take on the aroma of the tea. He modestly told me that this was not a full tea ceremony, but his own simplified version. Still, everything was done with a sense of grace, as he folded back the top half of his sleeves.

I asked him why he had not rolled his sleeves up fully, folding the bottom half of his sleeves too. I recalled watching Kong Fu movies with old masters showing the white inside of their sleeves, fully rolled back and folded neatly.

He sighed. "It is a shame that people have forgotten the ways of our world, and people copy each other's mistakes. You see, a gentleman should never roll the sleeves of his robe fully. Normally, he would leave them down, covering his hands. That is the way."

We sat upright on the hard stools in the main hall, in front of the round table. The pot was small, and the cups were tiny. One would not have tea in big gulps, as if drinking from a mug, but slowly and delicately, appreciating the fine aroma and exquisite taste.

Over tea, Gentleman Na told me about Chinese history, from Pan Gu the mythical world creator, to the Great Yu the flood-tamer, then Xia slaves, Shang bronzes, Zhou rites, the chaotic Spring and Autumn and Warring States periods, with the Qin finally uniting the central plains and standardised writing, measurements and weights two hundred years before Christ. Then the Han Dynasty that took China's western frontier to modern-day Kyrgyzstan, the Three Kingdoms that followed, when Guan Yu lived, the general who became a god, whose statue I had in my room… I cannot remember all that he told me about China, for his history lecture covered over five thousand years, numerous dynasties and unpronounceable names of emperors and generals. It reminded me of my schoolmate, back in the Cotswolds, the kid who first opened my eyes to China. Although I could barely take it in, I wanted to know more, and Gentleman Na was willing to educate me in his calm way, recounting the peaks and troughs of China.

"Knowledge is like a circle. The more you know, the larger the area becomes. Its circumference grows too, and the length of that circumference is what you feel you don't know. Only a fool thinks there's no more that he needs to know, because his circle is so tiny. By the way, did you know that China knew π was something between 3.1415926 and

3.1415927 in the fifth century? The Europeans did not work this out until a thousand years later."

"That's quite a few digits. How do you remember them all?"

"I recall more than just those. I cannot say it in English, for I remember it in Chinese. Let me write it down." Gentleman Na took a pen. Seconds later, he handed me a piece of paper that read: 3.1415926 535 897 932 384 626 and smiled. "I remembered it as a child, as a test for myself, just for fun."

"Although China was advanced in the ancient days, things changed. China went to sleep," Gentleman Na signed.

"But it's more awake now, I guess."

"Yes, I think so."

"How do you think it will change in the future?" I asked, "For example, will it adopt a more Western style of politics?"

My question led him to recount a few millennia of history, comparing China to the West. To him, things today only made sense when they were put in an historical context. China had a unified writing system based not on speech but meaning, which had enabled an effective centralised bureaucracy to govern a large land mass for over two thousand years. In contrast, Europe was fragmented with its numerous written languages based on different speech. Because of China's unity, it was a powerful country. Within the country, the more centralised system of governance ensured a clear line of authority, most of the time, and even when the country fell into disunity, there was no doubt in people's mind that one day a centralised unity would be restored – that was the Mandate of Heaven, a matter of course, the default, the law of nature, how things should be.

In contrast, England's Magna Carter was a sign of the King John's weakness, but it laid the foundation of plurality, as nobles set up parliament, keeping the king's power in check. This political plurality eventually became a force for progress, as more people became part of the political system, enfranchised to become participating citizens rather than passive subjects. As small European countries competed with each other, political factions and schools of thoughts competed within them and strength emerged, culminating in the Renaissance, and leading to the Industrial Revolution. Meanwhile, in the East, China went to sleep, self-assured that its unity and size meant it was still the centre of the world, the Middle Kingdom.

Eventually, Britain knocked China's door down in 1840, after China banned British opium. The war ended with China handing Hong Kong to Britain. Fast forward, today, was the West in decline because of its plurality, under the influence of mass media, with people swayed by soundbites, with politicians more interested in scoring points and winning cheap laughs than seriously working to improve people's lives? Had politics there become a pantomime, a TV show? Was China on the rise because of its centralised system, with cadres rising through the ranks quietly, delivering reforms, liberating the forces of production, lifting millions out of poverty in record time? Maybe one day, having risen because of centralism, China would again decline because of it, and the West would rise again because of its plurality. Who was to know which system was better, or what was best? The present day was no indication of truth. A hundred years were but a fleeting moment in history from the Chinese perspective. Therefore, when he was asked whether the French Revolution was a good thing, Premier Zhou said it was still too early to tell.

Yes, Gentleman Na was quite a scholar. My learned reader, you will recall that his name was Bohan, as I told you. 'Bo' means 'broad or lots', and is typically associated with one's level of literary understanding and book collection. 'Han' literarily means the brush, but was typically used to conjure up images of the scholar. *Han Lin Yuan* meant 'brush forest institute'. That was the name of the highest school of learning in old China – the Imperial Academy – whose members were senior officials and advisors to the emperors. And 'Na'? Disappointingly, his surname meant 'there or that', he explained casually, without five thousand years of historical context.

40

Days went by quickly. I was pretty busy, teaching the kids and preparing lessons for them. In Class One, we focused on talking about jobs and society. I explained to them that most people did not work on farms or in factories in England, but in offices. Many of the kids expressed confusion about what people in offices created. They did not see how pages and pages of reports and presentation slides led to anything other than squabbles. Some of them also failed see the point of parliament. "Do you mean that in England, you pay people to argue with each other?" my top student asked.

In Class Two, our topic was food and drink. "What is your national dish?" one kid asked. I explained that perhaps it was fish and chips. Maybe I had become influenced by Mr Na and his habit of explaining everything with some historical context. I talked about the history of fish and chips. The style of frying fish was brought over to England by Jewish refugees fleeing Portugal and Spain in the seventeenth century, around the time of the Qing Dynasty in China, and the chips went back to either Belgium or France. At some point, perhaps in the mid-nineteenth century, yes, that was around the time that Britain had defeated China in the Opium War of 1840, either a Lancastrian or an Eastender brought together the fish with the chips, and that had somehow became popular throughout Britain. The kids listened to my story attentively.

I drew a deep fryer and took them through the steps of cooking. Some of them sat there with their eyes wide open and chin dropped. One of them screamed, "Bad taste!" Another followed, "Fish not fresh! Ruined!"

I also explained Sunday roast. Again, the kids did not seem to be impressed. One commented, "No taste!". Another one said, "Boil vegetables? No good!"

They got more excited when I explained curry. One exclaimed, "Hot! Good!" Another one confirmed, "Sauce, nice!" When I said almost every town had at least one curry house, the kids seemed amazed. The top girl from this class asked, "If curry house everywhere, why eat boiled vegetables?"

We talked a bit less in Classes Three and Four. I felt it was key that they were engaged and maintained interest in learning English. So, we did a lot of simple English songs, and did arts and crafts things like making model cars and houses using cardboards. Throughout these activities, we talked amicably; although they couldn't always understand me, I was certain they enjoyed themselves.

I continued the sports theme with Class Five. I introduced them to rounders, explaining the rules and they enjoyed this old English game that originated in the time of the Tudors, when it was the Ming Dynasty in China. Whenever I could, I related things back to China and the kids found it easier to understand that way. I was surprised that they seemed to have a good grasp of Chinese history.

"Yes, most kids know the key dynasties," Teacher Zhou explained to me one day when we were in the staff room, "at least in terms of roughly which one came before which. All those TV dramas about the ancient days help. In our country, history is very much present."

41

I did not see Mr Na as much, as he was often out and did not come to see me as frequently as when I first moved in. No Two Pot Heads or tea together for a while. It was coming up to the Chinese New Year, and so maybe he was busy seeing his friends and contacts in high places, attending parties and reunion dinners, making money for himself and the school.

In the evenings, I started an exercise routine. I would go for a jog in the alleyways near home, and come back to the courtyard and do stretches. I looked at the four koi in the pond. Perhaps they had their own exercise routines, which to the untrained observer looked just like their usual slow swim. I tried to decipher them, but could not. Maybe, if they looked at me, they would be curious about this strange foreigner looking at them. Perhaps they would not look me at all, utterly unconcerned with anything outside of their pond. Meanwhile, the four of them had plenty of issues to resolve among themselves, and that was keeping them busy.

One evening, I was in the middle of the courtyard when Mr Na came back. He was in his blue blazer and pink shirt, without his greatcoat, just like the time when I first met him at Beijing Hotel. Perhaps he did not have to walk outside much, travelling instead in a taxi.

"Want a drink?" he asked me.

"Sure."

We went into the main hall and sat down on the stools. He took out a bottle of whisky from the sideboard. I can't remember what the name of the whisky was. Mr Na explained that he had received it as a gift from one of his contacts who imported fine Scotch.

"Cheers." We raised our glasses. The drink had a nice aroma and taste, quite peaty. We had a chat about whisky and drinks in England. Mr Na enjoyed Indian Pale Ales when he was at Oxford, as well as whiskies and Champagne. We talked about Oxford, and how he enjoyed the independent Picturehouse cinema in Jericho, the various indie bands that performed in pubs, and he liked the old pubs, such as the Bear Inn, which dated back to the thirteenth century, and the Turf Tavern, which dated back to the fourteenth century. He enjoyed the balls and parties at night and cycling around town during the day.

Mr Na looked almost nostalgic about his time there. As we continued to drink, he told me about his friends from all parts of the world. By that point, we had probably had about over a third of that large bottle. I couldn't help but ask him about Isabel.

"Ah, she was a fine filly." He lit up a cigarette and casually chucked the packet to me. I took one out. "We had some really good times together." His eyes looked into the distance and puffed out a trail of smoke.

"Oh? Were you very close?" I did not know whether he knew about Isabel and me. This was my chance to find out.

"Erm… Hard to say. Sometimes I felt we couldn't be further apart, yet at other times, I thought we were terribly close." He sipped his whisky.

"Were you…" I finally picked up the courage to ask, "in a relationship?"

Mr Na looked at me, as if he had never seen me before and was baffled by this strange creature sitting opposite him. My face probably turned red at this point. He put his whisky down. "Time for bed," he muttered.

"Well, were you?" I persisted.

He gave me a cold glance through the corner of his eye, while stubbing out his cigarette. "Don't think so." He stood up and walked off.

I sat there by myself. I poured more whisky in my glass and took out a cigarette from the packet he had left on the table. My mind went blank.

42

I did not see Mr Na for days after our whisky-filled evening. Although he was not at home, I felt his presence. It was a cold presence. I became increasingly anxious as I recounted our final exchange that evening, but was not sure whether he was angry with me or not. Perhaps he felt I was intruding on his privacy, especially when I was at his home, his sanctuary that sheltered him from the outside world, this quiet courtyard of old-world elegance. Perhaps he never knew about my relationship with Isabel, otherwise surely he would have understood why I asked him. I guessed that Isabel never told him about me. That thought was quite upsetting. Maybe she had a fling with him, leaving him confused about their relationship? I desperately wanted to probe Mr Na again. I wanted to confront him about his relationship with Isabel, whatever that was, and I tried to encourage myself to so do when he returned home at some point. However, I deliberated and debated with myself on whether that was the right thing to do. If he was just an ordinary guy, then perhaps I should ask him again, but he was not just some random acquaintance – he was my boss, my provider of accommodation and food, and my bailer from my drunken purposeless existence at that kindergarten.

No, I could not ask Isabel. That would be just sad. No! She would not have betrayed me. She was my girlfriend then, and so she would not have been with him. Surely, she would have broken up with me if she was with him. But… did she care? Did she think that I was her boyfriend then? Did she love me? Perhaps that was the most important question. What was more, did I understand her, or even myself?

I sat at my desk. I wrote and wrote, drawing flowcharts to establish the possible relationships between all those involved in this confusion, and all the hypothetical causes and consequences. Nothing became clear at the end of that analytical session – just sheet after sheet of paper on which rested the ruined spiderweb of ink.

43

"Help," Chun'er called out. I followed her voice to a room that I guessed was Mr Na's study.

There were lots of books on the shelves, volumes in Chinese, and a few in English. I looked at the English ones – guide books to the British Isles, academic books on economics and international relations, poetry books with works by Auden, Byron and Shelley, a few by the Russian émigré writer Vladimir Nabokov, and even George Orwell's *1984*. There were some notebooks too.

While Chun'er busied herself with bags of stuff on the floor, I took one of the notebooks off the shelf. It was a sketch book. Sloping roofs and pagodas, mountains and rivers, dams and power stations, accompanied by writing in Chinese, the Radcliffe Camera of Oxford, the Big Ben of London, the Royal Crescent of Bath, thatch-roofed cottages of… the Cotswolds? Mr Na was pretty good at drawing.

She called me over and picked up one of the bags, and so did I. Inside the bags, there were wrapped gifts. I guessed maybe Mr Na had received these from his acquaintances, but did not like them and, hence, they had to be stored somewhere, even if just temporarily. I wondered if he would give these things away, as his own gifts, and then the same items would work their ways through the circles of gift-giving relationship-builders before eventually returning to the original senders. She led me to another room, where we put the bags down and went back to the study.

As Chun'er sorted the various bags, my eyes wandered around the room. Old black and white photographs were framed on the walls, depicting imperial dignitaries in their long robes and beards sitting outside a hall with a sloping roof, Chinese men dressed in smart Western suits standing with Western men dressed in similarly styled suits outside a hall with Greek pillars, Chinese men dressed in Mao suits waving banners and distributing leaflets on the streets, Chinese men and women, dressed in grabby military uniforms with a barren hill behind them on top of which stood a lonely pagoda… A Chinese man dressed in smart military uniform, with stars on his shoulders and wings on his collars, flanked by lesser-looking men, and behind them a MiG fighter plane… Then, in a corner, I saw a few colour photographs, tucked away, almost sadly compared to the proud display of black and white photographs from decades ago, some perhaps even a century in the past. I picked up these unloved coloured photos – a little boy dressed in the fashion of Biggles in front of a museum-piece MiG fighter, an older boy proudly riding a large town bike, a young man sitting next to a young Eurasian-looking woman in front of a lake with a pagoda behind them, the same couple at the airport with other youngsters, the young man in front of Oxford's Radcliffe Camera, a party shot of him and a foreign woman holding champagne glasses in their hands, both laughing… Wait, that was Isabel…

44

Mr Na was wearing his blue blazer, the one he wore when we first met in the lobby café at Beijing Hotel. He was all smiles. His hair was somewhat windswept, or just wild with the party. He held a bottle of Champagne, and with one pull of the cork, he opened it. The cork shot up, and the foam splashed out. He let out a happy cheer. Isabel put her champagne flute in front of him and he poured her some. She was wearing a little black cocktail dress, plus a good amount of make-up, all in the festive spirit.

There were lots of other people. I did not know any of them, but somehow, I knew that they were Isabel's friends from Oxford, perhaps a few from her old school too. They were all rather debonair – the bon vivants, the silverspoons, the rah-rah, the Hooray Henries. Some gave me a glance, carelessly. More people did the same. However, at the same time, it was also as if they had not seen me at all. They talked, laughed and cheered among themselves. Mr Na and Isabel did not notice me.

He was sitting comfortably in a big wingback leather armchair, sipping his Champagne, so at ease with the world around him, as if he owned it all. I noticed that under his shirt collar, rested a red cravat, nonchalantly tied. He was puffing on a cigarette. Isabel was standing next to the armchair, holding her champagne flute, chatting and giggling with him, as if she was one of the people he owned, there to entertain him, to flatter him. She leaned over, as Mr Na offered her a cigarette from his slim silver case. He lit it for her as her face almost touched his. Then, she perched on the arm of Mr Na's armchair, cosying up to him like a purring cat. He did not put his arm around her waist, as his hands were occupied with his champagne flute and his cigarette. As they talked, they looked somewhat amorous as they looked into each other's eyes occasionally, smiling and giggling, perhaps they had noticed that some of the people in this party were amusingly timid, rigid, out of place…

Then the music grew louder. It was some sort of dance music, but not the sort of cheesy tunes that I had grown accustomed to when I was at university. People started dancing. Mr Na and Isabel danced too. No one was dancing particularly hard, as if that would not have been a cool thing to do. But clearly, no one was stiff or holding back either. Everyone looked so merry, thoroughly enjoying themselves and each other's company.

I had a pint of beer in my hand. I did not know where I had got it from. It was a pint of Green King IPA. No one else was drinking beer. I did not dance but merely looked at these unknown dancers. Why was I at this party?

The music grew louder and louder. It was deafening. Everyone got closer and closer, including Mr Na and Isabel…

They kissed.

I woke up.

45

Spring festival descended on the city of Beijing. Red lanterns were everywhere. Our school locked its metal gates. They would not open until a month or so later.

It was customary for Mr Na to hold a party for his staff at his residence. Chun'er cooked for what seemed like a week before that. I was busy too, helping her to chop this and that. I was sure that even if I had returned to England there and then, at least I would be returning with a new skill, chopping. I could now slice potatoes so thinly they were mere shreds, dice aubergines into perfect cubes and cut pork up into stripes. As I chopped, working with Chun'er, I joked with myself that I had become Mr Na's servant, like Chun'er. I started to hum *Rule Britannia*, satisfying my sense of humour, a sort of ironic and self-depreciating inverted snobbery.

Chun'er took out all the utensils and grabbed some woks from the back. I was ready to chuck the pork in, but she leaped over and stopped me. She took out a whole new set of kitchen equipment. "No pig. No pig," she said to me. That was one of the very few times she spoke English to me. She led me to the sink and grabbed my wrists under the tap – "Wash," she said. She put some lamb on a different chopping board and gave me a different knife and led me to the opposite side of the kitchen. I was puzzled by all this. Perhaps she realised that I was confused. She said, "Mrs Na. No pig."

Mrs Na! That was the first time I'd heard about her! I was excited. Finally, I was going to meet Mrs Na! No pork? Did she not like pork? Did she not eat pork? Was she a Muslim? Was she Hui?

Ouch! Blood! My finger! Thankfully, it was only a small cut...

46

Night fell early in the winter. Chun'er had already hung up all the red lanterns – at the front entrance, at the second entrance, under the roofs of the courtyard. The main hall was transformed. I helped her cover the tables. The tablecloths seemed old, a little bit rough, but like the fine wool of an English gentlemen's suit, age could not erase the sense of quality and elegance. In fact, age added to it all. They were imperial yellow, with motifs of dragons. Texture, silky.

We arranged the chairs around the table. These were heavy chairs of hardwood. Dark.

Chun'er went to the switch. On. Red lanterns. So warm. So festive. Then, she disappeared. I sat down, taking a deep breath, enjoying the decorations. She returned with a wind-up gramophone. She put it down on a side table, then put on a record of soft yet cheery Chinese music, perhaps from the 1920s. We smiled at each other, then hugged. For the first time, I had some physical contact with Chun'er. I guessed she was just so happy that everything was in place for this party.

We opened the door of the banqueting hall. Meanwhile, Mr Na got out of his room and entered the courtyard. He was in a long gown, over which he wore a furlined vest jacket. He greeted people as they entered. Teacher Zhou arrived first. She was all smiles.

I was relieved of my household duties. Chun'er was serving everyone. She was a busy little girl, but she seemed more delighted than ever.

Unlike Western parties where everyone kissed on the cheeks, in the air, there were no kisses here, a few hugs between people of the same sex was as physical as it got. The only exception was Teacher Zhou, she kissed Chun'er, as if the little girl was her granddaughter. Chun'er dashed around and greeted people. Had this been my first time in this courtyard, I'd have thought Chun'er was the proud lady host, not the servant.

Lady host... I mused... But where was Mrs Na? The real lady of the house? There was no empty chair to either side of Mr Na. He was surrounded by men I had not met before.

"Who are they?" I asked Teacher Zhou.

"Oh, these are Mr Na's friends. They have been generous to the school."

The night went on. A few people had brought along musical instruments, Chinese ones, which I could not name. A mini-concert started amid all the chatter and laughter. The musicians did not seem to mind, as if it would have been disappointing if everyone listened attentively on this festive occasion. There was a lot of alcohol everywhere, but not everyone drank. Mr Na and his friends were the major drinkers. The older women did not touch alcohol. Although, without alcohol, they seemed as merry as any old drunk in England, as they patted and teased each other.

I was getting quite merry over Great Wall Red, Moutai and Two Pot Heads. I had some good spouting sessions with some of Mr Na's friends, who all spoke very good English while toasting each other like there was no tomorrow. It turned out that many of them had attended universities in the UK or in the States, while others practically grew up in the Capitalist West.

"It's called Red Capitalism," one of them drunkenly whispered to me. "Mr Na hates the term, but he loves it really. He's one of us Red Capitalists! Don't tell him I said it! You don't know what he got up to in England!"

Then, another one joked, "Or who he had got up to!"

Someone else whispered to me, "Never mind England or English girls. Let's talk about the here and now. You should ask him to take you to Heaven On Earth!" My puzzled face led him to continue. "It's the best club in town, if you know what I mean..." He winked.

Before I could ask him or someone else what this club offered, the Red Capitalist tried to control his laugh, "Can you imagine Old Na in Heaven On Earth?! He'd be as stiff as a lamp post!"

The whisperer laughed uncontrollably, "Stiff as a lamp post! You bet! But which part of his body?!"

They both had a lot of fun at Mr Na's expense and my ignorance, indulging in their own company and jokes. So, I took leave from them to go to the toilet.

As I stood up, a shadow dashed across the room. Before I could fix my drunken focus, it vanished. I did not think much of it. Then the same shadow appeared again. Was that really a drunken hallucination? Or was that really someone whom I had not met yet? Maybe. I tried to hold steady, ready to catch this shadow. I was walking slowly, almost waiting.

But I waited and waited, it did not reappear. I got out of the hall, and went to the toilet via a passage-way illuminated by the red lanterns. The moon was so bright that night, matchless, the stars felt shy and had hidden themselves away.

A woman emerged under the lanterns. A long dark dress. Plain. She looked up. Her face, distinctive from the Hans, more Caucasian than Mongoloid. Her big, dark eyes. Her long nose. Her delicate cheeks and chin. Her peony lips held no smile. She was beautiful. A dash of crimson on her face, from the glows of the lanterns.

"Hi," she said.

"Mrs Na?"

"Halisa."

"Halisa… Hi…"

"You must be George." She did not have the accent of a typical Chinese person speaking English – her syllables were less rigidly delivered. She knew who I was. Perhaps Mr Na had told her about me.

"Yes…" I answered.

Like her long dark solemn dress, her face did not portray any festivity. She did not seem pleased to see me, but she did not seem disturbed by my presence either. It was just a matter of fact. We stood in the courtyard, with the sound of music and laughter from the hall in the background.

"See you at the school. I'm restarting after the holidays."

Before I could ask her anything like, "What do you do at the school?" or even, "Looking forward to seeing you there too," she gave me a quick nod and left me looking at the back of her solemn dark dress, as she disappeared into the hall. I gazed at the entrance to hall as I stood there in the courtyard. She did not stay in the hall for long. Soon, she came out from there. She wore a large fur hat and a long dark coat, as solemn as her long dark dress. She stopped and looked at me for a brief second. Her eyes looked straight into mine, expressionlessly. Her face, without a smile. She looked away and walked straight out. As she walked, a strong gust of wind burst into the courtyard, lifting the corners of her solemn long dark coat. Red lining.

Mrs Na had gone. I knew nothing about her apart from how she looked. The harsh wintry air cooled my festive head. I sobered up. Her icy words chilled my belly, which had so far been warmed by glasses of spirits.

I went to the toilet and went back into the hall. The Red Capitalist and the whisperer were still laughing together. Hopefully, they had moved onto something other than Mr Na and his stiff lamp post. Somehow, I did not want to continue with that party, especially when I saw those two looking at me. Not wanting to re-engage them, I said my "Happy New Year's" to people and left for my room at the back of this exuberant courtyard.

I went to bed hearing the cheers and the songs and the laughter from the hall. I closed my eyes and saw Halisa walking towards me, in her long dark dress, passing me, then walking away in her long dark coat... the gust of wind... the flash... the colour of fire...

47

All through the rest of the holidays, Halisa occupied my mind almost daily – her looks, her iciness, her absence from the Na residence, the lining of her solemn long dark coat, the colour of fire. It was clear to me that she and Mr Na were not together any more in reality; that they had separated. What happened? I guessed I would find out eventually, not from Mr Na, but maybe from Halisa? But she was so cold when she met me. Not even a handshake. Not even a smile. Would I ever find out?

I continued with my exercise routine in the courtyard in the evenings, involving various stretches and jumps. Afterwards, I would sit down and gaze at the koi in the pond. It was therapeutic to watch them. I wondered whether they remembered Halisa and everyone who had ever lived or visited this courtyard. Maybe they heard all the laughter and cries, cheers and jeers, music and silence. Perhaps they gossiped among themselves about the world outside their pond. If only they could talk, and tell me what they knew! Yet, when I saw them swimming so idly, so calmly, I thought they were maybe oblivious to the outside world, as the world to them was only the extent of this pond and that, to them, was more than enough.

I did not do much over the winter holidays. I took out my Chinese book and started from Lesson One again. I got to Lesson Three and got stuck, as I had before. I locked myself in my room and tried to overcome Lesson Three. After a few days, I succeeded. Mr Na was hardly home. Chun'er was the only other person in that complex of rooms. I tried my newly learnt words on her. Sometimes, she would return a reply I had expected, but quite often she just giggled. Maybe my pronunciation was funny.

Perhaps Chun'er thought I was bored when she invited me to her room. It was about the same size as mine, at the other end of the courtyard. Like mine, she had a metal framed single bed, some old furniture. Unlike mine, she had more stuff, which made the place look warmer and more homely than temporary accommodation. On the walls, there were cut-out pictures of flowers, gardens, mountains and rivers from magazines. On the desk, was a framed photo. I bent down and looked at it. There she was, standing behind her parents, with a younger boy standing next to her. I guessed it was not taken that long ago, as she looked pretty much the same as in that photo. We smiled at each other. I wanted to ask her why she had not returned to her provincial home, but I could not. How I wished I could speak Chinese!

On a low table, there was a TV. Chun'er turned it on, and flicked it to CCTV 9, the English channel. She looked at me, as if asking whether I wanted to watch this. I did not. But I still sat down. We watched something together. I cannot remember what it was. She sat in bed, and I sat in the chair next to the desk. We just sat there, even though she could not understand the English programme. Maybe she felt I simply needed company. She had always been kind to me, a kindness that transcended language.

I met up with Jillian again one afternoon, at hers. Danny had led the rest of the crew on a bar crawl somewhere. Apparently, there was a new area on the drinking scene. The lads had invited Jillian along but had not persisted. Perhaps they had given up on her. Well, they had certainly given up on me – but then again, I had not contacted them either.

Jillian had no plans to go anywhere outside Beijing, just like the crew and myself, together with most of Beijing's permanent residents. To go anywhere during the Chinese New Year would have been the result of either compulsion or voluntary madness, as the country's transport system struggled to cope with the mother of all peak travel seasons. Were the railways not expecting to carry three billion journeys?

Jillian's boyfriend had a lot of free time. However, she had never been to his place. She did not even know where he lived exactly. They did not plan things far in advance either. It was as if he was granting her an audience at times that were convenient for him, and she had to be available, always. Well, she was not exactly a busy girl, and so that was perfectly fine.

What did he do? He was a clerk at an insurance company. No, he did not have a car. Did he cycle? No. He just appeared whenever they met. His dress sense? Quite ordinary. Their time at the Mogao Caves?

"I couldn't believe it!" Jillian exclaimed, as we sat in her flat. "We flew there on an air force plane!"

I could not quite believe it either. Jillian explained that apparently, he had some low-level connections to the military, and that his friend told him that, as it so happened, there was a flight from Beijing to Dunhuang, and they might as well catch it, for free, as a gift from his friend.

The plane was a cargo plane, but it had seats. The two pilots were very polite, almost humble when they emerged from the cockpit to say hello. "This was during the flight!" Jillian was surprised. It turned out the pilots trusted the autopilot system enough.

One of the pilots was travelling from Dunhuang to the caves to see his cousin who worked there. So, he gave them a lift in his military Jeep. How very exciting!

He had lots of friends then? Well, she had never met any of them, not even this kind friend who had arranged for their flight.

And how were the caves? Her boyfriend sketched, copying the thousand-year-old murals. While some of the caves were busy with noisy tourists who casually came, saw and went, some of the smaller caves the couple visited were completely quiet. Yes, completely, as these caves were unlocked just for the two of them! Of course, this was thanks to his pilot friend's cousin, who worked there. What a privilege! Although Jillian was not sufficiently educated in mural arts to appreciate all the differences there were between these murals, she liked these quiet places where she could gaze at the art and at him studiously sketching away. Was she ever bored with him taking his time over his artistic pursuits? No! It was blissful beyond words to be in these thousand-year-old caves, just the two of them – so quiet that she could hear herself breathing and hear him breathing.

And by the end of the weekend, as luck would have it, there was another air force flight taking off from Dunhuang to Beijing. Of course, they could not believe their luck.

How very lucky. How very lucky. Was it luck though? I did not ask that question. Free flights and visits to locked caves. Yes, right… it just so happened that there were these cargo flights… What did they carry apart from these two lovers?

Had she told Danny and the crew about her holiday? No.

<h1 style="text-align:center">48</h1>

The Chinese New Year holidays ended uneventfully. I cycled to school, and in the staffroom, there was Halisa laughing with Teacher Zhou.

Halisa extended her hand. I shook her slender, soft, warm hand. I was bewitched by her smile, which I had not anticipated. She looked into my eyes for a brief second, and withdrew her hand. A draught came in. A shiver went down my spine.

"Halisa teaches English sometimes and helps with some admin," Teacher Zhou explained.

Halisa stood up and collected her things. She said something to Teacher Zhou and left the room. She looked back at me, before closing the door. She smiled again, so very briefly.

I stared at the door, now closed with Halisa gone, as if she was still there smiling at me. I hoped I did not stare at her, but Halisa's Eurasian looks captivated me – her pale skin, sunken eyes, long nose… Yet there was something Mongoloid about her, although I could not pinpoint what it was.

"Halisa is a Uyghur," Teacher Zhou explained. I did not respond. How did she know what was on my mind?

The bell rang and I went to my classroom.

All day, I found myself thinking about Halisa. Why did she appear so cold when I first saw her in the courtyard? Had she separated from Mr Na? I knew very little about the Uyghur people. Was she often mistaken as a foreigner in Beijing?

Lunchtime. I accidentally bumped into Halisa in the canteen. I wanted to know everything about her but, of course, it'd be terribly rude to just ask. So, we exchanged a few words of little significance, while my torrent of questions was stuck firmly in my belly. Although she did not appear as cold as when I first saw her, there was a wall between us, or a veil hiding her from me.

She did not have any of the meat dishes. She explained they were not halal. Was she a strict Muslim? No, otherwise she would not have married a non-Muslim man. I did not feel at ease enough to ask her how her marriage had come about.

Over lunch, Halisa told me she knew from Mr Na that I had moved into the Na residence, but she did not know how I had come to know him. I told her that my ex-girlfriend had given me his contact details before I left London. Yes, I said "ex". I was really glad that Mr Na was able to help me. I jabbered on through my nerves.

"I'm glad," Halisa said quietly, looking elsewhere.

Lunchtime was short. I had never felt it being so short before. Gone in a few seconds. I managed to get by in the afternoon, just about, while thinking about her and my torrent of questions.

She jumped into a taxi after school and I watched it disappear along the dusty road, as I slowly cycled home.

When I got home, dinner was ready. Mr Na and I ate together. He said he had a private appointment that evening, so we did not venture on to drink Two Pot Heads. He went to his room after dinner. I helped Chun'er tidy up. As I walked back to my room, I saw Mr Na leaving. He was not wearing his army greatcoat, but a plain, short puffa-jacket, plain blue jeans and brown shoes. No sharp blue blazer, no Mao suit, no long gown. Just an ordinary man, so plain that he could be mistaken for a common clerk, with no grand views or ambition, even though he might have a name burdened with aspiration…

<h1 align="center">49</h1>

I saw Halisa almost every day at school. Apart from her looks and her habit of catching a taxi every now and then, she was just like the other teachers, going about her lessons and admin tasks.

As luck had it, the seat opposite her in the canteen was occasionally free at lunch.

As luck had it, we would see each other as she came out from her lesson, with me busy picking up the books I had accidentally dropped all over the floor.

As luck had it, every now and then, I bumped into her, on her way out from the staffroom when I was looking for my keys that I was sure I had left there somewhere.

We only managed to talk briefly each time we bumped into each other, with our conversation not extending far from the basic pleasantries; how I was getting on with the teaching, and what she was up to. Now that I had become a teacher here, Halisa was no longer as involved in English listening and speaking as much, instead she helped Teacher Zhou with the reading and writing elements. She was quite busy outside of school too, helping her uncle to translate old Uyghur texts into Han Chinese.

Halisa's English was excellent. I asked her if she studied in England, but she did not, although she had always loved languages. She explained how she started learning English when she was five years old. Her mother was an English teacher. Later, she had private tutors and read a lot books in English.

While Halisa explained some of her life story to me, I did not feel comfortable to ask her about her absence from the Na residence. Having perhaps upset Mr Na with my intrusion on his privacy on that whisky-filled evening in the winter, I thought I must not run any risks with Mrs Na in the spring. Yet, the more I held back, the more I wanted to know.

I thought about her when I was in bed. Everything about her fascinated me. Every time I looked into her large light brown eyes, I wanted to create another opportunity to see her. Perhaps through all those lucky incidents, we were becoming more familiar with each other. The passing of time was lifting her veil to me. "Let time do the work," I said to myself.

50

The seasons in Beijing could change dramatically. One day, the winter was still harsh. The next day, I noticed some flowers had started to bloom. The sky was no longer permanently grey. Song birds called in the spring.

Teacher Zhou informed me that it was customary to have a day trip for the kids in the spring, and this year it was a long walk to a park called *Tao Ran Ting*. She explained that the park was named after the pavilion that was built in the seventeenth century, which had been a popular spot for poets to meet in the Qing Dynasty.

We set off from the school. The two hundred or so kids marched along on the pavements. It was like some military manoeuvre, the Long March, with the Head Boy leading the columns of kids, holding the flag of the school, which was simply a red flag with the school's name sewn on it. There were twenty teachers who walked along with the kids, to the sides of the columns, making sure that no one could run off and get lost.

I caught up with Halisa.

There was a gentle, refreshing breeze. I could smell the fragrance of the newly blossoming flowers. We walked at ease, next to each other. Although I could not say that we were friends by then, at least the winter chill I felt when we first met had gone. The ice had been melted by a degree of familiarity.

Halisa whistled a little tune. The way she put her lips together made her look like a little bird. She noticed me looking at her and her smile stopped her whistling.

"What was that tune?" I asked.

"Gulbita," she explained, "A Tajik tune about a common merchant falling in love with Princess Gulbita, but he could not be with her. So, he travelled along the Silk Road, singing this song, thinking about her."

"Where were the merchant and the princess from?"

"Perhaps somewhere around Kashgar," Halisa explained. I was inquisitive about that distant land and she was happy to tell me more. This was the first time Halisa and I had talked at length. I thanked the heavens for the opportunity that came through this long march to the park.

She explained that the city of Kashgar rose on the Silk Road in the mists of time. Closer to Kabul than Beijing, at times it was integrated with the rest of the Chinese empire, at times not. There, for thousands of years, the bazaars bustled with the traders' cries and the jingling sound of coins. Merchants came and went, to the sound of the camels' bells. Shamans, Buddhists, Christians, Muslims, Confucians and Taoists worshiped. Uyghurs, Tajiks, Hans, Huis, Kazakhs, Kyrgyz, Russians, Mongols, and all kinds lived there. Adventurers, spies, insurgents and peace-bringers operated there too.

This was the city where Halisa was born and grew up; the city of her ancestors, where they lived in large courtyard houses built using local earth and stone, several storeys tall, where grapevines climbed up the ornately carved wooden pillars, where the family gathered in the middle of the courtyard, drinking tea, telling children witty tales of Afanti's adventures from centuries ago, and how he helped the common poor folks while humiliating the rich authorities.

"I'd like to go there at some point," I said. Halisa's talk had inspired me.

"Kashgar is a beautiful place," Halisa explained. She then told me about her childhood, growing up in the old quarters, running about with other children freely, and only returning home when the moon had risen. "Everyone knew everyone else where I grew up. It was perfectly safe for children to be out and about. Maybe one day I will go back to Kashgar, or live somewhere else in Xinjiang."

I was about to ask whether she would relocate alone, so as to gently probe her about her relationship with Mr Na, but before I could utter the words, Halisa continued. I did not interrupt her.

"But you know, these days, people go everywhere, like us Uyghurs, everywhere, all over China, working in professional jobs, running restaurants, selling melons… Since the early 1980s, people in China had been allowed greater freedom to move, and so millions and millions of people moved to big cities, mostly in the east. If a city in China did not have a Uyghur restaurant, then it was not big enough to call itself a city!" Halisa laughed. She then explained that the presence of Uyghurs in eastern China was not only a modern phenomenon. Centuries ago, many of the forefathers of the Uyghurs lived on the Central Plains, just as there were ancient Hans in modern-day Xinjiang.

For example, in Hunan Province of central China, there was a large group of Uyghurs who had set up home in the fourteenth century, after they arrived to help the emperor in crushing a rebellion. One of China's greatest modern historians and educators, Jian Bozan, was a Uyghur of this descent.

Halisa sighed with the mentioning of her fellow Uyghur. Why? Having studied at top establishments in China, Jian went to the States and studied in California. He joined the Communist Party in 1937. He was the Deputy Principal at Peking University and the Head of History. Politically, he held seats, at parliament and commissions. During the Cultural Revolution, even when Chairman Mao did not want him prosecuted, the Red Guards humiliated him, both physically and mentally. In 1968, he and his wife overdosed on sleeping pills. They left two pieces of paper. One said they really did not have anything to confess; the other only had "Long live Chairman Mao" written on it three times.

"Was Jian religious?" I asked Halisa. I thought perhaps being a Uyghur, he might have prayed in his hours of need, using his religion to give himself strength.

Halisa did not know for sure, but she explained that Communists, by definition, were not religious, unless you counted the ideology itself as a religion – certainly many of the Red Guards were comparable to the worst and most fanatical religious fundamentalists. Anyway, Uyghurs like

Jian, who had lived in Hunan for centuries, were not as Islamic as the Uyghurs in Xinjiang. But just as not all Hans followed the teaching of Confucius, why should all Uyghurs follow the Koran? Should all English people be Protestants? No.

"Yes, I think when it comes to China, many Westerners are confused between ethnicity, religion and the broader political identity," Halisa reflected. "Well, maybe it's like people in China getting confused between what is 'English' and what is 'British.'"

"Yes, maybe, and most people in England would say Hans are Chinese, but you Uyghurs are not."

"I see, a confusion between ethnicity or race and political or national identity." Halisa explained further that Uyghurs were officially classified as Caucasian by the Chinese government. The reality of the genetic mix was more complex, with some Uyghurs having more Mongoloid traits than others. After all, the region of Xinjiang had always been a crossroads between the East and the West. The concept of Chinese, as an inclusive term for the people of China, was a relatively recent development. In ancient days, there was little conception of what it meant to be a nation. Loyalties to your clan, to your regional governor and to your emperor were the bonds between people instead of abstract concepts, such as nationhood. Of course, people had some ethnic self-identification, but that should not be confused with the modern conception of nationhood, especially the multi-national nationhood of today's China.

Halisa then went on to tell me more about Xinjiang and the Silk Road. I enjoyed learning about that distant land, and imagined myself travelling in ancient times, finding Halisa in Kashgar, the princess of Kashgar…

Although our conversation did not follow a tight structure, I enjoyed Halisa's seminar. "You are such a great teacher and scholar," I commented, "just like your husband." After saying that, I realised I had made a slip of the tongue. Oops…

Halisa fell silent. I did not know whether I should apologise. I fell silent too. How long we stayed quiet for, I cannot recall. Our preceding enthusiastic chat made the silence only the more awkward.

Finally, Halisa sighed. "Yes, Bohan is thoughtful and eloquent. That's why we got on so well at the start. Perhaps thoughts and eloquence are like the pattern on the surface of a vase. The vase has to have flowers in it to fulfil its purpose." Halisa stopped there and did not elaborate.

I thought perhaps that I should not probe her, even though I thought I had barely started. Then, while I was thinking over her metaphor, Halisa started singing quietly, just loud enough for me to hear. It sounded like this, in transliteration:

Ay pari, nozuk pari
Az bargi gul cambuk tari
Akajon i dilbari az inqigho yan digari
Gulbita, dar naz mima dare z acal xiren param
Mislikay vi harg guzal homoridor ran, Gulbita

Then, she translated the lyrics for me:

Oh angel, beautiful angel,
The fragrant flowers are no match for you.
You are so delicate and beautiful, and your beauty is beyond words.
Gulbita, your words are sweeter than honey.
Your red lips intoxicate me, Gulbita.

As she sang, I daydreamed about the young merchant travelling along the Silk Road, from Xi'an, with its magnificent bell tower and drum tower, its great city walls with tall gatehouses. They headed to the west, their camel-trains loaded with silk and porcelain. The camels' bells echoed along the ancient highway. They exited the Jade Gate or the Pass of the Sun, at the end of the Great Wall, then took a rest in the oasis town of Turpan, perhaps commissioning a mural in the caves, praying for a safe journey.

After having recited sutras and burnt incense, they set off, leaving the vineyards behind them, trekking along the edge of the Taklamakan Desert. They stopped by at Kucha, another oasis town in the ocean of sand. There, they drank in a dusty inn, spending some of the money already earned on entertainment. A group of local singers and dancers walked to the middle of the carpet. The merchants were already intoxicated by sweet wine and the subtle aroma of incense that was slowly burning around the edge of the hall. They enjoyed the delicious mutton and dates, the exuberant lyrics and melodies, and the midriffs of the dancing girls... Yet, in the morning, the merchants had to leave. Setting off again they travelled over the silent dunes...

Perhaps some of them would see a distant mirage of an oasis, and mistaking it for reality limber on towards it, as the vultures circled above them, dispelling that mirage, that hope, that dream. The unlucky ones would meet their end that way, all the while thinking that soon they would reach an inn, where wine flowed freely and beautiful ladies danced...

But for all the disillusions and hardship, those who were pious would have their prayers answered when they reached Kashgar, the ancient town where people lived on a man-made plateau. There, the traders from Xi'an discussed prices and brokered deals with the traders from Persia and India. Kashgar... where the princess lived, where the young Tajik merchant sang about his princess, where dreams started, where hopes were dashed...

A merchant was a merchant. He had his own life to lead, his own mission to fulfil. That was his fate. Maybe the princess felt something for him, but she had her fate too. He remembered his good times, as he travelled with other merchants, battling against snow storms and wolves, crossing the Heavenly Mountains. Some of them met their destiny and rose to the heavens, leaving the rest to go west and come back east, to the courts of the Central Plains, bringing with them the magicians of music and dance from Kucha, bringing with them musical instruments that were then adapted and became the backbone of the standard Chinese orchestra centuries later...

I looked at Halisa, the profile of her face, pale, smooth. Her long thin nose, her large light brown eyes. Her hair in a single long braid that ran halfway to her waist. I bent down to tie my shoelaces. She walked on. Her narrow waist. Her womanly hips that swayed so slightly with each step. She wore plain clothes, just an ordinary jumper and a pair of ordinary trousers, yet they could not hide her beauty, like a plain vase could not hide the blossoms of freshly picked flowers...

I caught up with her. She smiled at me – a smile that was sweetened by the fragrance of the spring flowers, as a butterfly fluttered, and in its fluttering, pollen flew into the air, falling on the flowers... I felt the entire world around me had vanquished in a split second when I caught her smile, and all was void, apart from that smile.

Then her face turned away from me, as her smile ended, as the world returned to me, that real world, that harsh world, despite the spring, that cruel world, in which she was my boss's wife, my patron's wife, my landlord's wife, my master's wife. George, stop your foolish flight of fantasy! It was just the spring air doing the devil's work in your heart, tickling your hormones! I told myself all this. I took a deep breath and felt normal again, just fine. Gosh, that was close... imagine where my fantasy could have led me if I had just let it run wild!

Our long march to the park finally ended. The kids were very excited. After some instructions from the teachers, they went off, freeing up Halisa for me again.

Boats floated on the lake by a marble-railed bridge. The willows wept along the banks. An exquisite house stood there on the bank. Halisa explained that Emperor Qianlong of the Qing Dynasty came here to write and paint, while enjoying the view of lake with its lotus flowers in bloom.

"Emperor Qianlong?" I asked Halisa, "Is that the Manchu emperor who had a consort from Xinjiang?"

"Yes, she's famously known as the Fragrant Concubine. She's from Kashgar. Some say she led a good life and enjoyed being with the Manchu emperor, while others say she committed suicide as she could not bear being taken by the emperor. Still some others say she was poisoned by the jealous empress. Maybe she lived like a prisoner in the Forbidden City... Well... did the Uyghur consort and the Manchu emperor love each other? Only they would know."

"I can't quite imagine what it would have been like for this lady, in those days, before trains and planes, to travel all the way from Kashgar to Beijing. Well, I guess having been given to the emperor as his consort, she's practically imprisoned in a harem," I commented.

Halisa sighed. "The world is full of cages. Let me tell you about the nunnery over there."

The nunnery was built seven hundred years ago. Ironically, the atheist communists used it as a secret meeting place in the early days of the movement. One of the attendees was an organiser of the labour movement in the early twentieth century. He was buried here.

The activist was forced by his father to marry someone. He later met a free-thinking woman who was also of the Left, but as a modern woman, as one of the most renowned writers of that age, she could not accept him because he was a married man, even though it was not a love marriage. Finally, he gained a divorce from his wife for her with the agreement from his father-in-law, in an era when divorce was legally permitted but socially taboo. However, almost as soon as he had announced his divorce, he died in 1925, at the age of twenty-nine. Three years later, she died too. Their union was finalised only in their burial.

Halisa looked at me. "Cages," she said quietly, "The world is full of cages for us to live in."

Society... Circumstances... Fate, even. What if he had not first married? What if they had lived in a different era? Then he would not have been forced to get married in the first place. What if she had not been a liberal woman, but someone submissive to the ancient ways of the accepted norm and became his concubine? But if she was such a woman, would he have loved her? Did he die from the curses he received for breaking his marriage in an age when divorce was taboo? Did she die of a broken heart after him? What if, they had simply run away instead of breaking taboos? Would that have been the right thing to do? Would his wife have been devastated? Would he not have become a villain in everyone's eyes? But was it not a person's right to love? But would she have run away with him? While they would then be together, in name, he would still have been a married man, running away in shame with another woman? Reality… Name… Honour… Rights… Wrongs…

As we spoke about this sad story, we occasionally looked at each other. Sometimes our eyes met. They dwelt on each other for a second, or even two, and then shied away. This meeting of our eyes was too long, seconds too long. Halisa was not like any woman I had ever met. Not just in terms of looks, but also in terms of mind. When was the last time that Isabel and I had an in-depth discussion over life's mysteries and moral dilemmas? But I had been so captivated by Isabel. If Isabel took me to Madeira, then Halisa had transported me to another world – one of poetry, songs, legends, distant lands in time and space, and romantic tales from such lands that were fuelled with more questions than answers. Was this why I had left London?

51

After that school trip to the pavilion, I felt closer to Halisa. She warmed to me too. We talked a lot after work. I felt she enjoyed my company and talked to me sometimes as if she had not talked to anyone properly for a long time. Instead of jumping into a taxi, she would walk with me, while I pushed my bicycle along. Sometimes, our walk would last an hour or so, sometimes even longer when we stopped by some low-key eateries for supper. There were many halal restaurants run by Uyghurs and Huis. I felt like asking her why she was not rushing home, and indeed where she lived, but I let her tell me when she felt like it.

I told her about my experiences growing up, from the East End to the Cotswolds, then to Bath for university, and wasting time in Clapham. I did not mention Isabel much. I don't know why. It was as if the existence of another woman was inconvenient when I was talking to Halisa. Maybe I was subconsciously suppressing my thoughts about Isabel, when my attention was on Halisa.

Halisa was born a few years in Kashgar before I was born in London. She attended a mixed school, where some lessons were taught in Han and some in Uyghur. Her father was a prominent local official. Her grandfather was a well-known local thinker, and one of the key people who helped to keep the peace in the land that marked the western-most edge of the People's Republic. Some local people used to joke that her grandfather was the reincarnation of Yusuf Has Hajib the much-cherished, eleventh century philosopher. Did Muslims believe in reincarnation? No, but once upon the time, religion was not so much of a hot topic, and things were mostly quite easy, so Halisa told me.

Her grandfather lived through a turbulent time, when various factions fought each other during the last part of the nineteenth and the first half of the twentieth century.

In Xinjiang, the Han warlord Sheng "did not blink when killing people," as the old Chinese saying went. Russia was getting a foothold there. To the east, the neighbouring province of Qinghai was ruled by the Hui warlord Ma, who invaded Xinjiang while trying to oust Sheng and get rid of the Russian influence. To the south, Tibet increasingly came under the influence of British India. While foreign powers and Chinese warlords played a great game of chess with each other, local rebellions and counter-rebellions came and went, with various flags flying and then falling.

When the People's Liberation Army entered Kashgar, her grandfather did not know what to do. He had heard some good things about them, with their soldiers sleeping on the streets of Shanghai instead of disturbing the local people. However, there were rumours that these Communists ate babies and believed in the sharing of property, including wives. Once enough people were talking about the end of Kashgar, one could not help but wonder if there was some truth in these rumours. Some people fled to save their babies, wives and possessions.

When well-intentioned friends tried to persuade her grandfather to run away with them, he was stubborn as an ox, refusing to leave his home. Flashing his dagger, made in Yengisar, the county south of Kashgar famed for its blades, he said, "This is my home. If friends come, I have good tea. If bandits come, I have this…" Yengisar daggers had helped to settle feuds over many centuries, putting wrongs right and bringing justice as God had intended.

"He's quite a character, your grandfather."

Halisa smiled. "Yes, he was strong-willed. Maybe I take after him…" She then continued her story about the old man.

So, he waited, dagger in hand… One day went by. One week passed. One month. Then two months… He no longer tucked his dagger under his belt when at home…

Then, one day, when he was sitting in the courtyard, drinking some tea, there was a knock on the door. Could this be it? He thought to himself. But where was his dagger? He rushed around and found it on a table in the corner of one of the rooms. He tucked the dagger under his belt and opened the door.

An army officer in yellowed uniform and knee-high horse-riding boots bowed to him, in the Central Asian style, with his right hand on his heart. When he straightened his body, Halisa's grandfather realised that the officer was not a Han person, but a Tajik! The Tajik people were the least Mongoloid and the most Caucasian of all ethnic groups in Xinjiang.

The officer smiled and spoke to Halisa grandfather, saying that the new government would like to invite him to a tea party, to discuss the future of Kashgar.

From there on, the wise man no longer carried his dagger. He hung it on the wall. When friends visited him, he used to tell them the story of how he was prepared for the worst, but that things had turned out for the best. Of course, not everything went well, during the Cultural Revolution, he was pushed around by the Red Guards, like old wise men elsewhere in the country. But nothing prevented him from encouraging his son to be part of this new China.

Halisa's father joined the Communist Party. He could not be a proper Muslim and a proper Communist, but he was not dogmatic about religion and ideology. He was a pragmatist. And that pragmatism, combined with his hard work and good connections, led the family to Beijing when Halisa was a teenager. She later went to the University of the Nationalities, located north of the Purple Bamboo Park. The university was originally set up to train ethnic minority students, who were then meant to return to their ethnic homelands and help to rule this vast country of over a billion people of fifty-six nationalities. However, like many of her peers, she did not take the intended path. Instead of becoming a cadre returning to Xinjiang, having studied literature, she became an assistant to her uncle, who was a notable translator between the Uyghur and Han languages here in Beijing.

It was while she was at university that Halisa met Mr Na.

"So, he went to the University of the Nationalities as well?" I asked.

"No, but he was from a prominent Manchu family..." Halisa explained. "He hasn't told you much about himself, has he?"

"No. Hardly anything. He enjoys talking about other things, history stuff."

"Very typical of him." Halisa smiled. It was a cold smile, perhaps.

It turned out that she met Mr Na for the first time was at a conference to promote political participation of students from ethnic minorities. Mr Na was a speaker at that conference. He, by then, was already a young blade in the Communist Youth League. She was one of the few Uyghur youngsters in Beijing close to the Party. Their first exchange was when she asked him a question while he was on the podium. His main argument was that true welfare should not be sought along ethnic lines, and that it was dangerous to base politics on ethnicity. She asked him how, unless one was conscious of oneself, could one be conscious of others. She argued that the work towards greater welfare must be first based on the realisation of oneself, and ethnic affiliation was not something that one could deny, even though theoretical identification would always be in a state of flux.

"Did you win the argument?" I asked.

"He was good in his response. No one won any arguments at that conference. Everyone was too busy trying to convey their own views. It was lively, yes. Fruitful? No. We were just young students, and most us were more eager to voice our views than listen to others. It was as if every single one of us was so well educated that no one could be wrong at all, even in the slightest. I dread to imagine what our guardians from the Communist Party thought. Probably some laughed at us behind our backs, while others had serious concerns about the quality of people coming through the Youth League!"

I was quite surprised by their frank discussions, which contradicted my previous perception of China being a country where no debates were held. Halisa assured me that they had to go through a lot of rather dry stuff at the beginning. However, once the floor was open to the delegates, the speeches were more interesting, some even provocative. Of course, those who would speak on the podium were selected beforehand. Nevertheless, there was a lot of freedom for people to speak their minds, to exchange views, and more importantly perhaps for their views to be heard or monitored. After all, it was among these people that the future leadership of China was most likely to emerge, even though at the most senior level, there were very few ethnic minority leaders. It was the same in the UK, I informed her. By population, the proportion of ethnic minorities in the UK was similar to China.

Mr Na apparently liked Halisa's challenge, and their debate went on after his time on the podium. They talked over dinner, then over drinks. She had a few too many cups of tea that night and could not sleep. It was either the tea, or the conversation, or Bohan himself, as she confessed that she was quite captivated by him – his charismatic style of speech, the power of his reasoning, and perhaps, to a certain extent, his unquestionable sense of self-belief. It was down-to-earth, open, but at the same time self-assured in a way that meant it did not diminish his own manliness when he agreed with his challengers' views. This was the sort of confidence that many men lacked.

When Halisa spoke about Mr Na and the start of their relationship, I could tell that her reminiscences about that bygone era brought her a sense of joy. I encouraged her to continue her revelations about Mr Na and herself. It satisfied my curiosity about him, and at the same time, I felt as if I was undertaking a spot of espionage on her, to see who she was. She gladly continued to recount the story.

When she first told her father about Bohan, he was delighted but worried at the same time. Delighted because Bohan sounded like an intelligent man who could go on and do big things. Worried because *his* father would prefer her to marry a Uyghur for cultural reasons. Although the old man was progressive in his outlook about society out there, inside the home, he perhaps preferred a degree of convention. While the grandfather did not mind too much about his son's pragmatic approach to his professional life, as per his compromise between Islam and Communism, it would be quite something else if Halisa were to marry a non-Muslim. Although she had just met him, her father could not help thinking about their possible marriage. Who was it that said courtship was hooliganism if the intention was not marriage?

What about Mr Na's family? Well, apparently, he did not tell his parents until many months later. Then his father was delighted.

While at the beginning they courted only in private, and never accompanied each other to parties, they were later open about their relationship. And it was almost the talk of the town. Well, among a certain a section of society at least – that section being the sons and daughters of the Red Establishment. News spread quickly to the parents of those sons and daughters.

They enjoyed each other's company while studying at different universities. Bohan went to Peking University to study Economics, a rather boring subject in Halisa's eyes, and in Bohan's eyes too.

Bohan was an artist. He drew very well. Halisa had shown his drawings to an acquaintance who was an examiner at the Central Academy of Fine Art, and the examiner said he should apply. It was likely he would have been offered a place.

Bohan was also quite a poet. His poetry in Chinese had won him a small but national level award. He also wrote poetry in English and was well versed in the classics of Chinese literature. He had some knowledge of Auden, Byron and Shelly too. Perhaps he could have studied literature, which he would have enjoyed hugely.

In addition, Bohan was a first-rate musician. He studied the piano under one of the most renowned pianists in the country. He was a natural improviser, and could just sit in front of a piano and churn out a mini-concert without any preparation. He was a prolific composer and was known to many young musicians of the Red Establishment. He had many friends who later went to the Central Conservatoire. He used to arrange for these top musician friends to play his chamber works. Once a professor at the Central Conservatoire said the fact that Bohan was not studying music was not only Bohan's loss, but the Conservatoire's loss too. During his late teens, he fell in love with music so much that while preparing for his mock exams, he spent most of the time composing a symphonic piece.

Because of his pursuit of music, he perhaps did not study Economics as hard as he could have. His exam results were respectable, but not as high as he had hoped or could have achieved. In a moment of rage over his lack of discipline, over his love of music, which he believed was poisoning his mind and ruining his 'proper' future, he took a sledgehammer to his piano and smashed it to pieces. And he had never touched a piano since.

Why then, Economics? Because that could lead to a real job. Bohan was down-to-earth in his views, at least back then. He wanted a stable job, like his father, and indeed her father, and then to rise through the Party hierarchy. He did not want to be a melodramatic artist – visual, literary or musical. How life had its funny ways, I thought, as Mr Na was hardly a man of the Party machinery these days, with his main role being that of the headmaster of a small charity school for the kids of migrant workers.

It turned out Bohan changed after his time at Oxford. Before leaving for Oxford, he held a pragmatic and boring set of views on what life should be, just work, home, kid. Yes, kid, singular. People from ethnic minorities were exempt from the One Child Policy. Nevertheless, as the son and daughter of the Red Establishment, they should lead by example, despite the exemption.

Did they commit to each other before he set off for Oxford? Yes. They made a vow on top of the Fragrant Hills, in northwest Beijing…

She wondered what his life was like in Oxford. That was in the mid-2000s. In the beginning, they used to write long e-mails to each other every day, sometimes twice a day. In these Bohan told her about his observations of England as a country where young people did not seem to give way to the old, and the old were invariably dressed in beige; where there were more restaurants serving foreign food than traditional British dishes, and when he first tried deep-fried fish, he nearly threw up because of the grease; where it rained most days, yet there were still water shortages in the summer; where in the evenings, people would drink pint after pint, without any accompanying snacks, then as the night progressed, even some of the most civilised looking people turned into chundering werewolves. Halisa enjoyed his e-mails, but he began to write less often. Maybe he was getting more used to life in Britain and fewer things amazed him. Halisa updated him on what was happening around her and in Beijing in general. He responded less and less enthusiastically, as if everything seemed to have become more detached from him. Finally, they only wrote to each other once a week. It was Bohan who started this downward spiral first. As a proud woman, Halisa felt it was the man's duty to keep his beloved happy, and that she would not be the pitiful woman chasing after his replies.

Why the downward spiral? Halisa did not know. For a second, I thought about telling her my dream in which Mr Na and Isabel kissed at a party, but I did not. It was just a dream. Why should I elaborate on the fact that Isabel had given me Mr Na's contact details, a fact which I had already told Halisa, by painting it over with some random dream? I guessed Mr Na and Halisa had simply grown apart, or rather that Mr Na had grown apart from Halisa. Who said that distance created beauty and that absence made the heart grow fonder?

So why did they not simply terminate their relationship? Yes, Halisa had thought about it. However, she believed she had to be true to her words, and she trusted that he would be true to his – that they would hold hands together till death. She believed that once he came back from Oxford, life would return to normal, but of course it never did. Still, they went ahead and got married after he graduated, with Halisa thinking that time would do its work and bring them back together…

Halisa fell silent. She looked down. Was there a small drop of a tear lingering in the corner of her eye?

"Why the final break-up?" I could not help myself asking.

Words. Words were like swords. They were deadlier than swords. In a few seconds, words could poison, could kill…

52

Of course, I could not ask Mr Na what those poisonous words were. As far as he was aware, Halisa and I were simply colleagues, who would not be talking about anything personal behind his back, and I would not have the slightest of feelings for her. I did not want to ruin that illusion, for that illusion was the screen between him and me, the screen that protected me. A Great Wall. Yet, my Great Wall was fragile. It could be overcome easily, through her revelation to him. No… She would not open the gates of my Great Wall to him.

Perhaps, instead of overpowering my Great Wall, he would go around it, like Genghis Khan's army did, attacking the Tanguts first, then the Jurchens – the Jin Dynasty of northern China, the forefathers of the Manchus.

Perhaps he would work it out all by himself. Through what? The look in my eyes? He earned his living by building relationships and using relationships. So he knew a lot about people. Could he see through me? I avoided his eyes. Perhaps that avoidance was ill-advised. But what could I do? I felt as if my Great Wall was becoming more and more useless, the longer I stayed under his roof. I could lose the war if I looked at him, and I could lose if I did not look at him… My pain! So, I spent less and less time at home. But that in itself perhaps was revealing to him. I felt helpless.

53

Halisa disappeared. I did not find her at school one day, then the next... I looked for the tell-tale signs of her return in the staffroom. However, her shawl was not dangling from the coat-hanger. I did not catch a glimpse of her shadow at the school gates. I did not see her jumping out of the taxi outside. I did not hear her speaking outside my classroom. I wanted to see her again. When would she reappear?

At night, I stayed in my little room, in self-imposed solitary confinement. I did not turn on the radio or play any CDs. I listened to what was happening outside. That was Chun'er leaving the kitchen. Those were Mr Na's footsteps. That was Mr Na closing the front gate. That was silence. Silence. I could even hear the stars as they twinkled. I could even hear the moonlight. I listened. Hours of silence. Nights of silence. Years of silence...

That was the inner gate being pushed open, gently, just a couple of squeaks. Those were the footsteps of Mr Na's return. There were also someone else's footsteps. I had not heard these footsteps in this residence before – the footsteps of a woman in high-heels. Could they belong to Halisa? No... The woman's footsteps followed Mr Na's closely, too closely. I heard them holding hands. I heard them breathing in unison. I heard them entering, not the living room hall, but Mr Na's bedroom. I heard the woman's laughter. It was not Halisa's. I heard nothing after that...

54

For all I knew, Halisa would never return to the school. Days went by… Weeks went by, years, decades… Eternity! Did she not know I had so many questions for her? But then why should she satisfy my curiosity? Was I really interested in her answers, or perhaps just her – with or without answers, with or without words?

"Are you okay?" Teacher Zhou asked me.

"What? Why would I not be okay?" Really? Did I really look fidgety? Did I really look unsettled? Why did she carefully examine me? Or was I so obviously going mad? Maybe yes, as I charged into a classroom, only to find Class One with protractors and compasses on their desks. As I stood there puzzled, the maths teacher came in. Wrong room. I hastily gathered my stuff and walked out, embarrassed.

Teacher Zhou smiled at me, gathered her books and walked out of the staffroom.

The little stove had plenty of coal and wood in it. The kettle sat on top of the stove. Steam charged out. It was ready for my tea. With enough heat, water would boil, however unwilling the water might be, and once boiled, it was only natural to see the steam. That was nature. Was I the water and Halisa the stove?

55

I wanted to be out and about, so as not to spend too much time with Mr Na; and not leave him sufficient time to notice my steam. I had to find various activities for myself after school.

I cycled a lot, often aimlessly. I did not contact Jillian, nor did she contact me, for months. I guessed she was busy being with her boyfriend, and I was busy being with… Halisa, at least in my mind. I hummed *Gulbita* while thinking about her. The more I hummed, the more I longed to see my princess from Kashgar. Sometimes, I thought that maybe around the next street corner, I would see her crossing the road. Maybe when I turned into that alleyway, I'd find her coming out of a little shop. When I stopped at a random low-key eatery, I imagined she would walk in minutes after me… I was searching for her aimlessly, as if the divine would reward me for my efforts and send her to me; that in this city of nearly twenty million lonely souls, we would simply chance across each other.

Yes, cycling, cycling. It was good exercise, especially when the wind was strong. I enjoyed every minute of it – the wind slapping my face, cutting my lips, drying out my eyes, deafening my ears, freezing my hands, pushing me back, pushing me over… On the ground, I laughed. I refused help from kind passers-by. I laughed. How long would this go on for? I lost count of the seconds, the minutes, the hours, then the days…

56

Then, one day Halisa returned to school. I could not hide my joy. I walked quickly over to her and asked, "Where have you been?"

"Oh…" She did not respond straightaway, then in her cold manner, the same manner as when we'd first met, she said she had been helping her uncle again, translating another book. I did not know if this cold manner of hers meant that our relationship had returned to Day One, and we were strangers again.

Fortunately, my suspicion was proved wrong. After school, we walked out of the gates together just as before. I thought we would walk and talk, then perhaps have some simple food together, parting afterwards.

"Can we go somewhere else, please?" Halisa asked.

I thought maybe she just wanted a change of scenery, to take a different route home. I was wrong. She told me to see her in front of Beijing Exhibition Centre in about two hours' time.

"Okay, I suppose I will be able to cycle there in two hours…" I wanted to ask her why, but before I could speak, Halisa had flagged down a taxi.

"See you there!"

I wondered what was going on, why Halisa had asked me to see her somewhere so far away from the school. Anyway, I was glad I was going to see her in the evening. I cycled northwards, towards central Beijing, humming *Gulbita*, excited that I was going to spend some time with my princess from Kashgar again.

I waited outside the closed cast iron gates of Beijing Exhibition Centre. The complex was built in the typical Soviet style, with a tall spire in the middle of the building, on top of which stood a golden star. There were motifs of hammer and sickles everywhere.

A taxi pulled over, and Halisa jumped out.

"You see, I've got here on two wheels ahead of you on four wheels!" I joked.

"You don't think it has taken me two hours to get here do you?" Halisa asked.

"Traffic can be bad." I smiled, knowing that Halisa must have stopped over somewhere between leaving the school and now.

Halisa smiled back and led me to a small Hui restaurant nearby.

The start of our conversation was cordial. Having not seen each other for over a month, and having not known each other for that long before her brief seclusion, we needed a little bit of time to warm up again, to refamiliarise. Fortunately, that did not take long and soon, I felt we had caught up and so confided in her how I felt that Mr Na was going to overrun my Great Wall. She laughed. Yes, he might be able to, if he so wished.

What did I have to hide behind my Great Wall? The same thing as she was hiding from him. I knew that through her smile. Her confirmation came with that sparkle in her eyes…

Gradually, we started a conversation about Mr Na and her. Start? Or just resume what we had started over a month ago.

After Mr Na returned from Oxford, they married and moved into his courtyard residence. They started living as a proper couple, keeping to the vows they made on top of the Fragrant Hills. However, having grown apart while he was at Oxford, growing back together seemed difficult. Halisa did not understand this at first, thinking that time would do the work for them, and all she had to do was to be the nice wife she thought she was meant to be. As far as she was concerned, she did everything right around him. She kept their courtyard home clean and tidy. She cooked meals to the best of her ability. She accompanied him to various functions. She supported him when he was setting up the school, using her network of contacts to raise funds, get the volunteers, source the building materials and secure approvals from local officials. Yet, the more she tried, the further apart she felt they became. He was often quiet around her. Besides the procedural things, like what they should next do about the school, he made little effort to talk to her, let alone share his emotions, thoughts and desires. She tried to engage him, such as by suggesting she should teach him Uyghur or that they should learn a new language together, perhaps Spanish. At the weekends, she suggested trips out to the hills and valleys. She wanted to restart their relationship and reignite their passion for each other. However, nothing could change the quiet Mr Na. He stopped returning home in the evenings. He stopped talking.

Then one day, Halisa could not take it anymore. She burst into tears and asked him why had they become the way they were, why he was so cold towards her, and what the point of their marriage was.

He was silent for a while, then revealed that it had been pressure from his father that made him marry her in the end. What was Mr Na's father's argument? Bohan did not tell Halisa, but she knew.

Bohan's father would have said that things would surely work out, and what would other people think? They had been together and it was only honourable that they should marry. Face, that was so important to the Chinese…

How hurtful! Did he not have a mind of his own? Yes, about politics, philosophy, literature, the arts… about everything; everything apart from family affairs. His words. His poisonous words were more harmful than swords.

But that story could not just be a story about two people, or a few people. It was the story of a civilisation rooted in the Confucian sense of social order, in which respect and obedience were perhaps more paramount than heart-felt love. Mr Na's ancestors adopted Confucian ideals when they left the White Mountains and Black Waters, which were their Manchu homeland north of the Great Wall, and became part of the ruling elite of China during the Qing Dynasty.

No, their surname was not originally Na, but Yehe Nara, one of the most powerful Manchu clans. It was also the surname of the Empress Dowager who ruled the final decades of the Qing Dynasty. Following a series of losses at the hands of the Western powers, starting with the British over the Opium War of 1840, and plagued by internal strife, including several rebellions, the Manchus lost their Mandate of Heaven to rule China. To keep their heads down, many of the Manchus, especially those living on the Central Plains, changed their surnames. Na was one of the Han surnames chosen by the Yehe Nara clan.

Despite the republican revolution of 1912 that overthrew millennia of imperial rule, the New Culture movement of the 1920s, the Communist victory in 1949, the Cultural Revolution of the late 1960s and early 1970s, nothing could erase the Confucian sense of social order from the fabric of Chinese society. Consciously, subconsciously or unconsciously, so many people conformed to this order, their rights, wrongs, good and evil defined by it. To them, living like this was almost as natural as breathing, with Confucian ideals running through their veins. Even though Bohan was educated as one of the next generation of Communist leaders, and even though he had spent time in Oxford with not so much as a whiff of Confucianism, he was at heart a loyal son, and the father's words were more irreplaceable than the emperor's decree… It was in his blood.

But Halisa did not have generations of Confucianism in her blood. She was born in a city built out of Central Asia's earth and sandstones, in a house that was closer to Kyrgyzstan, Tajikistan, Afghanistan and Kashmir than the distant heartland of interior China. She did not hear the recitals of Confucius's analects as much as prayer calls from Id Kah mosque. Her communist father was pragmatic not dogmatic. She understood the multitude of world views, whether they originated from Confucius's Qufu of eastern China, Muhammad's Mecca and Medina, Marx's British Library in London and Engel's textile factory in Manchester, or Chairman Mao's cave houses on the dusty plateau of

Yan'an, where a lonely pagoda stood on barren hills. Her only dogma was that one should be true to one's own feelings. And she believed in love, not living with lies, or living in a certain way due to pressure from one's parents.

In the end, Mr Na and Halisa could not reconcile their differences. He had his values and she had hers. Neither felt they could change their morality and virtues, as that would be akin to changing their blood or changing the very meaning of being them.

True to one's feelings. I thought about her words long after we said goodbye. She waved down a taxi. She looked back at me before she got in. I saw her beautiful eyes, her smile, her wave. Then, she disappeared into the darkness of the night, as the red tail lights of the taxi vanished in the distance. Then, I started cycling.

True to one's feelings…

57

At night, I would sometimes sit by the fishpond and watch the koi, swimming slowly, in perfect serenity. Were they really at peace with their lot? Did they dream of freedom from this pond? Did they know about the world outside it? Perhaps, they did not realise their own sorry state, but were content as this was all they knew – their entrapment, in this little pond with its delicate water lilies.

After sitting by the pond for a while, I would go for a stroll on the dimly lit streets. For a twenty-first-century city with perhaps twenty million people, parts of the old city seemed to have been forgotten by the march of time. There were no tourist bars near the Na residence, no local eateries, just a little hole of an internet café and a tiny shop nearby, where the shopkeeper slept on the divan at the back, only to wake up when I entered to buy a packet of Big Front Gate cigarettes. This part of the city went to bed at nine o'clock. I walked on my own with a trail of smoke above me and behind me, passing gatehouses with their sloping roofs, on top of which some grass had grown. Spring was warm in Beijing, but only during the day. At night, under the cover of the darkness, winter returned while I walked, cold and alone, only disturbed by the crisp ring from a bicycle bell, as an old man rode past me slowly, as if he wanted time to stand still.

During the day, at the weekends, I did not want to spend much time with Mr Na. I rode out when he was home, and stayed in when he was out, spending time in the courtyard with its many flowers. Peonies were my love. I put my nose to them. I watered them. I watched them bloom, and when the rain was heavy, I saw their petals fall.

Although I tried to avoid Mr Na, living in the same courtyard meant we still saw each other almost every other day. While most instances led to little more than exchanging a few sentences, sometimes Mr Na invited me for supper or tea, although these invitations became less and less frequent. Ever since that whisky-filled evening, when I asked him about Isabel and he walked out of the hall, I had avoided talking about him, his life or his personal relationships. Instead, we talked about other things, things that happened a long time ago, seemingly distant from us. Sometimes, as Mr Na spoke, I wondered if he had any knowledge of my time with Halisa, and whether it would be honourable for me to tell him.

Back in my room, when sitting at my desk, I would gaze at my little Chinese warrior statue. The god of loyalty… Loyalty… Truth… What if the two become conflicted?

I bought a large map of China, an English version. Mr Na joked that I bought it because I was becoming patriotically Chinese.

I stuck it on my wall. Beijing was marked with a red star, with the land to the west of the red star gradually becoming browner, the colour code of mountains and highlands. Then, a bit of green surrounded Xi'an. West from there, it was mostly brown again. Further west, I traced the Great Wall on the map. The end at Jiayuguan, the Pass of the Brilliant Valley. Westwards… Turpan… Kucha… Kashgar…

Oh angel, beautiful angel,
The fragrant flowers are no match for you.
You are so delicate and beautiful, and your beauty is beyond words.
Gulbita, your words are sweeter than honey.
Your red lips intoxicate me.

I closed my eyes and rested in bed while humming *Gulbita* to myself. In the back of my eyelids, that black canvas on which I could paint the most kaleidoscopic of dreams, I saw Halisa walking towards me. I saw her smile. I heard us talking about her and Mr Na, satisfying my curiosity about the self-styled princeling of Beijing. I heard us falling silent, as there was nothing else she had to say about him. Instead, she talked about us, the two of us; how she would like to invite me to her city of the west and show me the grapevines that climbed up to her bedroom window, wave to me from her bedroom window, appear like a princess, my princess…

58

Appearance was important. The wearing of blazers and tweeds in England portrayed one's class, or preference for class. In China, one's appearance always had a profound sense of importance, since ancient times. The ancient Hans believed that one's hair was gifted from the parents. To cut one's hair was to cut ties with one's parents. Buddhist monks, upon joining the sangha, would shave their hair, to symbolise their detachment from the earthly world.

Clothes too were important. Confucius once said, "Guan Zhong had been supporting the king to fight against the barbarians. Had it not been for him, we would now all be wearing our hair loose, and have the right front of our robe covering the left." Here "loose hair" and "right over left" were symbols of barbarity.

After the Manchus marched south of the Great Wall, the Prince Regent Dorgon issued an imperial edict – the Queue Order – in 1645, that any male subject must shave the front of his head and tie his hair at the back into a long plait, following the Manchu style. Resistance meant death. The choice between submission to the new regime and loyalty towards one's parents through the Confucian doctrine meant that hundreds of thousands of men chose death.

Later, the cutting of one's queue was symbolic in the defiance of imperial rule, of support to the new republic. For officials, mandarin robes gave way to what became popularly known in the West as the Mao suit. Actually, Mao himself did not design it. It was designed by Dr Sun Yat-sen, the founder of the Republic of China. Mao merely popularised it, especially in the Western media coverage of China after 1949, long after Sun's death. Then, after the Cultural Revolution, the solemn Mao suit gave way to the Western suit and tie. Today, an official wearing a Mao suit would look odd – it would be as if he was stating that he preferred the old order of Mao, rather than the new reform-minded Deng and his successors. Oh, Mr Na had been my great educator in Chinese things!

And my educator came home one day while I was watering the flowers in the courtyard. He did not say hello but went into his room. He came back out, without his coat.

"Let's have supper together," he said, then went back into his room.

Later, I was laying the dinner table with Chun'er, when Mr Na came into the main hall. He sat down. He stood up. He sat down again. He stood up again. He walked to the sideboard and took out a bottle of Moutai, and poured some into his shot glass. He downed it. Then again.

He saw me looking at him. We froze. Just looking at each other.

"What is it?" I asked.

"I'm sure you have met my wife, at the school." He spoke in a matter-of-fact way, rather than as an accusation.

"Yes…?" I wondered where this was going.

"What do you think of Halisa?"

Oh, what was I to say? But more importantly, what had prompted this question? Oh no, I should not have hesitated. Damn. Now, he must be suspecting something.

"Don't worry, just say whatever you feel."

"Okay, ummm… She's a nice person… Quite strong-willed, so she seems… I don't know why, but I just get this feeling that she is…"

"Strong-willed? Damn right, strong-willed!" He downed his shot.

"What has happened?"

Mr Na poured another shot for himself, and one for me. Apparently, there were some riots in Urumqi, the regional capital of Xinjiang, between the Uyghurs and the Hans, and some people have been killed, mostly Hans.

"But how does this relate to her?" I had not heard about anything, and was a bit confused.

"Halisa, since this riot, has been wearing her Uyghur dress out on the streets of Beijing. After 9/11, when much of the world turned to look at Muslims with suspicion, as if everyone could be a terrorist, Halisa wore her Uyghur dresses every day. She went to the mosques more often than usual."

"Perhaps she was just praying for peace?" I suggested.

"Maybe, but it is a political statement that she is a Muslim."

It was a time when Muslims in China walked with their heads down, as if there was some sort of collective guilt, even though the vast majority of Muslims in China were good citizens, just like everyone else, and in any case 9/11 took place in America, not here. The Chinese government joined the US and the other countries in condemning the attacks and placed further pressure on Xinjiang to quash its Muslim Uyghur separatists, under the banner of counter-terrorism. It was not a good time to publicly profess Islam. Of course, in principle, why should some terrorists blacken the name of Islam? But also, in principle, one man's terrorist is another man's freedom fighter. Rights or wrongs, principles aside, one had to live, and although such a provocative display of religious and ethnic ties was not absolutely incorrect, it was ill-considered, insensitive, or just stubborn.

Now, after people in Xinjiang had been killed and more could be killed if violence escalated, Halisa had chosen, once again, to display her identity. What timing?! If her display had happened any other time, then it would have been perfectly fine, but now... This was like rubbing the authority's nose in it, when she knew full well that her actions, like many of her peers in the Red Establishment, would be watched by those who had an interest in the next generation of leaders toeing the right line, and that line was of understated pragmatism, rather than statement-led showing off.

"Is Halisa in trouble?" I asked.

"No. Of course not. The wearing of Uyghur clothes is not a crime. Going to the mosque is not a crime. So, no one would do anything to her, no one in officialdom anyway."

Mr Na downed another shot. "She is selfish! So very selfish! She does not care about her own future. Fine. But she does not care about me! My future! What do you think people would say? Anything good? 'Oh, look at Mr Na's wife. How beautiful she looks in her dress! How devout she is to her Allah!' Would people say that? Or would they look at her, this Muslim Uyghur, and think of the killing that has been taking place in Urumqi, with most of the attackers being Uyghurs and the dead being Hans?! This is Beijing and most people are Han! There is enough of an anti-outsider mood in Beijing already, with all these housing shortages and petty crimes, without things taking on a religious and ethnic dimension as well!" Mr Na downed yet another shot after his rant.

"I'm sure things will pass, Mr Na." I tried to comfort him.

"Yes, sure, things will one day pass, but the damage could last a long time."

We sat down and had dinner. After a few more shots, Mr Na seemed a lot calmer. China, he explained, was a country of fifty-six ethnic groups. It was a big family. Like all large families, there had been quarrels, and sometimes the family had split, but later, the family had always come back together at some point. Harmony was important. One could not get carried away by emotions.

Some Uyghurs were not happy about things. Sure. Many people in many parts of the country were not happy about things. The right way would have been to resolve problems peacefully. Now, hundreds were dead on the streets of Urumqi. This was not a good way to behave in this family.

How did all this violence start? A factory in southern China had hired some Uyghur workers. This was a good thing. It was good for people to move, to see different parts of the country, and to earn some money. But there was an incident. A Uyghur man accidentally walked into a Han woman worker's room. She screamed. Other men heard her scream and rushed to the scene. In the confusion, the Uyghur man was accused of trying to rape this woman. Fighting broke out. Perhaps three Uyghur men were killed. Then, the police arrived. The matter should have ended here.

The police would round-up the suspects and take them to court, which would deal with the criminals who killed their fellow workers. This criminal investigation was taking place as we spoke.

News spread to Xinjiang, where the Uyghur men were from. If this incident had not involved people from different ethnicities, then nothing more would have happened. Just because the criminals were Han and the murdered were Uyghur, this had taken on an ethnic dimension. It was certain that as the news spread, different people would have added more inciting stuff – a game of Chinese whispers with deadly effect.

Sure, there had been some grievances in Xinjiang among the Uyghurs concerning a range of issues, but this incident had acted as a catalyst. Now, Uyghur mobs were rampaging the city.

What was the underlying discontent?

Some Uyghurs said the influx of Hans to Xinjiang was diluting the Uyghur culture. Okay, that could not be denied. When the Manchus passed the Great Wall and entered the Central Plains, the Han culture was 'diluted'.

Was it diluted?

No! It was enriched! Today's Mandarin language was precisely the product of that dilution! Of course, dilution or enrichment, that was a matter of personal perspective. But, in this age of freedom, how could you prevent people from moving? No Hans in Xinjiang? Then no Uyghurs on the Central Plains? Could no one move anywhere and be tied to the land? That would be ridiculous! It would roll back the progress that China had made in the past three decades. The state today was not the all-controlling state of Mao's era, when you required a letter from your employer to come to Beijing, explaining your visit.

So, were some of the Uyghurs' grievances completed unfounded? No, the government should have been a bit cleverer and seen that apparently 'normal' problems could take on an 'abnormal' ethnic dimension. Ethnic dimension, like its cousin religious dimension, should be avoided at all cost, as they could turn nasty, very nasty.

How nasty?

Think about the Partition of India. Conceptually, how strange that it had led to the inheritor of the name of India not holding the supposed cradle of the Indian civilisation – the Indus River – but the rival Pakistan did instead. Should Pakistan not have been the inheritor of the name of India given the location of the Indus River? Then, what should India have been called? Conceptual mess was nothing compared to the real mess suffered by ordinary people. How many people died during the partition? There was the suffering of the people then, and the problem remained unresolved to this day – only now Pakistan and India were both armed with nuclear weapons. Could separation really lead to happiness?

"But living a lie is also a problem…" I murmured.

The air froze. What did I say? Oh no…

To avoid embarrassment, I quickly poured him some Moutai and some for myself. I was too afraid to look at him, thinking my comment was just a bit too much of a dig. I expected him to get angry.

But he did not. He took out a cigarette and handed me one.

"George. What do you think?" His voice was calm, but somehow his words carried some sort of weight. They were heavy with expectation. I had to give a good answer.

"Problems need to be resolved, Mr Na. Separation is the last measure. Perhaps problems could only be truly resolved if people's heartbeats could be felt, their true views heard. Pride must not stand in the way of future happiness – pride must be put aside. And with everyone having shared their views, an arrangement could be put together, which would reflect the wishes of the people, guiding towards a most agreeable outcome. Maybe, if it must be that separation is the only answer, then that separation needs to be managed peacefully and calmly, even amicably, so that everyone would be happier in the end, being true to their own hearts." I said all that in one breath, without looking at him.

I did not look at him after I had finished. I simply smoked. He simply smoked too. What would he say? Would he agree? Or would he see me as yet another Westerner hellbent on seeing China's demise?

"You're an idealist George." He laughed a little. "People are not animals. People are proud creatures. If pride was not at the core of our soul, would the Chinese nation have stood up to the British over their smuggling of opium? Would the Chinese nation have stood up to the Japanese, fighting on for years without any allies? You, the British, were you not a proud nation, fighting on your own after the fall of France?"

"Yes. We are a proud nation. Interestingly, Churchill said that the independence of India would only happen over his dead body. But Churchill lived on after India's independence. He then went on to win another election in Britain with another generation." Maybe I had too many shots of firewater giving me too much Dutch courage. Maybe I could no longer live with this feeling that I had to please Mr Na all the time.

Mr Na fell silent for a few seconds. He brushed aside the comparisons between British India and Xinjiang, even though he was the one who brought up the Partition first, and our conversation slowly died down after that. In a way, I was thankful that it died that way, without a fuss.

<h1 style="text-align:center">59</h1>

I told Halisa about my talk with Mr Na. She laughed a little. It was a very cold laugh.

"Yes, he is a very proud man. And I am a very proud woman. Our pride…" She sighed a little. I wondered if she was sad that they were not together, yet not separated either, bound together by some form of pride. Or was there something else besides pride that was binding them together? I wondered if they had ever talked about their own feelings, frankly and unreservedly, or admitted their own mistakes.

We finished another simple dinner at a simple restaurant. She was in her brilliant silk dress, a Uyghur dress of many colours, with different stripes all over the place, almost like something that was seen on *Top of the Pops* in the 1980s. Yet, of course, this was no passé fashion, but a traditional costume. She wore a little square skullcap, embroidered with shiny bits. Her hair was braided in a single plait. Her festive attire provided a sharp contrast to our down-to-earth noodles.

"I feel we are being watched," I whispered to her as we left the restaurant.

"Perhaps you're right. Let them watch!" she replied, speaking normally, almost loudly, as if to make a statement.

"Perhaps you should be more pragmatic," I whispered again.

"Thanks for the advice, George, but what's the worst that could happen? I have done nothing illegal. No one could persecute me. At most they could send me for 're-education' in a labour camp, but that's nothing, and it's highly unlikely anyway."

"Really?" I was quite surprised, as the term 'labour camp' conjured up an image of Siberia to me.

"Really. A friend of mine was involved in the Falun Gong thing a while back. You know Falun Gong?"

I replied that I had heard of it, as some sort of cult, which told ill people not to take medicine.

"She was sent to a labour camp. It was not that uncomfortable. The food was okay. The inmates went to lessons to repent their mistakes and made socks afterwards. If I get to go, perhaps it'd be a refreshing break from all this."

I tried to convince her that her words were chosen out of ill-temper and that it was best if she did not end up in a labour camp, however comfortable it might be.

"Are you working for Bohan here? Of course, it would do Bohan tremendous damage if people hear about his wife having been sent to a labour camp. I might just try to get myself sent there, just to annoy him." She laughed a little, then reflected, "Maybe not, as he wouldn't be able to command the respect needed to raise funds for the school. Okay, okay, I'll be more cautious, not for him, but for the school."

She waved down a taxi. I watched the back lights of that car disappearing into the dark night.

60

The next day, Halisa came to school in her ordinary clothes. Perhaps she felt she had made enough of a statement and annoyed Mr Na sufficiently. Teacher Zhou greeted her. Somehow, whenever Halisa and I were in the staffroom, Teacher Zhou was always there too. Just as Halisa and I were in the middle of talking about something, I would hear Teacher Zhou's gentle footsteps approaching and her entry to the staffroom would terminate our talk of things that were best kept private.

Yes, private… How happy I was that Halisa whispered to me. Feeling her breath on my ear sent shivers down my spine. I knew, then, that we had taken a step along a new path.

PART FOUR

61

Halisa did not invite Teacher Zhou, or anyone else from the school, to her birthday party. Not a single person from the school, apart from me! Joy oh joy!

After school, Halisa waved down a taxi and I got in with her. We watched the streetscape of Beijing in the rush hour. Millions of cars piled onto the streets, moving block by block. I did not care about the speed at which the vehicle moved. I was just happy to be with her. We chatted in this little space of ours over matters of no consequence, relaxing and enjoying our time alone.

Halisa said there was no need for me to dress up for this party, as it was informal. She was not wearing anything fancy either, just a smart knitted dress, tights and boots. She had a rucksack with her.

"What's in there?" I asked.

"You'll see," Halisa smiled.

The driver took a right turn at a set of lights. He stopped and Halisa paid. We got out.

We walked through the gatehouse, which had little minaret-like stubs at the top. Built of dark yellow sandstone, the main house looked like something that had been transported from Central Asia, with its beautifully carved arches and Islamic-style geometric patterns adorning the top of the arches, above the smoothly carved pillars.

"This is the Xinjiang representative's office," Halisa explained. Since the ancient days, each part of China had its own office in the capital, helping the communication flow between the centre and the provinces, and between the provinces as well. They were also reception centres for events and hostels for people visiting the capital from their home provinces. Some of them took on a cultural significance too. For example, Hu-Guang had a magnificent opera house, probably one of most renowned venues in Beijing. It still put on performances to this day. "Bohan loved Peking opera," Halisa commented, while explaining all this to me. She stopped speaking at that point and cleared her throat. It was the last time she mentioned him that evening, and for a while.

We walked into the building and entered a small hall. People stood up and applauded as we entered. I did not recognise anyone there. Amid the applause, I felt like a star, a celebrity… Wait? What did celebrities do? I recalled my conversation with the kids on Day One at Mr Na's school. Nothing. They just looked pretty. And here I was, thinking I was receiving applause for nothing but my association with Halisa. She was the real star.

The hall was filled with colourful people, in their festive clothes. A tall black fur hat – Tajik. A red embroidered skullcap – Uyghur. A white skullcap – Hui. A white pointy hat – Kyrgyz. A blue headscarf – Halisa couldn't remember that lady's ethnicity. No headwear – Han or most ethnicities, or 'nationalities'; as it was commonly termed in China.

I sat down next to Halisa. Those two seats were left free for us. What did her friends know about us? Had she ordered that the seat next to her should be free without her friends knowing why? Whatever the reason, I was delighted.

There were massive skewers of lamb cubes spiced with ground black pepper, red chillies and cumin seeds, and giant naan breads, piping hot, fresh from the tandoor. A huge plate of chicken with green peppers and onions and a huge bowl of rice mixed with shreds of carrot, dotted with chickpeas and lamb, as well as hand-pulled noodles with lamb, chopped peppers and onions, and chillies. Just as I thought the feast could not get more elaborate, the waiters brought along a whole roasted lamb!

Many of the party attendees were Halisa's friends from her time at the University of the Nationalities. Most of them lived in Beijing, working as officials, business people, teachers, scholars, musicians, artists, dancers and sole traders, and there was also a professional wrestler! He was a big Mongolian chap, built like a brick house. He toasted my good health and insisted that I downed the shot of Mongol firewater he had poured me.

"This is from my home! My father made it!" he said in English, with a thunderous voice.

Well, how could I refuse? Refusal would have been not only an insult to him, but his father and his homes people!

"Aargh!" It burnt like… mad! He laughed like thunder and I laughed too.

I enjoyed many shots with the Mongol wrestler over the course of that festive evening, as well as drinking with other people. Some men particularly enjoyed toasting to each other, walking from one table to the next, including a Tibetan, who had brought along some firewater made of hull-less barley native to the plateau. By the time I got to taste his firewater, my mouth had been desensitised – I could not remember the taste, but it must have burnt. While my mouth and belly were both on fire, my senses were heightened. Friendliness filled the little hall with laughter and cheers, as people toasted over firewater, poured pomegranate wine, downed beers and enjoyed fruit juices of all colours. I had never felt so great. This was not the drunkenness of London, not the drunkenness with the crew, nor the drunkenness at the Chinese New Year party at the Na residence – this was nothing but exalted bliss! Gosh, I was so drunk that I started to forget where I was… Was this heaven?

As the evening progressed, some people started singing, and some started dancing, then gradually everyone turned to Halisa as they applauded, and some wolf whistled. Halisa laughed. She picked up her rucksack and disappeared out of the little hall. A little bit later, she returned…

She was in her long Uyghur silk dress, which was mostly red but with a myriad of colours. She wore it with a little embroidered black waistcoat and a red skullcap. The background music stopped and a waiter put on a CD.

After the intro, some people started singing, in at least three languages – Uyghur, Tajik and Han, I thought…

Meanwhile, Halisa danced. Her arms waving, bending and straightening. Her shoulders shook up and down. Her neck shifting left and right. Her fingers waved to the tune, above her head, around her face and around her waist as she twirled. Her dress flew upwards and outwards in her twirl which became more and more rapid, the stripes of colours of her dress mixed into one beautiful rainbow…

Captivated… was an understatement of my state as I watched her dance. She glanced at me occasionally. Each of her glances spoke to me, as if saying, "Look at me. I am so beautiful. Do you not love me? Would you not die for me?"

In my heart, I sang with the others…

Oh angel, beautiful angel,
The fragrant flowers are no match for you.
You are so delicate and beautiful, and your beauty is beyond words.
Gulbita, your words are sweeter than honey.
Your red lips intoxicate me.

Her performance drew the wildest of cheers. Others joined the dancing as the music continued, echoing in the hall, with songs of various languages and styles. I took to the floor too after a while, dragged on by the Mongol whose dancing style seemed more like exercises before a wrestling match. I danced with Halisa. How clumsy I must have looked compared to her… She smiled at me, teasing me with her eyes, as she danced away from me, then leaping back. Oh Halisa, beautiful like a flower…

As the people thinned out that night, I waited with her to see them off, and then we walked out too. Between the party hall and gatehouse, there were no lights. A comfortable darkness engulfed this little space that was ours; no one else's but ours.

As we slowly walked, our bodies gravitated towards each other. I could feel the warmth of her body on that cool evening, coming closer and closer towards mine. Our arms briefly touched, then parted, but soon retouched. Below the arms were our hands… Timidly, the fingertips found each other. Then, the knuckles… Between mine, hers, and between hers, mine, intertwined. The palms… The pores opened. Moisture gently oozed out, one tiny particle from my palm, then another from hers, to mingle with each other, and to be sucked in by other pores, to be exchanged, to be shared, to be one of the same body. The pores kissed. Their kiss glued them together, in that subtly humid environment – the little universe of mine, hers, ours… born amid nothing but the blissful darkness that was the back of my eyelids, to the sound of nothing but my own breath, and hers, in unison. Were we still walking? Or had our slow walk turned into a gentle shuffle of feet and eventually hardly any movement at all? There had been no stars in the heavens before this moment. The night had not been separated from the day yet, and all had previously been a state of wantonness. That night, the moon was carved, brand new…

62

Halisa and I jumped on a train. She was in her colourful dress, wearing her little square skullcap. Instead of one plait, she had countless today. As she stood up to get some hot water for our tea flask, some of her plaits brushed against my cheek.

She turned and gave me a sweet smile. I smiled back.

The train moved, gently rocking. We opened some instant noodles and I filled them with hot water from the large boiler in our carriage. Our neighbouring passengers opened up various items, and we all shared. A cucumber, a tomato, some ham, which I had and, of course, Halisa did not. One guy took out some beers from his bag and we shared those and, of course, Halisa did not drink alcohol. We had a little chinwag with our fellow passengers. I surprised myself that I was able to hold a half decent conversation using a mixture of English, Chinese and hand gestures.

After that simple supper, I went to the space between two carriages for a smoke. There was just me. Night fell and I could see my reflection in the window, against the dark night. Every now and then, there was a flash of light passing by, gone before I could tell what it was.

Having brushed my teeth, I returned to our carriage and Halisa had already washed and climbed into her bunk bed, at the very top of a three-tier bed set-up. Mine was at the top too, facing her, with a gap of perhaps a metre between our beds.

There we gazed at each other. She did not look like a mature woman, but a young girl, so in love, as she smiled at me sweetly, almost giggling with excitement. I too was smiling, almost giggling with excitement.

We did not say anything, just stayed like that, facing each other, as the train rocked on, gently. Then the light went out.

Somehow, I could still see her in the dark, and I was sure that she could still see me. I reached out to her, and she held my hand.

We fell asleep.

When we woke up, we were travelling on the Central Plateau of China, the barren landscape of yellow earth.

Later, we sat on little foldable chairs in the corridor space, facing each other, enjoying the view of the open landscape under a sapphire sky. We held each other's hands occasionally.

A young man suggested that we play some music, and took out a guitar. An old man had a little hand drum. A young woman took out a bamboo flute. They started playing. Halisa stood up in her beautiful long dress and danced, while singing a song from a distant past, the stuff of myth and legends before today's troubles, before the clash of civilisations, when men and women composed poetry and drank sweet wine:

Gulbita, as attractive as a goddess, no flower could compare to you.
There's no language in the world that could describe your beauty.
To gain your love, I would happily surrender my life.
Gulbita, your sweet smile is like honey, but no honey could be compared to you.

To Bukhara or to Kabul, the distant journeys do not worry me,
Now, I have seen the goddess on earth, I am so happy.

Gulbita, Gulbita, I give you my heart.
Gulbita, Gulbita, I give you my heart.
I give you my heart, I give you my heart.

My beauty, do not get upset, I am just a visitor.
I have brought the lights of Bukhara. I am the bright moon.

I have travelled through all of Bukhara, and have taken in Kabulstan.

For the beautiful Gulbita, I am willing to abandon all my wealth.

Everyone says that Gulbita is sweeter than honey.
Drinking is a habit. To get rid of it is hard.
Gulbita's beauty surpasses the blooms of a hundred flowers.
Poems of praise can never run out. For to describe her, there are not enough words.

Why are the flowers so red?
Why so red?
Gulbita
Gulbita

Gulbita
I see you coming,
From the beautiful icy peaks,
Coming towards me,
Your long hair,
Your dark eyebrows.

In between your lips,
A red rose.

Gulbita
I see you coming,
From the distant Gobi,
Coming towards me,
Your golden veil.

A snow-white feather
On your head you wear.
Black and shiny eyes
Affectionately gaze
At your lover far away.

Ah, Gulbita,
Gulbita.
You are a flower.
Why are you so red?

Are you waiting
For the moon to rise?
So that you can be with your man
And together drink that sweet wine

… …
… …

We arrived in Kashgar in the early evening. Against the fading light from the setting sun, I saw the silhouette of the city – the spires of the mosques, the houses built on a man-made platform, rising one after another, made of the earth of Central Asia.

We arrived at Halisa's house. It was made of mud bricks, so plain from the outside, but as soon as I entered, I was dazzled by the colourful geometric patterns painted on the wooden panels and the delicately carved railings and pillars. There was no one there, apart from us. In the middle of the courtyard, under the grapevines, there was a little table on which rested a white pot with dark blue patterns. Two cups waited by the pot. I sat down on a stool and poured myself a cup of green tea. I sipped. Meanwhile, Halisa went up to her room. She reappeared from her room, leaning forward at the railings, smiling at me, her long wavy hair dangling down.

The new moon has risen, yee-lah-lah, has risen,
It shines over the dressing table of my girl,
Yee-lah-lah, her dressing table.

The new moon has risen, yee-lah-lah, has risen.
Please open your window.
Yee-lah-lah, open your window.
Yee-lah-lah, open your window,

And pick a rose for me.
Gently, throw it down to me…

… …

… …

I climbed up the squeaky wooden stairs to her room. A little breeze came in through the open windows, lifting the soft curtains slightly. It was all so quiet as night fell. Her bed, facing the nascent moon…

And I woke up.

I sighed.

I got up from my iron-framed single bed. It was utterly silent in my room, at the back of Mr Na's courtyard. But in my heart, the songs echoed, endlessly. It was still the middle of the night, just like in my dream. I went to the window.

The main hall stood outside my window. There was only so much of the sky I could see from my room. I gazed at the moon. Like in my dream, it was a new moon, so beautifully curved. Nothing could compare to the beauty of the new moon, so perfect, especially as this brand new moon was carved on the night of her birthday. I opened my curtains completely so as to let the moonlight pour into my little room. On my face… My moon… Our moon…

63

Zhuangzi, who lived three hundred years before Christ, had a dream. In this dream, he was a butterfly, flitting and fluttering around very happily. This butterfly enjoyed its flight, its existence as a butterfly. It was definitely not Zhuangzi. Then, Zhuangzi suddenly woke up and there he was, unmistakably, Zhuangzi, not a butterfly. But was he Zhuangzi who had a dream in which he was a butterfly, or was the butterfly now dreaming that it was Zhuangzi?

Where was I? My mind? Everything? Was all this a dream of mine? Was I, in fact, still living in Isabel's flat in London? Did Zhuangzi write this novel for me? Or I had merely dreamt of Zhuangzi? Or perhaps the butterfly?

64

I had never thought that I would want schooldays to last for a few more hours, but I did as it meant more time and more opportunities for me to catch a glimpse of Halisa. At the same time, I could not wait for the day to end, as after school, we could meet, even though such meetings were never long enough for me. Whether it was during the working day or the resting night, my mind was with her, in her classroom, in her taxi, in her room. Meanwhile, I dreamt about her, while lying in my cold bed under the shadow of Mr Na's main hall… I dreamt at night. I dreamt during the day. In my dreams, she was with me. I cycled. She sat at the back of my bicycle, on the rack. I taught. She visited my class. I ate at school. She ate with me. I walked. She talked to me. I dined with Mr Na. She waited for me. I retired to my room. She opened the door to the room. I got into bed…

I woke up… I went on dreaming…

<h1 style="text-align:center">65</h1>

I reasoned with myself that while I had found her fascinating from Day One, I could not have just fallen in love with her. I was not in love with her at first sight, or second sight, or third or fourth, not even on the night of her birthday party. We were colleagues and she was someone's wife. I was simply foolish to have felt that way. After all, I was no longer a hormone-driven teenager, but an adult, a man, a man of reason…

But as much as I tried, I could not fool myself. I was a man of passion. Passion led me to China. Passion led me away from that kindergarten. Passion led me to work at this school for migrant workers' kids. And as I gazed at her, with her being miles away from me, in this city of twenty million lonely souls, no distance was too great for my fire-like passion, which burnt the whole city of Beijing, then all of China, the entire world! My world! And she… did she catch one flare?

Of course she did! She was burning just like me, ever since that night when the universe was created anew, after her birthday party. Every night, she went to her cold bed and in the morning, as the sunlight entered through her window, like on my own bed, there would be nothing but a pile of ashes from which she had to painfully arise again for her day, just like I had to for mine.

Yet, every morning, I could see Mr Na's main hall right outside my window, with the sun's rays blocked by that big grey building, with my entire room under its shadows…

Did I see or talk to anyone? No. I did not meet up with Jillian, let alone the crew. I enjoyed my solitude, my melancholic state of mind that Halisa had occupied.

66

"Form is emptiness, emptiness is form," so the Heart Sutra read.

Love, then, was no love, and no love was in itself love. I was not myself, but that non-being was precisely myself.

"It is not the flag that is moving. It is not the wind that is moving the flag. It is your mind that is moving," so the Gateless Gate master Huineng said in the thirteenth century.

Love... Halisa... Nothing was anything... Everything was nothing... It was not Halisa in love or me in love, but my mind in love... Not with love or Halisa... For love was no love... Passion was not passion...

I burnt at the stake...

67

Knock knock.

I went to the door and opened it. It was Chun'er. It was a Saturday afternoon. Chun'er led me to the main hall, where Mr Na was reading a book. I went in and Chun'er left. I closed the door behind me. Mr Na lowered his book. He was sitting on a chair with the painting and the calligraphy behind him. He was in his long robe, looking stately, like a statue of a scholar-official of the imperial days.

"Please," Mr Na gestured quietly. I sat down. Between us was a table, on which there were two cups of tea. He put his book down, then lifted his cup and took a sip. I drank my tea too.

We went through some unanimated chit-chat, almost depressingly. Our conversation did not flow as usual. It was almost contrived – the questions and the thanks and the answers. I thought perhaps he was going to break into something more substantial than these mundane topics of daily life.

And he did.

"I advise you not to see Halisa in private." He spoke slowly, firmly, authoritatively. Of course, it was not an advice but a command.

My first instinct was to ask why, but something held me back – I should know why. Mr Na's face was stern.

"Do you want to ask me why?" he asked.

"Yes." Now, the word 'yes' was much more positive and comfortable than a confrontational 'why'. Thanks Mr Na, for this more amicable break-in.

"I will tell you frankly. Two reasons. One is that her current behaviour, given the riots that have been going on in Xinjiang, is frankly unacceptable. Although she has stopped dressing for a statement, she has gone one step further – she has been making statements publicly!"

Had Halisa really been making public statements? I was not aware of this. Was this true? Or was this just Mr Na's lie?

He continued, "Now, I know that Xinjiang is thousands of miles away, but here in Beijing, it is as if every part of the Middle Kingdom is next door. Things are sensitive. To be too close to Halisa is against your interest, which is to have a safe time fulfilling your promise to teach at the school, for the benefit of those poor kids."

Very comforting, I thought in mockery, that Mr Na knew exactly what my best interest was!

He continued, "I do not want your work and life to be jeopardised by that self-centred woman. I do not want to go into the matter any further, but simply advise you to keep away from trouble. Now, that is the first reason. I advise you as a friend and as your employer.

"The second reason is more private. People see things, and people talk. Some of the talk that I have heard lately has not been too pleasing. If you have a wife, George, then you are her husband and she is your wife, however your relationship is, until you have divorced her. As such, there are standards and respect to be maintained here. I do not wish people to whisper behind my back and dishonour my name. It is dishonourable for Halisa too – also, my parents and her parents, as well as the wider clans and associates." He paused and sipped his tea.

My fists were clenched, not because I was ready to punch him, it was just a nervous reaction to his words. My palms were sweaty. I wondered if my forehead was sweaty too. Anyway, as he spoke, I felt my body turning cold, from the crown of my head through to my face, neck, chest, belly and legs. Inch by inch, section by section, muscle by muscle, bone by bone, until my entire body was almost shivering from the chills. I sipped my tea, avoiding his eyes, hoping to warm myself up, back to life. I did not know what to say, as whatever I said now would later be turned against me in this court martial. I simply wished this torturous meeting could end as soon as possible, even though I wanted to ask him who he was seeing! I knew he was seeing someone!

He put his cup down and continued in his calm and stately, soft yet firm voice. "I'm sure there is nothing between you and Halisa. I believe you are a man of honour and dignity. I know that, and that's why I invited you here, to live here and to work at the school, which was what you wanted. I trusted, and still trust, that you are a respectable man, and you will not act to dishonour me or my wife, or betray my trust. However, while I trust you, other people are less trusting. Gossip spreads and can take a life of its own. Some rumours have already started. You may not mean any harm when you meet Halisa, but it fuels gossip. Often reputations are ruined, not because of true intentions, but other people's interpretations of innocent actions. This is the second reason why I suggest that you stop meeting Halisa in private. Privacy? Well, nowhere is private. Understood?"

I accepted his reasons and took leave from him. He took up his book again and started to read as I closed the door behind me on my way out.

I wanted to see Halisa immediately. What did he mean by "nowhere is private"? Did he mean to say, "just don't do it" or that he had spies everywhere. Was my room bugged? I checked up and down, high and low, top to bottom, wall to wall, ceiling to floor, but could not find anything. I wanted to continue my search again, this time more thoroughly, but suddenly thought that if he saw me looking for his hidden camera, it would only make things worse. Then I thought how foolish I had been, checking my room top to bottom, for I did not have the habit of talking to myself!

Why was I so frightened?! I tried to kick myself out of this mode. I whispered *Mad Dogs and Englishmen* and *Rule Britannia*. Nope, that did not work. My reader, you must be laughing over my silly fright. You probably think this is all ridiculous. But have you been living under some strange foreigner's roof, in a distant land, where you hardly knew anyone, where your livelihood was owed to someone, where you had thanked that person for having granted you a new life, whom you were indebted to but could hardly repay, where you thought the rule of law could be weak or unfavourable towards you as the guns were controlled by those with connections? Think *1984*, think *Animal Farm* – was I being neurotic? What was more, what if you suspected him of being able to click his fingers at one of the largest military forces in the world?!

68

It so happened that there was no one else in the staffroom apart from me and Halisa. So, I grabbed this opportunity to tell her what Mr Na had said. As soon as I had finished, Teacher Zhou walked in. I did not think she could have heard any of my whispering words.

Halisa walked out of the room. I was left wondering what she had thought about it all. Meanwhile, Teacher Zhou marked a few exercise books and we had a cordial exchange of words that actually held little content.

Was Teacher Zhou a spy for Mr Na? No, she looked so nice and genuine. She was just an old teacher. Well, a great spy would not look like a spy and so maybe she was one. Yes, she was! That look in her eyes just then, as she moved her focus from her exercise books to me, then back to the books – surely, she looked shifty then! How clever of you, Teacher Zhou, to try and hide your true intentions behind these apparently cordial chinwags! But you do not fool me! Although most of the time, you can disguise yourself, it will take only one telltale sign for you to be exposed!

At the end of the school day, I walked with Halisa out of the school gates. I whispered to her my suspicion.

"Bohan does suspect us, I think," she whispered. She paused, "It would be terrible if he finds out."

We gazed at each other, just outside the school gates. I did not think much about what she had said immediately. She jumped into a taxi and disappeared.

It would be terrible if Mr Na found out about us. Yes, it would be terrible. The air suddenly froze on that warm day in late spring.

Wait... "finds out". I did not say "finds out", which of course meant that there had to be something to be found out. No, I did not say "finds out". She did!

The air suddenly turned into nothing but a fireball of passion. In a split second, my reinterpretation of "finds out" changed everything! The world disappeared and there was only the two of us in the universe, as I stood there by myself outside the school gates… Yes!

Zhuangzi was Zhuangzi. The butterfly was the butterfly. Zhuangzi was not the butterfly. Form was form. Emptiness was emptiness. Form was not emptiness. The flag moved. The wind moved the flag. The mind merely remembered the movements. It was clear to me in that split second… *Finds out…*

And the world was deafened with the silent roar of rejoicing in my heart!

69

Late spring in Beijing was getting hot, with the air gradually becoming more and more humid by the day. The wind had long ceased to blow from Siberia, instead the wind now came from the south, from the seas, over the plains, and was stopped from travelling further north by the hills. And so, the air in the city was gradually becoming suffocatingly still and the pollution from the millions of cars, increasing in number every day, was trapped. There was nowhere to go. Especially on days when there was no wind at all, when the smog started to form, sitting there like a blanket over everyone – if you breathed, you were killing yourself, but if you did not breathe, you would, of course, die. All I could do was to breathe gently, quietly, as stealthily as possible. I could be struck down at any moment, any one of my breaths could be my last. I could be caught. But I had to breathe…

She had to breathe too…

70

Beijing was littered with internet cafés for secret lovers to chance across each other. One would arrive before the other and sit in front of different machines, on random chairs, typing to each other. One would leave before the other, with nothing but a smile, having arranged their next meeting…

The city was filled with holes underground – makeshift hostels in dark dingy retired air-raid shelters – ran by migrants for migrants. One would arrive before the other. The other person was never stopped by the lazy receptionist who would be invariably be too busy watching pirated films – no attention was paid unless there were some keys or money involved. There, in the hole underground, they would spend a few hours together, and one would then leave before the other, with nothing but a little kiss, having agreed where and when to meet again…

This was urban warfare. They were the partisans…

On the open plains, partisans would be spotted easily and shot. So, they took to the hills. One would take a long-distance bus, and the other would arrive on the next service. One would walk up the hills from one path, the other would follow later on another path. They never met on top of the hill, the scenic spots, but would meet off the beaten track, in the woods. And one would leave before the other, with nothing but a sigh…

Thrill was the variable. Fear was the constant. No, they did not fear when they were together, even though one day, they would be caught…

But why should they be partisans? She did not want to be one. She wanted to stand proud with her comrade. She wanted the world to know that they stood together, shoulder to shoulder, heart to heart. She could not endure a life in hiding any more. There was nothing wrong with what they were doing. They were living their truth, rather than living a lie to satisfy other people's perceptions. If they had to go down, then she would rather be like a lancer of the light brigade, charging into the valley of death, proudly, gallantly.

To him, to live was more important than to die.

Coward! She shouted at him.

He hated being called a coward. When he returned to his solitary room, he confronted himself. Was he really a coward? Why did he not dare to face the enemy square on? Oh, my reader, this man had been a coward since he was twelve and a half, even when it came to writing an e-mail! The only brave thing he had done was to say goodbye to his first love. Even then, he dared not look back at her, to say goodbye. Now, facing a formidable adversary, what would you expect him to do, my dear reader, apart from hide?

71

How long could I hide from Mr Na? I did not know, but over the last three months, Halisa and I had developed something to hide from him. As the cool and gentle spring turned into a hot and passionate summer, I knew that at some point we could no longer keep a lid on things and carry on suppressing our desires. I longed for her to be with me and I knew she too wanted to release her true self, completely, from all the constraints of herself and society. Yet we could not rush each other. I needed time to come to terms with the fact that I eventually had to challenge Mr Na, and turn him from my benefactor into an adversary. She needed the time to acknowledge, once and for all, that Mr Na was her ex-husband, part of her past, and her future was with me. Meanwhile, we were still confused about who should say or do what to whom, and so we had to hide in order to give ourselves time to prepare. We could not be exposed before we were ready.

Yes, Mr Na could expose me if he wanted to. I was sure that certain looks he had given me were telltale signs that he knew about my feelings towards Halisa. What could I say then? I could not thank my benefactor by saying, "I have been liaising with your wife."

If Mr Na would not confront me himself, then would Halisa? As a headstrong woman, how long could she keep on hiding? And then, what would I do? Could I just be a follower of her? Would I then not be the worm that she had started to imagine I was? Would I then not really be a worm in Mr Na's eyes? What status would I hold then? Would Halisa really love a "yes, yes" worm?

But why had Halisa not already come out in the open? Was she taking her time to prepare her attack? Or were her words there to incite me to confront Mr Na, man-to-man? Or was there something holding her back, stopping her from confronting Mr Na herself? Or were her words merely said by her passionate heart, while her more reasonable mind had told her to keep calm and continue to hide? Could her feelings one day overrun her reason? Yes, she said be true to one's feelings… Yet, whenever I wanted to talk about our future together, she seemed passionate but confused, or constrained. It was as if something or someone was holding her back. Could that be Mr Na himself? Or her family? Or the network of the Red Establishment with its sense of order? I wanted to probe her, but she often fell silent. Was that her way of saying that I should be the man and challenge Mr Na?

Whichever way, one day we would come out in the open. I had to take the initiative – to be the man who was worthy of her love…

I looked into the mirror. Was that George looking back at me? What did 'George' mean? The dragon slayer? Was Mr Na the dragon? Could George take on the dragon? The dragon was in his throne room, in front of George's little room.

The dragon was mighty. George was weak. Could the weak ever take on the mighty face-to-face?

It was not the flag that moved or the wind that moved the flag; it was the mind that moved. The dragon was not mighty. George was not weak. It was me who thought that the dragon was mighty and George weak.

George was strong! George was strong! Halisa would not be with the weak! George *had* to be strong! For a start, George had to be strong in his own mind! George screamed in his heart in his little room, lit by a yellow table lamp that was surrounded by darkness, night after night…

How many nights? One, two, three… one thousand and one? George saw his shadow growing in stature, night after night. Finally, he became a giant! He was a giant to start off with – it was his own weak mind that had prevented him from recognising his own giant stature. Now with a clear vision, he saw his own strength.

Strength was not enough. George had to have a sword to slay the dragon. He searched for this sword – the sharpest sword in the world. He knew that there must not be a prolonged duel. It had to be a master stroke, one that would fatally enter the proud dragon's heart!

Night after night, George looked for his sword. No mountain was too high; no waters were too deep. From the land of the White Mountains and the Black Waters, to the desert from which no one could return, from the frozen earth to the scorching rocks, George was tireless in his search, travelling one thousand miles in one night on the heavenly horse that was his mind… Night after night…

How many nights? One, two, three… one thousand and one? He found it! His roar of joy shook the world! But the dragon did not hear George's roar. It must not realise that George had found his sword. The dragon had to be ignorant. Let the dragon sleep. When it woke up, it would be its last awakening…

With that sword in hand, George the giant met his fair lady. He held his head high. He explained his plan of action.

No. George must not take on the dragon.

What?! Did the fair lady not have to be saved from the dragon? Why not?!

"Look George, let's just carry on like this," the lady pleaded. Was it not she who had accused George of being a coward?

She was temperamental. She was out of her mind. She had let her passion overcome her senses, the fair lady explained. But her explanation left George only more confused. Did she not have faith in George's victory? Did she think the dragon would not be slain, but George would? Was it a matter of timing? Or didn't she actually want George? What was holding her back? Did she still hold something for the dragon? Did the dragon hold something for her? Did they hold something together, which meant that the fair lady could not disappear into the sunset with George?

Was the fair lady out of her mind? George was out of his mind! George presented his sword to her time and time again. His plan of attack would surely work. The dragon would see that he was nothing but a worm – a hypocritical, pretentious, face-loving, self-centred, self-righteous, pig-headed, schizophrenic worm – and as such, was no match for the fair lady and so had to let her go, and the worm's only option would be to crawl in between the cracks in the earth and disappear forever out of their sight, and they would be free to live and free to love!

George's torrents of passion were returned by the fair lady with the drops of her tears. No… George must not attack.

George was losing his mind. "What was it?! What's holding you back?!" George asked. Silence, answered Halisa…

George lost his battle with the dragon before the battle had even commenced. George could not even win over the trust of the fair lady. What was the point of George's plans? What use was George's sword?

The worm did not crawl in between the cracks in the earth. George did, back to his little room, under the shadow of the dragon's throne room.

72

I kept up my pretence of being amicable with Mr Na. I mimicked being a guest or a servant, it was confusing which I really was. I had to try to disguise myself – I was the thief. A thief was a worm, for he dared not let people see his face or his actions. He had to be sneaky, had to hide.

The school broke up for the summer… Beijing's summer was hot, suffocating. The air stood still. After having done some cleaning with Chun'er, and working up a sweat, I sat down by the fishpond. I looked at the koi. They swam so slowly, almost as if they were still. Even though they were in the water, perhaps they felt it was too hot to move about much.

"Have some tea. Chrysanthemum tea – it's very cooling." Mr Na invited me into the hall. Chun'er went to the kitchen and soon emerged with the tea. She poured.

"Gosh… This is good…" I let out a groan. "Beijing's summer is so hot. Unbearable." I tried to keep up my old appearance of being a good person for Mr Na to talk to.

We moaned about the heat, and somehow our moan developed into talk about which part of China was cooler than Beijing. Did Mr Na steer our conversation this way? Before I knew it, I had said yes to his proposal, request, or command to escape the heat with him. Why did I say yes? I did not want to, but somehow my moan earlier had left me with no choice but to say yes – it was not as if I could have provided a good reason not to escape this steam room of a city. What excuse could have been sufficiently well-sealed to not arouse his suspicion that I wanted to stay here to see his wife?

So, I found myself packing a bag and preparing to spend just under a week in the cooler northeast with Mr Na.

73

The next day, a Jeep arrived. It had a white registration plate – the plate of the military. A young solider jumped out and loaded our luggage onto the back. We jumped in. Well, I did not jump in joyfully, but perhaps dragged my feet a little.

The Jeep travelled at an amazing speed down the streets of Beijing. It ignored all the speed signs, overtaking and undertaking other vehicles, while sounding its horn. To say it was a horn was an understatement. The honk was broadcast through a loudspeaker, a hundred times louder than the average car horn, in a baritone thunder. The traffic police, upon noticing this military vehicle approaching, all turned their backs to it, as it jumped several ambers. In Beijing, jumping an amber was not allowed; it was almost as big an offence as jumping a red. I grabbed onto the handrail. Mr Na had his eyes closed, head back, seatbelt idle.

We did not arrive at Capital International Airport. We did not arrive at Beijing Railway Station. We arrived at a small airport, beautifully named Southern Garden.

We got down from the Jeep and the young soldier carried our bags. There was nothing garden-like about this airport. It was austere, solemn, with only a few passengers dotted around, mostly in military uniforms. We went straight through the side entrance of the lobby and then exited the building in no time. In front of me, a medium-sized plane was fired up, its propellers in motion. The captain greeted us. He was not in a typical civil aviation pilot uniform. He had shoulder straps with stars and stripes on them. He shook our hands and guided us onto the plane. There was no one else on the plane apart from the two pilots and us. The interior was barren. It had seats, but they looked somewhat temporary, as if the plane's primary duty was not to carry people but cargo. *Bing.* It approached the run-way. *Bing.* It started to take off. The engine shook the plane violently and roared as it thundered into the sky.

Once the plane had stopped ascending, the two pilots came over to greet us. They chatted to Mr Na in a very courteous manner, nodding their heads, as if they were the princeling's servants. Throughout the flight, Mr Na did not look at me – he did not invite me to speak. I was speechless.

We landed after nearly two hours. We walked out of the plane, down the steps and jumped straight into a waiting Jeep. *Bang.* The boot slammed shut, with our luggage having been loaded into the vehicle.

We travelled at breakneck speed down the streets, even on the wrong side of the street. Common cars gave way to our Jeep, which had established its hegemony on the roads. The traffic police saw us but did nothing. One could almost imagine that they should have saluted us.

After an hour or so of driving, during which time Mr Na had his eyes closed, we arrived somewhere in the heavily forested mountain ranges. A white building appeared in the distance. The driver put up a sign against the windscreen. He slowed the vehicle down and drove past two soldiers standing to attention, who upon seeing the sign behind the windscreen, saluted promptly. The Jeep approached a hotel-like building and drove up the ramp.

Two doormen came out. They opened our Jeep's doors. We jumped out. Another doorman unloaded our luggage. An attractive young woman led us to two rooms that were next to each other.

"See you at the lobby at four-thirty," Mr Na said, without looking at me.

My room was of the typical hotel type. A bathroom to the right of the entrance. Twin beds. Two armchairs under the window. An ashtray on the table between the chairs. A dressing table at the end of the beds, with a TV sitting on top. Four-thirty was in half an hour. I unpacked. Went for a wee. Sat in the armchair. Had a smoke. My hand shook a little, and it was uncontrollable. I stubbed my cigarette out, stood up and walked out of my room.

I waited for Mr Na in the lobby. It was not as grand as the lobby of Beijing Hotel where we first met. In its attempt to look grander than it was, it failed miserably. The four tacky, gold-rimmed clocks on the wall displayed different times, supposedly in different countries. The pillars pretended to be marble, but were not. The plants were decidedly plastic. Yet, there was a sense of pride here, as everything was neat – perfectly aligned sofas, chairs around the tables evenly distributed, and the floor so polished that I could see the outline of my face.

Mr Na emerged. He led me out, and we walked. He did not speak. I did not say anything either. We arrived at a shooting range. A young soldier was there, who appeared to be waiting for us.

"Ever done any shooting before?" Mr Na asked, without looking at me.

"No."

"You're in luck – pistols, light assault guns, sniper rifle, semi-automatics, machine guns… Take your pick."

The young soldier led us to the arsenal, which was big enough to arm a small contingent. Mr Na took what appeared to be a classic Kalashnikov. He handed me one. "Have a go. Type 56. Similar to the famous Soviet AK 47."

We took our rifles and walked to the range. The targets appeared miles away. I could barely see them. Mr Na put his rifle to his shoulder. *Bang! Bang! Bang!*

He looked at me, as I stood there looking like some frozen statue on this temperate day. "Have a go," he encouraged.

I slowly lifted the heavy rifle to my shoulder and put the sight to my right eye. I squeezed gently on the trigger. Nothing happened. I squeezed harder… *Bang!*

My right shoulder nearly came off as the end of the barrel shot back in the recoil. Mr Na smiled. "Go on." His encouragement sounded more like a command.

Bang! Bang! Bang… My shoulder hurt like hell. Was I holding it correctly?

The targets came back. His target – seven, eight, eight, nine, nine, ten, ten. Mine – one. Okay, at least I had hit the target. Two. I was impressed with myself. Five! That was very lucky. The rest? Not on target at all.

"Not bad!" Mr Na commended me, quietly and dispassionately.

"Beginner's luck." I was modest.

"I saw your eyes blinking with each shot. That's natural. A real shooter does not close his eyes. He always keeps his target in sight." Mr Na instructed. For a split second, his eyes looked piercingly into mine.

Mr Na went back to the arsenal. I said I did not want to try any more. He shrugged his shoulders.

He brought over what looked like a machine gun. He got down on the floor and put up the stand. *Bang bang bang! Bang bang bang bang bang bang…* It was deafening. Like a lion, the gun roared in anger. Empty bullet cases flew out from the side. A straight continuous line linked the end of the barrel with the target. It was maddening, as the cartridge seemed to hold countless bullets. The target came back. It was just a frame. The middle had been ripped to oblivion. To be on the receiving end of that was unimaginable. Nothing of your upper body would be left. They would not even be able to gather enough flesh for a decent cremation. Your bones would have vanished into the ether… My legs were stiff. I felt cold…

74

Although I was away from the suffocating heat of Beijing, the cooler air of the northeast brought me little comfort. I endured five days with Mr Na. He insisted on me coming with him to the shooting range every afternoon. I occasionally shot a few rounds, just to be polite, while he pulled the trigger on guns large and small, and each time returned shredded targets. Every morning, he insisted on me coming with him for hour-long jogs in the woods. I could not keep up with him. At times, I fell onto the ground, gasping for air. He would command me to get up and carry on. He also insisted on me coming swimming with him in the little lake, which appeared like an ocean once I was in the water. He rested on the opposite side, while I was only halfway across at most. His body in the sun looked like a bronze statue of perfectly formed Greek art… I dragged my tired body out of the water, skinny and pale.

Instead of being a holiday in a retreat, it was a torture session, deliberately set up by Mr Na as an unspoken showdown, to make it clear to me that he was the master, the winner, the man, and I a mere underling, a loser, a worm…

What if I had turned my gun on him on the shooting range and pulled the trigger before he could react? What if during a jog I had grabbed a fallen branch, come up from behind, and bashed him on the head as hard as I could? What if when swimming, I had jumped on top of him and pressed him to the bottom of the lake? As I looked at my blank target, as I struggled to lift myself up in the woods, as I crawled up the bank of the lake, I knew my wild thoughts were nothing but fantasies. What did I have but fantasies… Yes, Mr Na, you had put your point across, without saying anything. I understood.

75

We got back to Beijing. I walked into my room and dumped my bag on the floor, then sat on my bed and stared straight into empty space. How long I stayed like that, I do not know. Eventually, using some unknown force, I catapulted myself up from the bed. I looked around. The little Chinese warrior statue caught my eyes. The god of loyalty… Loyalty, one of the most important virtues of a gentleman of the plains, as well as the grassland. I recalled Mr Na's informative stories when I first moved into this room, when he came to see how I was settling in. The grassland… the Mongol steppes… What was the reward for betrayal? Genghis Khan, ordered the execution of the men who betrayed Jamukha – his greatest adversary – for they had betrayed their master… Death…

I ran out of my room, sprinted through the courtyard, and jumped into a taxi. I kept on looking behind me to see if there was a car following us. Yes, there was! Mr Na was following me. I bit my lip and kept on looking back. Oh good, the car had disappeared. Maybe it was not Mr Na. We turned the corner and there it was! He was following me! Then his car was gone again.

I paid and got out of the taxi and started running, taking a detour, constantly looking over my shoulder to see if anyone was following me. No, there was no one. I went up to my old block of flats to see Jillian.

She opened the door and I charged in, madly circling around in her flat, shaking uncontrollably. She insisted that I sat down. I did, but I jumped up again. I tried to tell Jillian everything as quickly as I could, but my words got muddled up and my sentences confused both her and me. Eventually, I thought I had put my point across…

"No. That could not possibly be true," Jillian laughed at me. "Mr Na and Guangxuan could not possibly be the same person. Don't be silly! Guangxuan is as ordinary as any guy could be. I cannot for a minute imagine him shooting all those guns and getting them on target. He is not a solider but a peaceful art lover…”

Yes, right, peaceful… To protect the peace, war was sometimes necessary. Art lover? A crafty lover would be a more befitting description of that man – that hypocrite who told me to back off from his estranged wife while he was sleeping around himself, and deceiving Halisa and Jillian by inventing this Guangxuan character. “You think I’m a fool, Mr Na? You do not fool me!” I spoke madly. Jillian tried to reason with me, but I did not have the time to explain to her. I dashed around like a lunatic.

As I was still without a mobile phone, I demanded, “Give me your phone please, quickly, quickly!” Jillian was confused but handed me her phone. I grabbed it and called Halisa. I ran out of Jillian’s flat to see Halisa.

Shit! Shit! Shit! Why did I use Jillian’s phone?! I ran back and asked Jillian to delete the record of the call from her phone. She did not understand why I was charging about crazily, insisting on the deletion. How clever I was!

Even cleverer, I had never told Jillian about Halisa and me. Imagine if I had not figured out who Jillian was seeing, and I had confided in her, then she had spoken to her Guangxuan casually about it all…

Although Jillian was not sure what I was doing, only that I was out of my mind, she duly deleted the call record. I ran and jumped into a taxi, heading to one of underground hostels that Halisa and I had used once before for our secret rendezvous.

Once again, I hopped out of the taxi, perhaps half a mile away from the rendezvous point. Instead of walking, I ran. I was out of breath. Halisa was already there when I arrived.

She gave me her bottle of water. I gulped and gulped. Finally, my spirits caught up with me.

“What is it?” she asked.

I explained it all to her, everything that had happened, including the bit about Jillian and the person she thought was an ordinary insurance clerk named after a pile of paper.

Could she not see that a pile of calligrapher's paper was a game of words that Mr Na had played with his name, from Bohan – a large collection of brushes?!

Footsteps outside…

Mr Na's footsteps!

I started shaking. My trembling hands found Halisa's hands and gripped them. Halisa tried to ask me what was going on, but I froze there, sitting on the bed, like a frightened chick, staring at the eagle, as it was diving down for its prey – its eyes never leaving the prey in this hunt… The footsteps came closer and closer… I knew he was holding a pistol… I knew he would fire one round at me and one round at Halisa…

The footsteps came closer and closer… I shook uncontrollably in fear… I saw nothing else but black.

Bang! Our locked door was kicked open – my Great Wall had been finally overrun by the Manchu princeling. A pistol was lifted, aimed at my head – between my eyes.

Everything flashed before my eyes… The urban jungle of the East End and the mirrors on that girl's dress as I had supper at Jameel's… The rolling hills and the trickling streams of the Cotswolds… The crisp sound of leather on willow that accompanied my first meeting with Isabel… The Madeiran stars that witnessed my love for her… My time wasted in drunkenness with her in London… My grandfather's final words on his deathbed… I wished I had looked at Isabel once more before I finally left London… My time with the crew… Even they were my brothers now… My first meeting with Mr Na… How he saved me from purposelessness… Those great conversations we had… The knowledge I had gained from him… My first meeting with Halisa, whose hand I was holding now, my sweaty hands… My time with Halisa, even just a trivial supper at a nondescript eatery was as precious as… as precious as anything that could be imagined – I had lost my ability to visualise. Oh! All of these had sealed my doom! Did I start my life for the purpose of Mr Na's shooting?! No! No!! No!!!

Bang!

I woke up in cold sweat… My whole body was as cold as ice… Had I dreamt all of that? Or were my moments of being awake merely a dead man's dream?

76

Whether I was a living man who dreamt of death, or a dead man dreaming he was still alive, I no longer cared. I knew that I could only live once. Since I could already have died, I no longer cared if Mr Na was going to shoot me, or shoot me again. Finally, I emerged from his shadows and became my own man, after my death.

"Where shall we meet?" Halisa asked.

"*Tao Ran Ting.*"

"Where in the park?"

"Near the nunnery."

Now the partisans emerged from their hiding. No more underground holes. No more dense forests. I insisted that we came out in the open, under the heat of Beijing's scorching sun. Our time in the sun. Halisa was not keen at first, but finally agreed.

And there, we met, under the midday sun.

"Sing for me."

"What song?"

"*Gulbita.*"

Oh angel, beautiful angel,
The fragrant flowers are no match for you.
You are so delicate and beautiful, and your beauty is beyond words.
Gulbita, your words are sweeter than honey.
Your red lips intoxicate me.

I moved myself close to her. I opened my arms. I captured her in my embrace. Our first embrace under the sun, in the open air. She initially hesitated, but accepted. I closed my eyes and took in the scent of her hair, toasted by the heat of the sun and steamed by the moist air. The leaves did not quiver. The clouds refused to move. The flowers stood still.

All were awed by our firm embrace, as we pressed each other into our flesh, moulding each other into our bones. Look! If the only way the two of us could be united was in death, then so be it.

"Let's go," I requested quietly, my lips near her ear.

"Where?"

Anywhere, Shanghai, Dunhuang, Xi'an, Urumqi, Kashgar… Anywhere, as far away from here as possible! We could have our lives together, without being under his shadow. Then, we would be free! Free to live! Free to love!

No, not any fantasy places. Instead, we would be realistic. She would go with me to England. We would first stay with my parents. All three of my siblings had left home, and so there was plenty of space in our Cotswolds house. My mother was a kind woman and she would like Halisa. My father was out touring most of the time. He would like her too when he returned. We would then go to London where I would find a job – no more messing around – and I was sure she could find something too. If she could not, I would support her. If one income was not enough, I would take on two jobs, three… as many as was required. I would work hard, and we would be happy together, in a land so distant from Beijing, in a land of freedom!

Our embrace ended. Halisa's eyes were full of tears. She looked at me and touched my face. She looked down. Why was she so sad? Did she not want to stop being a partisan, constantly in hiding? Did she not want to come out into the open? Did she not shout at me once, not long ago, for being a coward?

Okay, the fair lady did not want George to slay the dragon. So, George did not. But could the fair lady not just jump onto George's horse and ride away with him, leaving the dragon asleep? By the time the dragon had woken up, the fair lady and George would have travelled thousands of miles. The dragon would not know where they were, and then it would be too late for it to react.

"No George…" her voice trembled, as she looked at me with her beautiful, large light brown eyes, two ponds of crystal clear tears. The tears filled the ponds, and one drop slid down her cheek, running slowly at first, then gathering pace once it slid past her cheekbone. I wiped that teardrop away from her delicate jaw. She smiled, a bitter sweet smile, as if she had enjoyed listening to my plans of how we two lovers could become free, yet silently she mocked me, letting me know that my take on our future was nothing but fantasy.

Suddenly, she pulled my face towards her with both hands, holding tightly the sides of my face. A kiss. Lip to lip. Tongue to tongue.

The sun scorched the earth.

We scorched the sun.

She let go as suddenly as she started. She looked at me once more, fixing her eyes to mine. She pushed me away as hard as she could, then ran away.

It took me seconds to realise what was going on. I started to run after her.

"Don't! George. No! I can't! I can't!" She looked back, while still running. "Goodbye! Goodbye…"

There was no one around us, then. On midsummer's midday, only a mad man would go out.

There was no one in the park at all.

There was no one in Beijing.

There was no one in the world.

I stood there. I saw nothing but darkness, cold and boundless, from here to eternity…

77

If I had doubts before, that afternoon, I knew I was dead – the walking dead, a ghost – as I entered my room at the back of the courtyard. I packed my bag. I did not rush – the dead were not bound by deadlines. Nevertheless, it was not long before my worldly belongings were stuffed into a bag – funny how the dead still cared about the worldly. Did he care, or was this packing exercise merely done through automation, as if the ghost still kept the habits of the living?

Just as I thought I had finished packing, as I was swinging the straps onto my shoulders, I saw the little Chinese warrior statue on the desk. The god of loyalty. I picked it up. He gazed at me with his fierce eyes, as if they could penetrate my soul. But did I have a soul left? Loyalty… To whom? Myself? Isabel? Mr Na? Halisa? For what? Destiny? Love? Fantasy? Brotherhood and purpose? Love? Even the dead could feel perturbed. I put the little statue down gently, back on the desk, and turned to go.

Before I exited my room, I looked at the map of China on my wall…

Beijing was marked with a red star, with the land to the west of the red star gradually becoming browner, the colour code of mountains and highlands. Then, a bit of green surrounded Xi'an. West from there, mostly brown again… Further west, I traced the Great Wall on the map. The end at Jiayuguan, the Pass of the Brilliant Valley. Westwards to Turpan… Kucha… Kashgar…

Gulbita, as attractive as a goddess, no flower could compare to you.

There's no language in the world that could describe your beauty.

To gain your love, I would happily surrender my life.

*Gulbita, your sweet smile is like honey, but no honey could
be compared to you.*

*To Bukhara or to Kabul, the distant journeys do not worry
me,*
Now, I have seen the goddess on earth, I am so happy.

Gulbita, Gulbita, I give you my heart.
Gulbita, Gulbita, I give you my heart.
I give you my heart, I give you my heart.

My beauty, do not get upset, I am just a visitor.
I have brought the lights of Bukhara. I am the bright moon.
*I have travelled through all of Bukhara, and have taken in
Kabulstan.*
*For the beautiful Gulbita, I am willing to abandon all my
wealth.*

Everyone says that Gulbita is sweeter than honey.
Drinking is a habit. To get rid of it is hard.
Gulbita's beauty surpasses the blooms of a hundred flowers.
*Poems of praise can never run out. For to describe her,
there are not enough words.*

Why are the flowers so red?
Why so red?
Gulbita
Gulbita

Gulbita
I see you coming,
From the beautiful icy peaks,
Coming towards me,
Your long hair,
Your dark eyebrows.

In between your lips,
A red rose.

Gulbita
I see you coming,
From the distant Gobi,
Coming towards me,
Your golden veil.

A snow-white feather
On your head you wear.
Black and shiny eyes
Affectionately gaze
At your lover far away.

Ah, Gulbita,
Gulbita.
You are a flower.
Why are you so red?

Are you waiting
For the moon to rise?
So that you can be with your man
And together drink that sweet wine

I closed the door to my room behind me and walked into the middle of courtyard. I sat by the pond and looked at the koi. They were still their calm selves, swimming so slowly, gracefully, sometime coming together, sometimes parting, sometimes circling around each other, other times keeping their distance from each other. The water lilies were in full bloom now. Their petals were of different shades of pink against the backdrop of green leaves that floated on the water. A koi hid under the leaves, as if it was ashamed, then re-emerged as if nothing sorrowful had ever happened. This was their world. Their tranquil world, sheltered from the torrents of mighty rivers or fishermen's nets. It was their comfortable world, perhaps a meaningless world of ideal grace, nothing more, a hollow grace, a pretence of perfection, a beautiful centrepiece of vanity…

I felt someone coming from behind me. I turned. It was Chun'er. She looked at me, while I looked up at her. There was something in her eyes that told me she knew everything, although she said nothing. I stood up. She led me to the study.

By the entrance to the study, Chun'er stopped. She looked at my packed bag firmly lodged on my shoulders. She gave me a hug.

"Goodbye," she murmured in English.

"*Zai jian*," I murmured.

She left, looking back at me once more, before disappearing into the kitchen, quietly.

I stood there in Mr Na's study. Compared to the outside that was almost overwhelmingly bright and scorching, the study was dim and cool. The sunlight was tamed here – a hint of brownish yellow, echoing the shades of the teak and mahogany furniture, and the faded yellow photographs on the wall.

Most things had remained the same since the last time I was here, just before the Chinese New Year. But not everything had.

On the writing desk, there were two parcels, sitting next to each other. Tags with my name on them but in different handwriting. I unwrapped one parcel. Three books in English – *Private Lives* by Noël Coward, *The Analects of Confucius*, and *Quotations from Chairman Mao*. I flicked through the books for a little while, reading fragments of passages, mixing the lines from a Western playboy, an Eastern gentleman and a Communist revolutionary. I put them down on top of the torn wrapping paper, on the desk.

I opened the other parcel. *A Concise History of China*, written in English. It was not a proper book but a set of manuscripts, printed on sheets of A4 paper. The original author was the Hunan Uyghur historian who committed suicide during the Cultural Revolution – Jian Bozan. I looked at this set of manuscripts. I flicked through them, again reading fragments of passages. I wanted to read. I wanted to sit there and read it from beginning to end. I wanted the person who had translated the original and given it to me to be there with me, to answer my questions as I read it… No. Like the other three books, I put it down on top of the torn wrapping paper, on the desk.

On the bookshelf, where Mr Na's sketchbooks were, there was one that was not tucked in, but laid flat in front of the upright volumes. I opened it. There were drawings, made with a thin-tipped pilot pen, black, on cream-white paper. Copies of murals, the originals in the caves from a thousand years ago, from Mogao, *Mo* – never to be… *Gao* – surpassed. The murals recounted the life of the Buddha, his birth, youth and departure into the wilderness. His sitting under the Bodhi tree, enlightenment, preaching, nirvana, the realisation that all you thought was so real was nothing but a transitory illusion, that the material life simply went round and round on the dharmic wheel of endless suffering, that love's end was loss, happiness had to be accompanied by lament, and pride was the source of its own shattering… I touched the drawings and they came alive. The apsaras flew from the floor up to the ceiling, from corner to corner, playing their instruments, spreading the flower petals… I could hear a low accompanying sound of *Om*…

On top of the colour photographs that I had seen before was a new photo. A young man's face with sharp features, those of Mr Na. A young woman, with a tall nose and large eyes, those of Halisa. Between them was a little child with large eyes and long lashes, just like Halisa's, a little nose, but you could also see the shape of Mr Na's, a little mouth with lips slightly parted as if wanting to speak…

I glanced at the books on the desk, the sketchbook on the shelf and the photo of the couple with their child. I sighed, silently thanking Mr Na and Halisa, and indeed everyone I had come across on this journey, Chun'er, Jillian, the crew… I did not pick up the books… I left them on the desk, and perhaps in the past.

I walked out under the heat of the blinding sun…

78

The streets of Beijing were quiet, despite all the cars and people. The airport was quieter. The plane was silent. All the while, I could only hear my own gentle breathing, which confirmed that I was not dead, not a ghost, but alive. Zhuangzi was Zhuangzi. The butterfly was the butterfly. I was George, a different George, a new George, the true George.

One beer… Two beers… Three… They tasted refreshing. One mini bottle of wine… Two mini bottles… Three… They were not too bad. I closed my eyes and let darkness wrap me up in a comfortable blanket. There was no fire wolf, no struggle, just me on this plane, in my own darkness, my own peacefulness.

I woke up. I lifted the window shutter. The Millennium Dome. Big Ben. Buckingham Palace. Twickenham stadium. Landing strip…

Bus to Feltham. South West Trains to Clapham Junction. A little walk.

The door that I was so familiar with. The door that I walked out of. The door where Isabel stood, perhaps wanting to see me look back once more.

The doorbell. I stood there.

The doorbell. My finger.

The doorbell that I did not press. Let go. Let go…

I turned. I walked. I crossed the road.

Clapham Common. The summer. The warm sun, kissing the tender grass. The gentle breeze, caressing the green leaves. Young people in varying degrees of nakedness. Laughing. Drinking. Playing Frisbee. Playing play-cricket – not leather on willow, but tennis ball on pine.

A girl. In the slight distance. As she walked, the hem of her dress swayed with each step. A gentle breeze slightly lifted the hem. The soft fabric of summer. The smell of grass and the warm sun. The flowers in bloom. Her honey-coated slender legs.

The rim to the sides of her large straw hat dropped down, as if to hide her from unwanted attention. Her face would only be revealed if she chose to face me.

She looked, briefly, my way. Her thin nose. Slightly upturned upper lip. Slight freckles on her cheeks. Her eyebrows arched, as if puzzled by the world's business, intrigued by what all the fuss was about...

About the Author

Ed Zhao was born in Beijing in 1981. He was educated in Beijing, Warsaw, Chipping Norton, Bath and London. Since graduating, Ed has been working in London, mainly in the transport planning sector. He enjoys writing, painting and playing music in his spare time. *The Princeling* is his second attempt at writing a novel. It was drafted in 2012 at his home in Clapham Junction and in a café nearby. His first attempt at novel writing, a prose-like work of nostalgia and melancholy, *Catching the Snowflakes / Pass of the Sun*, lies buried for possible release in the future. He has many ideas for new works, including *Beijing, a Memoir*. Watch this space…

To find out more about Ed, please visit his website www.edzhao.com, where you can see his art-works. You can also see his creations on Instagram @ed_zhao_arts.

If you have enjoyed this book, please leave a review on Amazon. Ed would love to know what you thought of this creation.

ED WOULD LIKE TO THANK...

Apeksha Zhao, his long-suffering wife who has painstakingly read and re-read various drafts of this book, plus all the other stuff he has ever written, and will write.

Leila Green, founder of iamselfpublishing.com and editor who has been thorough and encouraging throughout the process, and the team for the project management and cover design.

Himself, for the illustrations in the book, and writing this novel.

His friends and acquaintances, whose names he has borrowed for this book, and whose characters and experiences have inspired him.

and of course...

You, my dear, soft-hearted and learned reader.